THE ENGLISH TEACHER

by Mick Le Moignan

ISBN: 978-0-6450566-0-0 (paperback)
ISBN: 978-0-6450566-1-7 (ebook)

Published by Bouley Bay Books, Sydney & Jersey
Tel: (+61) 403 039 164 MLM444@gmail.com

Typeset & printed in Australia by Image DTO
Tel: (+61) 423 360 883 imagedto@gmail.com

Cover Design and exercise book pages
by Derrin Mappledoram of Cambridge Marketing
Magpie sketches by Trish Le Moignan
Quotations from *The Love Song of J Alfred Prufrock* by TS Eliot
used by permission of the Estate of TS ELIOT and Faber & Faber

First published 2020
Copyright © Mick Le Moignan (2020)

Dedicated to the memory of
six students and teachers of English
who shared their wisdom generously:

Trevor Park
Chris MacGregor
Clive Hartwell
Richard Hutt
Ronald Youngs
T R Henn

After the presumed death of Mr Henry Barraclough,
seven school exercise books, written in his own
hand, were found among his effects. They hold
some clues as to the state of his mind, at and after
the time of his resignation from Effingham School,
but they do not cast any further light on his
mysterious disappearance in June 1996.

The accusation of sexual impropriety that brought his
brilliant teaching career to a premature close has not
been supported by any evidence. Later investigations
indicate that it may well have been completely
spurious.

These writings are offered to the public by some of
Henry Barraclough's grateful former pupils. We are
publishing them as a fond and respectful memorial to
a man who may, we believe, be more sinned against
than sinning.

Name: *Henry Barraclough*

Form: *-idable*

English (de)Composition

Book 1: For Sorrow

Effingham School
Effingham, Glos.

There he is again – the single magpie, swooping and fluttering among the trees at the end of my garden. In my younger days, I would have scoured the sky for another, mindful of the old saying: 'One for sorrow: two for joy'.

Not that I am truly superstitious – what hubris makes us imagine our petty human emotions might be so simplistically reflected in the cosmos? – but against all logic, finding the second magpie always struck me as a small victory over the malignancy of Fate. At the time, I had no idea just how malign Fate, in the seductive form of Miss Dorothy Pargeter, could be.

Now that I am more in need than ever of any small victories that may come my way, however insignificant – I find I can no longer be bothered to search for the second magpie.

This, then, is the state to which Miss Pargeter has reduced me: an impotent old pensioner, shuffling around the leaves in a small suburban garden, scavenging through the wreckage of his life, looking for a leftover fragment of purpose …

Forgive me: I over-dramatise – it is a grievous fault – *and grievously hath Caesar answered it'*. But I must be fair: Miss Pargeter did not, after all, hold a dagger to my throat and force me to *'make the beast with two backs'* with her. It was very much a matter of my own free will. I was masterful. I was strong. I recall distinctly that Miss Pargeter was far from disappointed.

I am not writing about Miss Pargeter: I am writing, if anything, to tear my mind away from that woman. I am trying to re-establish my own identity, after Miss Pargeter has ridden roughshod over my most cherished dreams. I am writing – such self-indulgence! – about myself.

But – asks a still, small voice – for whom to read? For no-one but myself. On that point I am quite determined. So I shall indulge myself further by being brutally truthful. It could be something of a relief, after a life spent playing the diplomat.

So. I have seven exercise books, the detritus of my curtailed career. I suppose the brutal truth is that they are stolen property. I have compounded my other supposed misdeeds by committing theft from my erstwhile employer. No matter. I am unrepentant. I glory in it. I shall inscribe each of the stolen books with one of those verses about the magpies. And then we shall see just how brutal the truth can be.

My name is Henry Ernest Barraclough. I am 49 years old, a teacher of English Literature. And I am now unemployed. I accepted what is euphemistically termed 'early retirement', rather than put the good name of my school at risk. That I was entirely blameless in the matter seems of supreme unimportance to all concerned, Miss Pargeter, the Headmaster, everyone.

I call to mind John Henry Newman, a Roman Catholic Cardinal of the Victorian age, who stood at a lectern for up to sixteen hours a day for many weeks, penning his *Apologia Pro Vita Sua*. So, the great man solemnised his own self-justification, his wriggling out of freely-taken, holy vows to the Church of England. I do not presume to come to this table so well informed on the wishes of the Almighty, nor does Western Christendom wait with bated breath for my decision. But at least I do not break my promises.

I am a humble man, meek, out of fashion. I have tried to share my joy in our greatest treasure – our language. I have tried to be kind, understanding, humorous, approachable. Where I have caused pain to others, I have tried to ease it.

But Miss Pargeter's pain would not be assuaged by anything less than human sacrifice – myself, for preference.

Absurdly, I begin to wonder whether teaching was the career I should have chosen. As if any conclusion I might reach at this late juncture could a lost hour recall....

I had a first class degree. Thirty years ago, that meant something. What? It meant I could probably have stayed at university and become a lecturer. I could have made a small but significant segment of study my own... But I did not.

Was I afraid? Did I suspect that my intellect, which had carried me so far, would finally expose its inadequacy at those rarefied levels? I doubt it. I told myself at the time that I'd had enough of educational solitary confinement: I wanted to deal more closely with other human beings, especially those who would shape the future. It seemed a noble and vital responsibility, to nurture the next generation. Or so I persuaded myself at the time.

At College I had friends. They were my contemporaries, kindred spirits, fellow-seekers after truth. They came to tea in my rooms. Fanshawe was in and out all the time, especially when I had purchased one of those excellent coffee and walnut cakes from Fitzbillies'. We toasted crumpets in front of the gas fire, melted a generous quantity of butter all through them and served them with Earl Grey or Darjeeling in a silver pot with Royal Doulton cups and saucers. Even dear Mother would not have been ashamed of the way I kept house there, all spick and span, with a place for everything and everything in its place. So, of course, I had friends, young men like myself...

Well. If I am going to be 'brutally truthful', as promised, I must admit, most of them were not at all like myself. They were gilded youths by comparison. They made me feel like Caliban, a strayed creature from the wrong species, a thing of earth, an impostor. I felt as if they had wafted into Cambridge on pure talent, whereas I had had to read and check and annotate and cogitate and work my way in, perhaps on false pretences. Results showed otherwise: regular alpha minuses proved that I deserved my Exhibition: but still Fanshawe stole the Scholarship – and the glory.

On one occasion, he managed to read Marlowe's Doctor Faustus while returning from a weekend in Oxford on the back of a motor-bike. I was puzzled to find myself so angry about that. I felt it demeaned study to make anything so dashing out of it. What would Marlowe have thought? I realised the creator of mad, despotic Tamburlaine, himself reportedly killed in a tavern brawl, may well have taken Fanshawe's view. Most galling was that he then dashed off a more searching and more polished essay than my own, between breakfast-time and our eleven o'clock supervision.

I learned a very valuable lesson, that day, which I hugged to myself: I learned that I could not achieve everything I desired by hard work alone. No amount of sheer hard work could put a ginger-haired, pasty-faced, nervous, bespectacled, grammar school boy quite on a par with those born with silver spoons in their mouths.

But it might, it just might suffice to snatch the same First Class degree that I knew Fanshawe would collect effortlessly. He would receive the news offhand, with modesty, tossing back his long, brown forelock and running a hand through it to emphasise its casual beauty. He would give a self-deprecating smile and only a slight reddening of his cheeks would show his pleasure…

How well I knew him, or thought I did.

Looking for patterns of error in my life, I observe that I have been too ready to rely on my own assessments of character, too quick to trust. It is ironic, for I have trusted completely only three times in all my years. However well we know our nearest and dearest, they can still surprise us – generally by stabbing us in the heart at some vulnerable moment.

Why can I not banish the image of Miss Pargeter from my mind? I see her now, as first I saw her, sitting on the leather armchair in the Staff Common Room, holding court, surrounded by Blake, Davies and Colonel Pepper. She uncrossed her legs and stood up as they introduced me, and offered a cool thin hand and a shy, fluttering gaze.

'So pleased to meet you, Mister Barraclough,' she said. 'I look forward to learning all I can from you.'

So I can't say she didn't warn me.

For the first year, Miss Pargeter was the very model of an assistant teacher. She coped briskly with the day-to-day business of the department and deferred to me on matters where she felt she lacked experience. At staff meetings, she had few proposals of her own to put forward, but was always generous in her support of others. She became a valued colleague: being a woman had nothing to do with it. Was she plotting my downfall and inveigling her way to power from the very beginning? I will not believe it!

I have snapshots of her in my memory: sitting on the grass at a picnic, that first summer, cheering for our house team on sports day, then utterly engrossed, a few minutes later, speaking with a senior pupil about Jane Austen's use of irony.

It was not until the performance of *The Hollow Crown* in the Autumn Term of her second year, that I began to suspect there was more to Miss Pargeter than met the eye.

I had been in the habit of indulging my long-lost dramatic inclinations by directing the school plays – a major Shakespearean production in the Winter Term, and something lighter in the Autumn. Our canon had included Sheridan, Wilde, Ibsen, Shaw, Osborne and Pinter. We gave two or three performances to appreciative audiences of parents and friends.

Miss Pargeter had bigger ideas. She saw our humble offerings as deserving wider fame. Under the watchword of 'Service to the community' she hired a small theatre for the week, sold nine hundred tickets at £3 apiece and was generally the toast of the staff room. To my displeasure, I was unfortunate enough at the Christmas party to overhear Blake and Davies, the Heads of Science and Geography, if you please, obsequiously praising her entrepreneurial skills.

'All credit to you, Miss Pargeter: a triumph, if I may say so!' offered Blake, pawing vulgarly at her elbow to steady her sherry glass as he refilled it.

'Absolutely' agreed Davies, practically breathing into the same sherry glass, 'Most innovative, taking over the Playhouse like that. I'm surprised no-one in your Department thought of it before.'

How Julian Davies managed to say that with a straight face, I'll never know. At staff meetings, I'd raised the possibility of hiring outside halls. If I raised it once, I raised it a dozen times. Every time, it was shouted down on grounds of cost by those who thought it more important to resurface the tennis courts! Now that Miss Pargeter had suggested it, however, it had acquired the cachet of divine inspiration. All this was galling enough, but there was worse to come …

'The fact is –' Colonel Pepper joined the paeon of praise: 'Frankly, Dramsoc's been crying out for a good kick up the backside for years! Glad you were able to oblige, my dear. No hope of persuading Barraclough to step down altogether, is there?'

This from a man who had personally congratulated me on every play I'd directed for the previous twelve years! They used to be grateful to me for keeping Dramsoc going: now that it was a rip-roaring success, it seemed I could safely be dumped.

'Everyone speaks very highly of Mr Barraclough's Shakespeare!' ventured Miss Pargeter, 'I'm sure he'll have his plans for next term quite advanced already.'

She knew perfectly well. I was doing *Othello*. I'd confided in her over some casting difficulties.

'I'm sure it won't be finalised yet.' Davies, who had never, to my knowledge, attended a Dramsoc meeting, was suddenly an expert on the procedural rules of the school's amateur dramatic society, which I had practically founded, or at least brought back to life after a long period of substandard, slapdash productions. 'They vote on it at the beginning of next term.'

'Why don't you suggest something? Might do Barraclough good to have a break from it – you know, give him time to recharge his batteries – think up a few new ideas.' I rejoiced in the school's good fortune, in having for Head of Science such a discerning theatre critic.

'Splendid idea!' chipped in Pepper, 'The only thing that worries me is how Barraclough would cope with getting the sack. I mean, being a bachelor, you known, with all that free time to fill... Matter of fact, I rather think he enjoys being the centre of attention once a year.' Colonel Pepper's diagnosis, coming as it did from that hotbed of psychoanalytical skill, the British Army, I felt I could safely ignore. Filling my time, indeed! If only he knew the amount of reading matter I had to catch up with at the end of a term!

Miss Pargeter would not allow their fulsome flattery to turn her head:

'You're all very kind, but I must say in all sincerity I wouldn't dream of taking over from Mr Barraclough. He obviously commands the loyalty of the senior boys, and I think it's up to him to decide when to pass on the torch, and to whom. I'm afraid I'm not really in his league at all.'

'You're too modest, Miss Pargeter.'

'I just know my limitations, that's all. But if there was any chance of working with him as an assistant, I'd jump at it.'

There was much harumphing at this from the three balding Heads of Department, but they eventually concluded Miss Pargeter's attitude was very right and proper for newcomer, however comely. I suspect Pepper was wishing he had a daughter like her: the other two were evidently experiencing that rare slavering vibration that passes in school staff rooms for lust.

The conversation had gone much too far for me to break the cover of my cloakroom and excuse myself. I had to stay hidden till they moved on. It gave me time to think out a foolproof strategy: brushing aside the gratuitous insult, I had no objection to lightening my load somewhat, but I did not wish to go to the Dramsoc hustings with Miss Pargeter. *Othello* was well in progress. Recalling Machiavelli, I chose to regain the initiative by inviting Miss Pargeter to assist me with the production.

I attracted her attention, later that evening and made the offer that I thought would please her. But she was strangely quiet. I enquired what was troubling her.

'Oh, nothing, I'm delighted you've asked me. Flattered by your trust. But...' The last word was almost inaudible.

'But, what?' I said, encouragingly. 'If we're going to direct *Othello* together, we must both feel able to speak freely.'

'Well, it's just *Othello* itself, really. I've never been able to believe in it – the wickedness. It's always seemed to me that no-one in real life could be as malevolent as Iago. That's why it's a flawed play.'

'Really, Miss Pargeter? I'm pleased to see you applying such high standards of excellence, in your judgment of our national playwright. If *Othello* is a failure, I'm sure I await with bated breath your notion of a successful play!'

'It's kind of you to ask me. I'll need to think seriously about that, but off the top of my head, I'd say something like *Oh, What A Lovely War* might be within their range.'

'Lovely war? Don't you believe it, my dear.' Colonel Pepper had returned to run a moistened finger round the bowl that had contained Salt and Vinegar flavoured crisps. 'No such thing! It's Hell on earth!'

'It's a musical, Colonel, on a military theme. A sort of light-hearted spoof, you know…'

'Musical, eh? Now, that'd make a change. Nothing against your highbrow stuff, Barraclough, but the rest of us wouldn't mind a few tunes to set our feet tapping. That's on for next term, is it, this 'Lovely War' show?'

'That's up to Mr Barraclough' smiled Miss Pargeter.

I was not outflanked as easily as that. On the first day of the Easter Term, up went a large piece of paper, on the Dramsoc notice-board, inviting volunteers for both *Othello and Oh, What A Lovely War*. I knew my stalwarts would not desert me, and so it proved. Twice as many signed up for auditions for *Othello*, and I made sure Miss Pargeter knew it.

Gracious as ever, she readily conceded the point, but felt it might still be interesting to continue our experiment a little longer. We agreed to hold parallel rehearsals for both plays, to give our budding actors a chance to practice two contrasting styles simultaneously. The decision on which play to perform could, I felt, safely be left until later in the term…

Miss Pargeter suggested holding joint auditions, which was not such a good idea. Several of the actors I had pencilled in for *Othello* mysteriously transferred allegiance, so in the end the two casts were roughly equal in strength and experience.

Rehearsals were difficult. The seething passions of *Othello* were not proof against the gales of noise and laughter coming from Miss Pargeter's production. In the end, I took my group to a classroom, while Miss Pargeter's used the hall. Several more actors changed sides. Then there was the difficulty of building two completely different sets in the Playhouse. So we decided to save *Othello* till the next year. Not that I minded, in the least. As I explained to several colleagues, I was glad of the additional time for writing reports.

*   *   *

Writing. So much of my life has been spent writing. I have left a vast paper trail behind me, from my childish scribblings to this present exercise book, one of seven remaining from what I used to think of as my career. I have measured out my life with scribble on pieces of paper. There was no point to it, none at all: nothing of all that labour will survive me. I can see now, it was all a defence, a retreat from situations I feared. Had I realised that at the time, would I have lived any differently? I doubt it. There are those who are born to action and those born to vacillate. I am one of the latter, as Miss Pargeter was good enough to help me understand.

I blame Mother for my writing habit. I know (since Dorothy made the observation more than once) that I should not blame others for my shortcomings, but it happens in this case to be the truth. Memories of the time when my father was alive are scattered and indistinct.

My earliest memory is probably of myself, aged three, sitting on the ledge of a dresser, watching my father cook bacon and eggs with fried bread. He loved fried bread. Mother was in bed with a cold. And my father was singing: it was part of an oft-repeated story about an Italian chef he had met in the war, but it is the song that I can still conjure up, *La Donna è Mobile*, his favourite snatch of Italian opera.

It would be many years before I learned its meaning in English: 'Woman is a Fickle Thing'. And many more years before I was forced to acknowledge the truth of that sentiment.

My father died of angina, no doubt aggravated by fried bread. He was a good deal older than Mother, and had eaten traditional English breakfasts most mornings of his life, cooked either by his mother or by mine. I hope he enjoyed them. The breakfasts, I mean. I have a shrewd suspicion that he rarely enjoyed the time he spent with the cooks: after all, it was I who inherited their close attentions after his abrupt departure.

They were a formidable legacy, for a five-year-old boy. Grandmother was much concerned with bowel movements and how they could be induced by various herbal or dietary remedies. She preferred to experiment on other people's bowels, her own being rather delicate, after a lifetime's service in the cause of medical science.

Both Mother and Grandmother needed always to have another living creature on which to practise their wiles. It could be a cat, preferably Siamese, which they both loved. For many years, it had been my father: now they focused on me.

Too much attention is as bad for growing boys as too little. Those raised under shelter are not as hardy and robust as the outdoor variety. And so it proved with me. I became bookish.

I learned to escape into the imaginary worlds of stories. It helped me to turn a deaf ear to Mother and Grandmother arguing over whether or not I should spend three days on a diet of senna pods and boiled rice.

I was not allowed library books: Grandmother swore they carried tuberculosis. Instead, I read every book in our tall, mahogany-veneer, glass-fronted bookcase. One, in particular, had a formative influence, a chubby, illustrated, well-thumbed volume called *Dickens' Dream Children*. It consisted of character sketches from the great man's work, collected by his daughter. But it was not so much the individual stories that caught my imagination, as the central thesis of the book. It had never occurred to me before that writers have the privilege of creating their own friends and families, in whatever images they choose. Now, there was a freedom worth aiming for...

But I am no writer: I am a reader. I write lists, that is all – shopping lists, bills to pay, Great Romantic Poets in order of significance. We cannot all be writers: readers are also a vital part of the process. I always took great pride in being a thorough reader: to do otherwise is to fail the writer – or, more likely, to compound the writer's own failure.

*   *   *

'You haven't read all this lot, have you?' Fanshawe gestured grandly towards the book-lined wall of my college sitting-room.

'Of course.' I said with some acerbity.

'Beats me why you want to go filling your head with other people's ideas, like that.'

'We're studying the art of criticism, aren't we?'

'Criticism's not art.' Fanshawe was in one of his Wildean moods, liable to break into aphorisms if not swiftly diverted. 'The proper study of literature is literature!' he declared, grandly.

'Look, you skip the major critics if you like, but see where it gets you. Out on a limb, that's where. Being fanciful.'

'Oh, I fancy I'm not too fanciful. Fanciable, perhaps, in a kind light…'

'Don't kid yourself.' I was in no mood for Fanshawe's public school feyness. 'You've got to read the major critics, to write a decent essay. You need to canvass the current state of informed opinion about a writer before you give your own evaluation.'

'You don't think there's an argument for just presenting your own honest response to the text?'

'Look here, the people marking the Tripos have written most of the books of criticism themselves! It's only common sense to read the damned things. Good manners.'

'Oh, do you think so?' Fanshawe was suddenly more interested. He took a pride in his manners. 'I wouldn't want to insult them. I suppose I'd better skim a few of their ramblings. Which are the least unbearable?'

'I'll draw up a list for you.'

'Would you? That would be awfully kind of you, Henry, if it's not too much trouble?'

'Not at all,' I said 'I've probably got most of them on the shelves, if you want to borrow them.'

'May I? It would save a trip to the library.'

'Would like me to read them for you as well? I could give you a quick précis, to save you the time …'

'Oh, sit the whole blasted exam for me, Henry, if you like! I'll buy you dinner afterwards.' Fanshawe could be devilishly beguiling at times: his zest for life was hard to resist. 'But do tell me, honestly, have you really and truly read all this stuff?'

'Of course. I don't have unlimited funds to spend, so if I'm going to buy an expensive book, I make damned sure I read it. And I don't allow myself to buy too many more until I've read the ones I've got. Simple.'

'Amazing self-discipline. I have masses of books where I liked the cover, hated the first chapter, and never went on with it.'

'Well, you can afford it, can't you?'

'As a matter of fact, I'm not sure that I can.' Fanshawe's finances were a constant source of mystification to him. 'That bank manager keeps on writing me very offensive letters. I said I don't mind paying interest on the money I've overdrawn, but that's not good enough. He wants more.'

'Have you started filling in your cheque stubs yet?'

'Well, not all the time, no...'

'How can you possibly know how much you have left in your account, if you don't keep a record of what you spend?'

'I know. It's very remiss of me. You've pointed it out before. But aesthetically speaking, don't you agree that the moment of unleashing a cheque should be fun? The last thing I want to do is write down the price of something. That would make me unhappy about it, later on.'

'You can't reduce everything in life to fun, Fanshawe. That's not what we're here for.'

'What are we here for, then?'

'I think it's a sort of testing-ground, somewhere to build up our strength and fortitude for a better world.'

'But what if you're wrong, Henry? What if this is all we've got? And you've wasted it?'

'I don't believe this is all we've got. There must be a purpose behind it all, a pattern – something eternal, that we're all too involved with our daily lives to appreciate.'

'So you're giving up all hope of jam today for the faint prospect of jam tomorrow, are you? Putting all your eggs in the basket of the afterlife, so to speak.'

'I believe there is some sort of existence that continues after death, yes. And I acknowledge Jesus Christ as my personal Saviour.'

'What on earth does that mean?'

'It means that Christ made the one supreme sacrifice of his own life, so that everyone else should live. He paid in advance for all our sins.'

'Very decent of him, I'm sure. So this means we're all excused going to Hell, does it?'

'Well I wouldn't put it quite like that, but you get the gist.'

'I think I found Christianity more satisfying when you still believed in the Devil. He's the ultimate villain, isn't he? Spices the story up a bit.'

'We still do have the Devil. It's just that congregations seem to prefer the carrot to the stick, these days.'

'But the Devil's definitely still around, is he?' Fanshawe seemed genuinely pleased. 'Do you think he'd consider buying my soul from me? I'd certainly be in the market for that. At the right price, of course.'

'I'm sure you find all this very amusing, Fanshawe, but to me it's no laughing matter. It may be dangerous to speak like this.'

'You can't be serious! Tell you what, Henry,' Fanshawe suddenly seized his gown and briefcase from where he'd dropped them and moved towards the door, 'If I ever do succeed in selling my soul to Lucifer, I promise you'll be the first to know! You can arrange my last-minute repentance…' And he was gone, in a flurry of black cloth and a welter of cake crumbs. 'Thanks for the tea!' came echoing down the corridor.

I laughed and shook my head and started to mop up some tea he had spilled by trailing his gown. Life with Fanshawe around was never dull. And there were still forty-five minutes for reading the Elizabethan essayists (that week's essay topic) before I had to change for dinner.

Then it would be coffee and a glass of port in a friend's rooms, more lively discussions, probably of literature, which was our passion, and then across the court to the Chapel for the short service of Compline at 9.30. Finally, if I could avoid the Chaplain's Madeira, a further hour in bed with the Elizabethan essayists. Truly, an idyllic life, as we realized at the time. A privileged life, when thousands were beginning to die in Vietnam.

When pupils ask me about Vietnam, I always feel like those people who lived through the nineteen-thirties in Germany:

'Of course, we saw what was going on, but we were powerless to do anything about it. We just went on with our lives. We obeyed orders.'

So we went punting on the river, ran up huge bills each term for wine from the college Buttery, listened to music and discussed romantic poetry. While our contemporaries in the leading nation of the democratic world threw away their lives – and with them, the last vestiges of any moral advantage that the Western powers may have gained by the sacrifices of two World Wars.

It was television that finally brought the Vietnam conflict to an end. It transpired that the American public did not like napalm in their living-rooms any more than the Vietnamese did. We were too busy to watch television. We were on our own front line, adjudicating between Keats and Shelley, between D H Lawrence and George Eliot. We were assessing TS Eliot's impact on the whole of twentieth century literature. We had the enthusiasm of fans at the football stadium. We had come to man's estate and were rather enjoying it. We should have looked more closely at the story of the Garden of Eden.

*   *   *

As far as I could see, Mother never really needed a replacement for my father. Given the choice, as she was, she preferred being a mother to being a wife.

I stood at her side as they lowered my father's coffin into the gash in the damp earth. I looked at her face and saw fear – not the true and certain knowledge of the life to come that we had been murmuring 'Amen' to, a few seconds earlier – but fear of the future and the pain of a loss that feels as if it will never end.

I feared death myself, then, since it had made my beautiful mother's face crumple in such utter hopelessness. And I went on fearing death for many years: it cast a long shadow. Since death was so monstrous, I concluded that life should be lived timidly, with circumspection. I have lived my youth and most of my maturity by that precept – and I am beginning to realise what a fool I have been.

'You're the man in the house, now, Henry.' said Mother, placidly, after the last funeral guest had left. 'I hope you're going to look after me.'

'How do you mean?'

'Oh, there are all sorts of man's jobs you'll be able to help me with – making sure there's enough coal for the fire, cleaning your shoes, switching off the lights when we're not using them…'

'Did Pa do all those things for you?'

'Sometimes. When he remembered. He took good care of us, Henry, we'll – we'll miss him so much.' And she cried again. She cried about every half hour, on the day of the funeral. It was as if she was washing out all the pain. And of course, I couldn't help joining in.

'Why can't he come back?' I blubbed for the umpteenth time.

'He can't, darling. He's gone to be with Jesus, now.'

'What about us? Doesn't he love us any more?'

'He loves you very much, Henry, he always loved you – he was so pleased and proud, the day you were born …'

'So why has he gone away?'

'He didn't want to go, he wanted to stay here, with us, and watch you grow up. But God wanted him. God called him. God made us all, you see. He calls us to Him when He needs us.'

'When will He need you?'

'Not for a long time, yet, I'm sure. I've got a very important job to do, here on Earth. I've got to bring you up to be a man, just the same as if your father hadn't – left us like that.'

'I thought I was going to do the jobs?'

'We'll do them between us, shall we? I'll look after you and you'll look after me, all right?'

'I'll always look after you, Mummy' I said solemnly, and knelt on the settee and put my arms around her neck. 'I will.'

I have always kept my promises. I still do, whatever the cost.

And we did comfort each other, as we both in our own ways worked out how to live in a world that no longer revolved around my father.

Mother celebrated him, created little pictorial shrines to him all over the house. Little by little, she changed him into the man she would have liked him to be. He developed strong opinions on the garden, on what flowers and shrubs should go into which beds. Debates on such matters were still finalised, years later, by a quiet affirmation:

'I'm sure that's what Pa wants.' Wants. Not 'would have liked'. Wants. Because he was still there, for both of us. Our images of him came to differ, but he was still a presence in the house, wrapped up with our lives like hot fish and chips in damp newspaper, the final authority on every important decision we took.

For my mother, he disagreed with her much less frequently and became more docile. For a few years, she let him spoil the happiest moments, because she always felt his absence most acutely when there was some family success to celebrate. I remember how she ruined my euphoria, that mid-December night, when the postman brought, with a bundle of Christmas cards, a letter from the College offering me my Exhibition.

Mother fled to the bedroom in tears. I followed, not sensing her mood, for once. I was mentally dividing the princely sum of £40 a year into three terms and then multiplying it by three years. She knew she was being completely illogical. She was begging God to take her own life and give back my father's. She said it seemed to unjust that my father's dream for me should be realised without him being allowed to see it.

I suggested that possibly he could see it, a thought which was generally a comfort to her, but on this occasion she was not to be consoled.

'It's not enough! Don't you understand? I want him here. I want him with me, to share this. It's wonderful news for you. It means you've survived – you've escaped. But for your father, well, it means you can do all the things he wanted to do and wasn't given time to complete.'

The effect of this burden of responsibility was immediate. My shoulders sagged, and with them my spirits. There was no real escape from grief and obligation, even at our moments of greatest joy.

I calmed Mother down with a cup of tea and the *Radio Time*s, and went out carol-singing with a group of people from the Church. Two hours later, frozen to the marrow, in the middle of the fifth verse of *Good King Wenceslas*, I suddenly remembered:

'I'm going to Cambridge!'

I threw my arms around the girl next to me and kissed her. She was very surprised. I suspect she had not been kissed very many times before, especially by virtual strangers without any preamble. So I had to explain why I was so uncharacteristically euphoric: her attitude underwent a subtle alteration. She said she'd never been kissed by a Cambridge undergraduate. I gathered she wouldn't mind being kissed by one again.

But by this time, as we walked to the next house, I had looked at the girl more closely, in the light of a streetlamp. There was something – was it her skin, or her nose, or perhaps greasy hair – I can't quite remember. I know it was enough to deter me from telephoning her, as she'd suggested.

I spent the rest of the Christmas holidays trying to avoid her, out of embarrassment. It was the only time in my life that I ever kissed a complete stranger, on impulse.

She cornered me on New Year's Eve.

'Hello, Henry! It'll be midnight in twenty minutes.'

'Yes? Another year, eh? All the best for it, then.'

'You expecting any more of your romantic impulses, round about midnight?' she enquired.

'I shouldn't think so, Susannah. You'll be quite safe.'

'So I should hope! After the way you behaved at the carol-singing. I didn't know what to think.'

'Sorry, Susannah. Put it down to youthful exuberance, eh?'

'Oh, for Heaven's sake, relax, Henry. I enjoyed it. Only you can't just take what you want from a girl and then leave her, you know. Didn't your mother teach you anything? For us to be at kissing stage, you're supposed to have taken me out. Wined and dined me. Otherwise it's not proper.'

'You'll be lucky. I can't go wining and dining. I'm still at school.'

'I thought you said you were going to get a job, till you go up to Cambridge.'

'So I am. I start next week – teaching assistant at the King's School. Until then, the most lavish entertainment I can afford is a cheap seat at the cinema.'

'Oh, all right, then. So long as I can chose which film we see.'

'What's that?'

'The cinema. Any day next week will be fine.'

And suddenly she was snuggling close to me. I felt a well filled polo neck sweater pressing against my sports jacket. I could smell some scent on her, a little flowery, but not unpleasant. I slipped my arms around her and felt her hair in my face. What with Cambridge and Susannah, it really did feel like Christmas. Whatever it was that had upset me about her appearance earlier was more than compensated for by the very surprising fact that she seemed to enjoy my company.

It was one of the happiest winters of my life. Susannah was still at school, so we were only allowed to meet at weekends. We were both interested in church architecture - well, I was interested and Susannah became interested – and we used to go on bicycle rides to some of the finest churches in the area.

Usually it rained. Which gave us ample opportunity to grapple beneath the shelter of a large umbrella left over from my father's time.

I often wondered what he would have said about Susannah.

'La Donna è Mobile!' I imagine.

I enjoyed the grappling, once I was used to the intimacy of it. I mean, I would have looked askance at taking a bite from an apple after someone else. The vigorous sharing of saliva that was unavoidable in the sort of 'snogging' sessions we had would have appalled me in any other circumstances, but came to seem quite normal, even highly pleasurable.

Some parts of our bodies fared better than others, under the rules of combat formulated by Susannah's group of friends at school. Not just for us, although I blush to think now how Susannah must have regaled them with every detail of our halting courtship. When she thought she could trust me, she told me they had discussed at length 'how far one should go'.

A girl in the Lower Sixth had become pregnant and left the school, so the subject was particularly topical. According to the educational tenets of the day, the girls were left to work out for themselves how and why this tragedy had occurred. Any literature on the subject was confiscated as soon as it was discovered. Susannah's friends had decided that the procreative urge was more easily avoided when standing up than sitting down – and they may have been right. They were also suspicious of pelvic thrust: it was said that things could get out of hand that way. So while our mouths aped every conceivable form of copulation as we stood and embraced, she was always slightly wary of a full confrontation below the waist. This could be quite frustrating.

One day in the Easter holidays, we were alone in her parents' kitchen. Emboldened by the unwonted privacy and warmth, I held Susannah against a dresser and pressed more intrusively with my thigh against her crotch. She wriggled away at first, but then relaxed. Soon, she was matching the gently rhythmic pressure from my hips, kissing me with a new urgency and clinging tightly to me.

I responded without thinking. We caught our breath and our bodies instinctively settled into a position of maximum arousal. I found I could stroke one of her breasts with my fingertips. She started to tremble. I ventured to put my hand under her skirt and, instead of pressing my thigh against her, I started to touch and stroke her, between her legs. Our eyes met for a moment: hers seemed to be hardly focusing. She gave a long, soft moan. I tried to make out what she was saying, but I could not.

She unzipped my trousers and slipped her hand inside. I felt her cool fingers press on my erection. I gave myself up to the sublime sensation. I felt I was on fire, bursting with longing for her. I went on stroking her and she responded. She opened her mouth, breathing faster, closed her eyes. I wondered if we should pause, for a moment: this was way beyond anything we had done before. I relaxed my hand and started to move it away. Still breathing hard, she said 'Don't stop!' So, naturally, I continued. And so did she, rocking back and forth, taking longer breaths at last, sighing. And then I, too, was swept away by several powerful convulsions that overwhelmed me and blotted out all other thoughts and sensations.

Neither of us really understood what was happening. We had both, I presume, experimented with masturbation, but we would have been far too embarrassed to discuss it. Our bodies simply took over where our minds lacked the knowledge they needed. For myself, I was still separated from her by several layers of somewhat sticky clothing, but I had experienced the most blissful sensation, that I found indescribably delightful. Slightly red in the face and dishevelled, she looked at me, smiled and kissed me, very slowly and sweetly, for some time.

In the brief period of post-coital calm, we had no time to discuss what had transpired between us, because her mother arrived home, also prematurely. We heard her footsteps, outside the back door and disentangled ourselves. I went quickly to help with the shopping bags and hoped her mother would not remark on our suspiciously flushed faces.

The next time we saw each other, she was completely different. I put my arms around her and gave her an affectionate squeeze, to renew our intimacy, but she just glared at me.

'Henry, if you're going to behave like that every time we meet, we'll have to stop seeing each other.'

'I thought you enjoyed us being together. I certainly do.'

'Yes, but there are limits. I don't like it when you paw at me like that.'

'Sorry. I won't to do it, then.'

It seemed the committee of Susannah's friends had ruled against our harmless little pleasure. And I was to be given a free transfer at the earliest opportunity, Cambridge or no Cambridge.

I was still positive she would over-rule her friends. If she had felt anything remotely similar to the sensations I had felt, I thought she would be bound to acknowledge it. While we had been apart, I had allowed myself all sorts of self-indulgent fantasies featuring week-ends in country cottages with large, comfortable beds and crisp white sheets. Susannah, it seemed, had been thinking along quite different lines.

Her conclusion was that we were 'beginning to grow out of each other' and should give each other the chance to develop new friend-ships. This act of generosity apparently involved ditching any old friendships.

I was very hurt: 'I don't know why you're doing this. I so wanted to talk to you about – about what happened last time.'

'Well, that's the last thing I want to talk about, thank you very much. I'm trying to forget about that. And I don't want you going round telling all your friends about me, either. I'm not that sort of girl.'

I did not know what to say. I had been rehearsing various ways of trying to thank her for the astonishing gift she had given me, but none of the fine phrases now meant anything. I was bereft. I had virtually made love with this woman. I had discovered in myself an unsuspected ability to respond to another person, a precious escape from the loneliness I had always accepted, even at school, as my destiny.

And now, before we could even begin to explore these precious, new feelings, she was pulling away from me.

I had never been very free with my emotions, at least since my father died – but that day, something vital just seemed to shrivel up, deep inside me. At College, I affected a dry, sceptical approach to emotional matters. It was part of the legacy Susannah left me, when she trod on my dreams.

*   *   *

So, when Dorothy Pargeter came into my life, I should have known what to expect. But for all my book-learning, I am surprisingly slow on the uptake when it comes to dealing with real, live, unpredictable human beings. Give me the Dream Children of fiction any day, preferably someone else's – they tend to be less trouble.

I like to keep the books I have read where I can find them, standing neatly on their shelves, in alphabetical order. Sometimes it is useful to be able to check a reference. I have never been a very enthusiastic lender or borrower of books. I am not mean, but my library is an extension of my intellectual work: I need to keep it complete and in good, working order. Dorothy could not see this at all.

'It's just a book, Henry! There's no need to make such a fuss about it. I don't know whether I left it on a bus or a train or in a public toilet somewhere. I'll buy you another one, if it's so important to you.'

'You can't buy another one,' I pointed out, 'Not like that. It was part of a set. They've been out of print for years.'

'Well, what do you want me to do – go traipsing around second-hand bookshops, searching for an antique of the right vintage?'

'Look, forget about it. It doesn't matter. I'll replace it myself.'

'Don't go all sniffy on me. I've said I'm sorry. I didn't mean to lose it, and I'll get you another one. I'd better get a copy for myself as well, so I can finish it without leaving an ugly gap in your immaculate library.'

'I'm sorry, my dear.' I reached across the kitchen table and took her hand. 'I'm not very good at sharing, I'm afraid. Too used to having my own way, all the time. But I am trying.'

In an unguarded moment, I had lent her my copy of Hermann Hesse's *Journey to the East*. I thought she would enjoy it – which she did: I thought she would look after it – but there I was mistaken. It is the story of a fellowship of spiritual pilgrims. They are scattered in space and time, but united in their common desire to uncover the spiritual wisdom of Eastern religions – and in their belief in the commonality of all faiths. I suppose I really wanted to probe Dorothy's agnosticism. I joked that I could not bring myself to believe in it.

We had been seeing each other regularly, out of school hours, unbeknown to the rest of the staff, who would have made our association impossible. It was quite out of character for me: the whole affair took me completely by surprise. But after a few weeks, we had established a routine. I loved our long Sundays together: I have never felt so alive.

I wondered where this particular balmy Sunday had gone wrong. I went to embrace her but she pulled away and marched up and down in front of the bookcases, with her arms folded.

'Did you manage to read any of it, before you …'

'Yes, of course I did. More than half. I loved it.'

'Well, that's the main thing…'

She was perversely determined to find fault with me that day, so she continued trying to justify her own carelessness:

'Books aren't doing anything when they're stuck in book-cases.' she insisted. 'They may as well not exist. Books are meant to be read, not admired, like wallpaper. You ought to be pleased that we've liberated that book: we've set it free, to carry its message to someone else.'

'Very community-mined, I'm sure.' I observed drily. 'You make it sound more like a pet budgerigar than a book.'

'Especially when you remember what it's about!' she was quite animated now: her eyes sparkled. 'Maybe I was meant to leave it on the train, so that whoever finds it learns about the League of Travellers to the East. Don't you see? This is how ideas are shared: it's a way of winning converts. I'd have thought you'd approve. It's quite mystical, when you think about it like that. I'm rather glad I lost it now.'

'Remind me to lend you some more of my books to lose. You could open a sort of literary soup kitchen, supplying reading matter to the needy.'

'Well, it's funny you should say that, but that's virtually what Hesse himself did, in the First World War.'

'He was a pacifist, wasn't he?' I half-remembered some story.

'Yes, but when they accused him of cowardice, he spent a lot of time providing books for German prisoners-of-war, all over Europe. He started a publishing company to run it. He adapted the classics, wrote original stories of his own, commissioned works from other writers, and even printed the books himself, sometimes.' Her eyes were bright.

'Good for him.' Curmudgeonly, I refused to give an inch.

'He was a man of action, you see. When the times required it, he got off his backside and contributed something that didn't hurt anybody, but probably gave comfort to thousands of homesick German prisoners of war.'

'Very commendable.' I smiled indulgently, taking care not to let slip that I was already aware of much of what she was telling me.

'Well, there's no need to look so smug! I suppose you're thinking that's just the sort of plan you'd have worked out, if you'd been in his position. But you wouldn't! Don't you see? Oh, you might have had the idea, you might have told one or two colleagues about it, over a glass of port, but you, Henry Barraclough, would never have organised a scheme like that in a month of Sundays! No matter how tidy you manage to keep your bloody bookcases!'

'My dear Dorothy, I made no such claim. And I can't imagine why you're getting into such a state. If you're still feeling guilty about losing my book, please don't. It really doesn't matter in the least.'

'So you say. But it does matter, to you. We both know that, so why pretend? You've got to acknowledge your emotions. It's not healthy, internalising your anger like this.'

'I am not internalising my anger. I was mildly annoyed at losing something irreplaceable – I'm very attached to my books, as you know. But if it's gone, it's gone. I don't say that a phone call in the morning to the railway station and the bus company might not pay dividends, but I'm reconciled to the loss. I'm much more concerned about your state of mind.'

'Look, if I'd wanted a confessional, I'd have gone to a priest. You're supposed to be my lover. Why don't you do something about it?'

'Gladly.' I went to sit beside her on the couch and put my arm around her shoulders.

She shook her head. 'No, don't. Leave me alone. I'm not in the mood.'

'Do you think you might be in the mood tonight? I've bought some steak and a bottle of red wine, You could make your Bearnaise Sauce ...'

'I'm afraid I can't, tonight. I'm having a drink with an old friend.'

'Oh, yes?'

'Stephen Green, the Head of History at Hampton. I told you about him. He's over for the interviews for Deputy Head, tomorrow.'

'Really?' I risked another smile, trying not to look smug. 'Well, may the best man win!'

I suppose I was sincere. I had no doubt about who was the best man for that particular job, and I fully expected to get it. The Head had told me unofficially that the interviews were practically a formality: the Governors were very impressed with my record at the school, particularly my Oxbridge entries and scholarships, and they felt I deserved some recognition.

'Your interview was on Friday, wasn't it? How did it go?'

'Very well. The Head played it straight down the line. He said I was obviously a strong contender, but they were going to appoint on merit: if by any chance I wasn't offered it, they hoped I'd take it as no reflection on my abilities, and continue as Head of English and Housemaster.'

'That's fair enough, I suppose. Stephen's just doing it for the experience. He'll get a Deputy Headship somewhere, soon. I don't know that he'd even accept this one, if it was offered'

'Why would he turn it down?'

'He's very ambitious. He's not going to agree to come into a school in a senior position, unless he can have full authority to make what changes he see fit. He's a mover and shaker, Stephen. He's no Headmaster's dogsbody!'

'I don't think that attitude will get him very far…'

'You don't know Stephen.'

'No. And you do. Where are you taking him for a drink?'

'Oh, wherever he wants. Stephen always has very strong ideas on where to go. You should meet him: he's a very lively character, like a great bear – and very good company. You'd like him.'

'I'm sure I would, but I'll have to forego that pleasure for tonight. Rather a lot of books to mark.'

Why did I not go, when she asked me? Would it have made any difference? Was there anything I could have said or done at that stage to alter the eventual outcome? I do not allow myself to believe it, feeling that way madness lies, but late at night, I sometimes catch myself recreating the situation, like some old General reviewing his campaigns, and trying to find some way of swinging the balance of power my way. And I cannot help wishing with all my feeble heart that I had been man enough to stand up and fight for what I wanted. On that and other occasions.

By nature, I am a watcher. I like to polish my spectacles – it is no joke – I really do insist on being able to see as clearly as possible. I have suffered from poor eyesight since I was very small, aggravated by copious amounts of late-night reading – a habit even more likely to cause premature blindness than other, more lurid bed-time diversions.

As a child, wearing spectacles was a two-edged sword. On the one hand, it made me look rather more intelligent than I was – and it excused me from all the pointless forms of ball-chasing so beloved of most small boys. On the other hand, it marked me as a potential victim and there were plenty of boys at my school ready to do the victimising. Until Cambridge, I always had a faint suspicion that my immediate circle regarded me rather as a figure of fun. Long afterwards, I still caught the occasional whiff of sniggering conspiracy in the staff room: whenever it happened, I made a point of polishing my glasses as if I had not heard – the very picture of unconcern.

*   *   *

'Men seldom make passes at girls who wear glasses!'

'Don't you believe it,' I replied, 'glasses can be removed! What other Dorothy Parker do you know?'

'Oh, none. I always stopped at that one. I found it so depressing.' The speaker was Celia Daniels, a pretty, bespectacled brunette I had met at the library just after I became Head of the English Department. I had to sit forward a little, to hear her, as the train went into a long tunnel. We were on the way 'home' to Mother's house, for half-term. Mother and Celia had not yet met, so the atmosphere was a little tense.

'Do you think your mother will put us in separate beds?'

'I'm sure she will. Sorry.'

'It's all right. I understand. I'd probably do exactly the same, in her position. I hope she likes me.'

'Bound to. She's always had excellent taste.'

'Henry! Be serious!'

'I don't feel like being serious. I get enough of that at work. I feel frivolous. I feel happy.'

'Is that so unusual?'

'Not since I met you.'

She blushed and squeezed my hand. I looked at her downcast eyes and felt as if I had come home from a long journey.

She looked out of the window at the English countryside streaming past, vaporised slightly by the heat haze of the train. 'I hope...' she said slowly and then stopped.

'Go on. I want to know your hopes.'

'It's not really a hope, it's a fear. And a hope.'

'Tell me.'

She looked around the carriage, making sure no-one was tuning in to our conversation. 'I hope it stays like this. I hope you don't ever – take me for granted. Get bored with me. Lose respect for me.'

I took her hands in mine. 'I can't imagine doing that. Ever. I waited so long for you. I thought you'd never come into my life. I'm not going to lose you now.'

She smiled a little smile and rested her head on my chest. I saw a little farm go by outside the window. The farmer was leading in some cows as his wife drove up in a battered station wagon and got out with two children in school uniform.

I looked down at Celia, pressing her face into my neck. Suddenly, I could see myself through the eyes of someone across the carriage. I saw a tall, lean, bespectacled man in his late thirties, pale and a little prematurely stooped, perhaps, but otherwise sound, with an attractive woman caressing him. A pair of lovers, undoubtedly. Not Romeo and Juliet. Nor yet quite Antony and Cleopatra. More real, more ordinary. With a better chance of surviving life's buffeting. I had always seen myself in the mirror of TS Eliot's *Love Song of J Alfred Prufrock*:

> *'No! I am not Prince Hamlet, nor was meant to be;*
> *Am an attendant lord, one that will do*
> *To swell a progress, start a scene or two,*
> *Advise the prince: no doubt, an easy tool,*
> *Deferential, glad to be of use,*
> *Politic, cautious, and meticulous:*
> *Full of high sentence, but a bit obtuse:*
> *At times, indeed, almost ridiculous –*
> *Almost, at times, the Fool.'*

Now, I saw a different scenario. Why should the mermaids not sing to me? I had made my own isolation, and made it well. I had papered over all the cracks with loaded bookshelves. I had hidden myself away, reading, pretending to be happy. But now this girl Celia had broken through the shell and found the raw human being inside, shivering for lack of warmth. I put my arms around her, but it was she who warmed me, from her plenty.

Mother was at the station to meet us. All through that weekend, she never insulted Celia. Far from it. If she had been rude, I should have been down on her like a ton of bricks. She insisted on calling Celia 'Miss Daniels', despite several requests to be less formal.

'No, no, bless you, my dear: I belong to the old school. It's much too late in the day for me to change my ways.'

'Mother! You're making yourself sound about ninety!'

She gave a pained, slightly distant look.

'Don't worry, Henry. I don't expect I'll be in your way for that long.'

'You're not in my way. I like you being in my way. I mean...'

'I'm sure you know Henry's very fond of you, Mrs Barraclough. He talks about you all the time.'

'Does he, indeed? Well, I'm glad I'm not a fly on the wall to overhear you discussing me.'

'We don't discuss you..' I broke in.

'Miss Daniels just said you did.'

There are some people who can always wrongfoot you in a debate. Parents in particular. They wipe your bottom and hold it against you for the rest of your life. Metaphorically speaking. They have an unfair advantage: they knew you before you clothed yourself in your adult personality and went to meet the world. Mother was invariably right.

'Do look it up in the Shorter Oxford, Miss Daniels. I'm sure you'll find it's M.I.L.L.E.P.E.D.E. – with an E in the middle, rather than an I.'

Celia had converted my inglorious D.E. into a triumphant Treble word score with a bonus for using all her letters, by playing in order: M, blank tile, L, L, I, P, and E.

'Three for the M, four, five, six, two doubled for the P makes ten, eleven, thirteen, fourteen, - multiplied by three, makes forty-two, and fifty for the bonus – ninety-two, please, Mrs Barraclough.' Celia had been keen to prove her mettle at this game and she was understandably delighted with the move she had made.

Mother left the scorepad where it was and looked at the board more in sorrow than in anger. She tutted quietly to herself and then delivered her bombshell.

'It's the same as millimetre and millilitre, isn't it?' Celia chattered away happily as she flicked through to the appropriated page in the Marl-Z volume of the Shorter Oxford. Her face fell when she found it.

'I don't believe it! You're right, Mrs Barraclough. It is "E". "I" is not an acceptable alternative. It's millepede.'

'Of course, if you want to look in one of the new-fangled dictionaries, you may find they allow it.' Mother was ever-gracious in victory.

'No, no, I wouldn't dream of it. If this is the dictionary you use for the game, its decision is final.' Celia was observing the English tradition of stiff upper lip in face of adversity, while seething privately. I judged it was high time for me to pour oil on troubled waters and resolve the problem.

'Why don't you swap the blank for the "I" in the middle?' I suggested, 'Your score will be just the same.'

Oh, no, Henry, that's not the move I played.' said Celia, rather thin-lipped, removing all of her tiles, 'What would your mother think of me, if I allowed you to cheat for me?'

'Come on, darling, it's only a friendly game. Mother won't mind at all, will you, Mother?'

The 'darling' was very experimental and rather daring. I'd been extremely annoyed with my mother for refusing to acknowledge Celia's Christian name, and I was looking for a way of emphasising our intimacy. I had the satisfaction of seeing Mother give a little start at the word.

'Please accept the score, Miss Daniels,' said Mother, with her biro poised inquisitively over the score-pad, 'You'll spoil our evening.'

'No, thank you, really.' Celia shook her head impatiently. She put down an inconsequential, three-letter word, worth about six points, and began to study the paintings with a new-found interest.

Mother wrote down Celia's score and put down the biro with an almost imperceptible shrug. 'Your turn, then, Henry, dear.'

I studied the letters in front of me and could make no sense of them. From the corners of my eyes, I could see Celia looking frosty and my mother with the merest hint of a smile and a shrug, for all the world like a detective whose entirely reasonable suspicions have just been proved conclusively. We did not play Scrabble again.

Sunday evening was the culmination of the weekend's quiet, understated, bourgeois hostilities. War had been declared over my live body. Yet a casual observer would have detected nothing amiss. Condiments and gravy were passed when requested. Small talk was minimal: neither combatant was interested in sniping or small arms fire. We had been to the old parish church for the morning service: by chance, it had been Mother's turn to do the flowers.

'I did so love your flower arrangements, Mrs Barraclough,' Celia said, sweetly.

'Thank you, Miss Daniels,' returned Mother, fearing heavy artillery on the horizon.

'One so rarely sees that style, these days. It's quite an art.'

'It's nothing special, I know. But I like to do my bit for the community.' ventured Mother from the depths of her bunker.

'Of course you do.' Celia could not have been more patronising if she had been the hostess and my mother the guest. 'I think you're wonderful for your – wonderful, really!'

I waited with interest to see if the reinforced concrete had sustained any damage.

'Do you attend your own church very often, Miss Daniels?' This, I knew, was more than a sighting shot from Mother.

'Not every Sunday, but I do go quite regularly.'

'I though you picked up our hymns very quickly.'

'Well, thank you, but I had sung most of them before.'

'Really? I thought you had quite a different set of hymns.'

'No, not at all.'

There was a silence then, presided over by Mother, as it had been her turn to speak. We all crunched thoughtfully on pork crackling while Celia checked for damage, thinking the bombardment had been surprisingly light. That particular time-bomb had not been meant for her, at all: the explosion came later, when I had persuaded Celia to go for a stroll in the garden while Mother and I did the washing up together. She made me dry the dishes, which she knew I hated.

'What was all that about Celia not knowing the hymns?' I blundered into the ambush.

'She does know them. She said so: she's heard them in the synagogue.'

'What are you talking about? – Synagogue!'

'Any children, you know – they'd have to follow her faith: it goes down the female line.'

'Mother! Celia isn't Jewish.'

'With a name like Daniels?'

'You can't just go by that.'

'I wonder when they converted.'

'It wouldn't matter, even if she was!'

'What does her father do?'

'He's a businessman.'

'There you are, then.' As if that clinched it. I decided to attack on grounds less likely to make me angry with her.

'Is that why you keep calling her Miss Daniels? It's very rude, when someone's asked you to use their Christian name.'

Mother sniffed. She had a very expressive sniff.

'I once heard Lord Hailsham on the radio,' I said, pressing home what I thought was my advantage, 'He was quite angry, telling off some interviewer for exactly that. The interviewer was obviously nervous and had been stumbling over "My Lord" and "Your Lordship" and "Lord Chancellor". 'Do call me Quintin' he said, 'It's my Christian name, it's the name I like to be called by fellow Christians."

'Christians, yes.'

'Don't start that again, please.'

'There's no fool like an old fool, is there?'

'Oh, look, what on earth's wrong with you? Most mothers would be delighted if their 38-year-old bachelor son came home in love with someone. Especially if she was bright, intelligent, charming, attractive… More than anything, she's such good company.'

'Oh, I noticed, playing Scrabble.'

'I just feel so much happier when I'm with her.'

'Then there's no more to say, is there? You didn't come looking for my approval. You came to gloat.'

'That's ridiculous! I came to introduce you to the woman I'm going to live with.'

There was a long silence. Mother looked at me and I avoided her gaze. 'You mean without benefit of clergy? In sin?'

'That's what it used to be called. Nowadays, it's something most young people do, for a while, before they get married. It's sensible.'

'It's a sin. Sin doesn't change with the fashion.'

I gave up then. I knew when Mother was immovable.

I went out to see Celia and tried to rekindle the childish joy we'd felt on the train. But she felt I hadn't supported her when she needed it. Of course, she still loved me. She just didn't like the hen-pecked person I became when my mother was around. Given that the spacious garden flat we were intending to share was a hundred miles away from Mother's semi-detached, the problem did not seem insoluble.

The following Wednesday, Mother was taken into hospital with acute appendicitis. To convalesce, naturally, she came to me. And stayed. And stayed. And stayed. Celia never moved in. Shortly afterwards, she became engaged to a rising young salesman in her father's company. Mother acted as if she had been proved right all along.

Name: *Henry Bee*

Form: *-ula*

Book 2 : For Joy

Effingham School
Effingham, Glos.

Joy! What have I to do with joy? I am a desert man, dry, dusty and disappointed. I am beginning to think I was wrong to label these exercise books with the old rhyme of the magpies: I may as well have named them after the days of the week, or the first seven months of the year, or the colours of the rainbow, or just numbered them from one to seven. It has no significance, other than to set a limit on my self-indulgence. When these seven books are filled with my ramblings, I shall make an end of it. But I shall fill them first. I take some pride in completing my allotted tasks.

I must not be so hard on myself, I hear Mother admonishing me. For I have felt joy – real joy – and I suppose that is one of the purposes of living. Joy is not happiness or pleasure, but something deeper, more exquisite. At times, even divine. Where have I encountered joy? – In the theatre, on rare and precious occasions. While walking alone in the Lake District. Sometimes in church – and of course when making love. Is that truly joy – I mean spiritually uplifting – or merely pleasure? At the time, it seems like joy, but then, recollecting the experience in tranquility, one wonders.

I may as well admit that I have made a rod for my own back. One of the purposes of starting to fill these leftover exercise books was to banish all painful thoughts of Miss Pargeter from my mind. But if I am to write about joy, and adhere to the standards of 'brutal truth' that I have set myself, then I must confess that before she destroyed me, Dorothy Pargeter led me to the very altar of joy and taught me its taste.

Her production of *Oh, What A Lovely War* was, of course, a great success, even with Colonel Pepper, who affected not to notice the anti-militarist stance of the piece. I would rather have had nothing whatsoever to do with it, but Miss Pargeter prevailed upon me, as President of Dramsoc, to attend the final performance and make some presentations. Imagine my surprise, then, when I took my place in front of the curtain, to find Miss Pargeter standing beside me. Before I could order my notes, she began to address the audience:

'Headmaster, Ladies and Gentlemen – I'm sure most of you know, Henry Barraclough has been an absolute tower of strength for the school's amateur dramatic society for more years than most of us care to remember. It's very largely thanks to him that I, in my first Main production, found such a wealth of talent to draw on. As a small token of our appreciation, we'd like to present him with this first illustrated edition of one of his favourite plays, *The Importance of Being Earnest.*'

I was almost speechless, an unusual predicament for me. I said as much to the audience, who were kind enough to laugh, while I recovered my wits and set about restoring order. The gift was a treasure, which still takes price of place in my bookcase. But when I think back to that occasion, less than twelve months distant as I write, the predominant impression is of the heady waft of Miss Pargeter's perfume as she embraced me on the stage.

It was the last thing I expected to happen. I had come, ready to find fault with her production. The loss of *Othello* still rankled. I was not prepared for so beguiling an olive branch. Naturally, I remained for the celebrations. Because of the presentation, I sensed, absurdly, that I somehow shared in Miss Pargeter's glory. Every man is supposed to have his price, and Miss Pargeter had found mine, with unerring aim. Colonel Pepper was at my elbow, pouring me a second generous measure of whisky before I could protest.

'Damn good show, eh, Barraclough? I like a good comedy!'

'Really, Colonel? You don't take offence at some of the sketches?'

'Not a bit of it, no! No point in being narrow-minded. She's got her head screwed on, that girl, you mark my words. Not to mention a damn fine pair of legs!'

I noticed that the decanter of whisky, which only Pepper and I were drinking, was already half empty. He gave me a nudge as Miss Pargeter approached. I noticed, perhaps for the first time, that she did indeed have attractive legs, and a most engaging smile.

'I hope I didn't embarrass you, Mr Barraclough?'

'Not at all, Miss Pargeter. It was more than generous of you. I really don't know how to thank you.'

'First edition, eh?' chimed in Pepper. 'That'll be worth a pretty penny!'

'Colonel, I think Mr. Davies wanted the whisky. Would you mind?'

Miss Pargeter's smile was frozen. Col. Pepper knew an order when he heard one. He trooped off meekly, refilling his own glass as he went.

'I'll give you a toast, Mr. Barraclough.' she raised her glass and I prepared to respond. 'The fact is, I've been feeling rather guilty about pre-empting your choice. So here's to *Othello* for next year!'

'*Othello* for next year!' I drank readily, just choking slightly when I realised that Colonel Pepper had not added any water to my whisky.

'I must say, I'm exhausted!' Dorothy remarked, with a beguiling smile, 'There are so many things to think of with a production like this.'

I had told her this before she started, but I refrained from saying so and found her a chair, which she accepted gratefully.

'Never mind, Miss Pargeter. At least we've broken up, now. You'll have the whole of the Easter holidays to recover.'

'Well, yes and no. I'm booked on the car ferry, tomorrow at mid-day.'

'Really? Where are you going?'

'Oh, just through France, down towards Italy for a week or so. I often do that, at the end of term. I don't pack, just throw everything in the back of the Fiat and go.'

'I envy you. But you're not going alone, surely?'

'Well, I wasn't. But a friend's just dropped out, at short notice. I don't suppose you'd care to join me?'

'No, no, I couldn't, really. But it's very kind of you to ask.'

'What are your plans for the holiday, then, Mr Barraclough?'

'Oh, quite a lot of reading to catch up on. Get to grips with the garden, you know, that sort of thing.'

'Well, you can't bring the garden with you, but you could bring the books. I wondered about asking Colonel Pepper, but I'm afraid he'd think I was propositioning him!' She chuckled at the thought. 'Do you do things like that, on the spur of the moment?' I confessed that I didn't. 'Well, you should! The unexpected is very good for you. Helps to keep you young.'

'I must say, it's a most tempting suggestion. I haven't been to France or Italy for years.'

'Good! That's settled, then. Don't bother to pack. I'll come at half past seven. Anything you can't get in the car by eight, you can do without for ten days. All right?

I could hardly believe it when I heard myself agree. Immediately, I thought of a thousand reasons why I shouldn't go – but it was too late. Miss Pargeter would have thought me an indecisive fool. And I was already beginning to care what Miss Pargeter thought.

I stayed up most of the night packing, of course, and by the time she arrived, I had breakfasted and prepared a flask of coffee and some sandwiches for the journey. I couldn't remember feeling so excited about a holiday since my childhood.

'I wondered if you'd have changed your mind, in the cold light of day.' There was something different about her; I couldn't place it at first, but then I realised: at school, she always wore her long, dark hair up or tied back in a braid. Now, it fell over the shoulders of a waisted pink and grey ski jacket. She pushed a pair of sunglasses back onto her brow and squinted at me, almost with a hint of shyness.

'I'm more reliable than you realise,' I protested, 'I've organised a route map and some emergency supplies, too. And I'll gladly do my share of the driving, of course...'

'No need! The car's only insured for me, anyway. I don't mind: it's my way of relaxing. You can just enjoy the view!'

I did. My noble charioteer steered us through lifting morning mists to the forbidding maelstrom of the M25. She was clearly a very competent driver: I soon had full confidence in her. She spoke little in heavy traffic but relaxed more when we were safely on our way to Kent. I knew how she felt, the inevitable anti-climax of finishing a production of a play. For a day or two, re-adjusting your priorities, you ask yourself if it was all worthwhile – all that effort, the time, the stress, the not inconsiderable upheavals in one's daily and weekly routines.

'And for what?' she demanded, gesticulating with one hand and controlling the steering-wheel with the other. 'Performance art just evaporates: that's its nature. Just think of all those parents and friends who came to see *Oh, What A Lovely War.* how many do you think will remember it in a year's time? Probably not one in ten of them! We may as well draw pictures in the sand: one wave, and it's gone!'

'It's the actors who benefit from Dramsoc, not the audiences,' I protested, 'they're the ones who'll remember it all their lives. They'll tell their grandchildren about it!'

She considered. 'That's a very positive way of looking at it.'

'Of course. Don't sound so surprised.'

'Sorry. I'm so glad you were able to change your plans on the spur of the moment, like that. I don't know how I plucked up the courage to ask you, actually!'

'Courage? What do you mean?'

'Well, you do cut a rather forbidding figure around the school, you know. Elder citizen, senior statesman, and so on. But you're really nothing like as old as you pretend: I keep getting flashes of someone quite young and hopeful inside. Is that the real Henry Barraclough, do you think?'

'I wonder,' I said. 'It used to be.'

We drove on in companionable silence through the flattening fields towards Ramsgate, gently fencing for our positions, redefining the boundaries between us. I was no longer her Head of Department, but her passenger and map-reader. We agreed that Christian names should be the order of the day.

Some people, on a long drive, feel the need to chatter, to fill the awful vacancies with the first things that come into their heads. But Dorothy and I rather enjoyed our long silences. I don't mean that we had nothing to say to each other: far from it – our disputation could be highly animated – but from the first, we both seemed to sense when conversation would be welcomed and when it would not. In this way, we allowed each other time for reflection as well as speech.

On the ferry, we went our separate ways, Dorothy to the top deck for fresh air, I to a reclining chair in the saloon in the hope of convincing myself not to be as seasick as I usually am on such occasions. I was almost nodding off when I felt her slipping something over my wrists.

'Eh? What on earth are these?' I enquired.

'Sea-Bands.'

'And what do Sea-Bands do when they're at home?'

'Stop you being seasick. I swear by them.'

'What is it, witchcraft?'

'Almost. It's acupressure.'

'Not acupuncture?'

'No. Acupressure. No puncturing of the skin needed.'

'I'm relieved to hear it.'

'Just gentle, regular pressure on the spot that controls sea-sickness - right there, under your wrists. That's what the little button is for. And the bracelet holds it in place.'

'You don't seriously believe in this sort of thing, do you?'

'It works! I promise you, I've used them for years, and I've never had the slightest trouble with sea-sickness.'

I accepted the kindness without great expectations. But, as we moored in Dunkerque Harbour, I had to admit that nothing had happened so far to disprove Dorothy's claim. As I came to know her driving better, I learned to wear the little Sea Bands for car travel as well, and could not fault them. We only stopped to buy cheese at the roadside and fresh bread in a village. Dorothy was making for a little pension she had stayed in before, on the outskirts of Paris. We arrived at nightfall. It was comfortable enough, and served an excellent dinner, if a little rich for the hour.

Dorothy made it very clear by her manner, had I been in any doubt about the matter, that I had been invited to share only her car, nothing more. After several evenings together, she trusted me enough to explain that she had become involved with a colleague at her previous school, and the thing had ended in tears. She was in genuine need of companionship, which suited me splendidly, especially when I realised what a seasoned and well-informed traveller she was.

We visited Versailles, picnicked in the Forest of Fontainebleau and toured the art galleries of Paris. *En passant*, Dorothy managed to deliver me to the tender mercies of a number of Parisian men's outfitters, who provided me with some very pleasant clothes at very unpleasant prices - just how unpleasant, I only fully discovered when I opened my Barclaycard bill several weeks later. She told me quite frankly that she was planning to give me 'a new image', clearly that of a much younger, more dynamic and possibly colour-blind man.

I've never cared much about clothes, but to Dorothy they were matters of great importance, not only hers, but mine. I was perfectly content to be told what to buy; in fact, I rather enjoyed not having to make decisions: I have always felt time spent choosing clothes could be used more fruitfully, on a good book or a brisk walk. Mother used to choose most of my clothes for me; she left me so well supplied that I had not been obliged to add to my wardrobe significantly for many years.

The leather coat Dorothy pressed me to buy rejoiced in the name 'bomber jacket'. I wondered wryly if this was strictly politically correct. Straight-faced, she assured me it was.

My new shoes were Italian; I offered to wait and purchase them in Italy, but Dorothy took the view that a better selection was to be found in Paris. The trousers surprised me, being rather shapeless and made of material that seemed less than serviceable. I consoled myself with the thought that for English wear, a sturdy pair of long combinations would supply any lack of warmth.

Dorothy professed herself delighted with my new attire. I must confess, I enjoyed the attention. We paraded around Paris and on several occasions she asked complete strangers to take our photographs, immediately seizing my arm and behaving as if we were rather more intimate than was the case. I entered into the spirit of the game; I do not think anyone could accuse me of dandyism, but I was flattered. It was only much later that I understood the dark purpose of these photographs.

Dorothy was anxious for more warmth, so we set off for the Mediterranean. I quoted Hesse's theory that every voluntary journey is towards the south and the sun; she agreed heartily. For myself, I find weather has only a peripheral impact: I grew up watching drizzle through a window and soon learned to turn my attention inwards. But I enjoy the seasons – and I have never seen them in such close proximity as on that long drive from Paris to Northern Italy. We fled from wintry showers and passed through spring into early summer in a few hours.

I have always loved Italy, and always felt at home there. Even the sunlight is different, warmer, freer, as if it were not obliged to obey the strict mathematical laws laid down by the pedants of Northern Europe. Had I undertaken a doctoral thesis (and I suppose that is an option not entirely closed to me, even now) my subject would have been the relationship between painting and literature in the High Renaissance.

In my twenties, as a young assistant master, I spent a number of summers preparing the ground for this grand endeavour. I learned modern and medieval Italian, to add to my school Latin, and spent a number of holidays touring Northern Italy, in a state of wonder. I wanted above all to capture the spirit of the Renaissance, to pin it down and say this is why it happened, these are the conditions that brought about the greatest flowering of our culture: if we can only learn the lessons of it, we will set our spirits free as the great painters and sculptors of the Renaissance did, to be creators rather than mere passive analysts and observers.

It is a subject about which I still feel a passionate commitment. In the end, ironically, I was overwhelmed by the weight of my research; I found that, the more I knew, the less able I was to synthesise it in any meaningful way. In blacker moments, I wondered if the whole Renaissance were not a hoax perpetuated by scholars to explain away the unexplainable. But it was some years since I had confronted this scholastic conundrum, and this journey to Italy had all the enthusiasm and excitement of my earlier trips – with the additional pleasure of a lively, intelligent companion with whom to share my knowledge.

At first, Dorothy was not a good listener. I began to speak of my love of Piero della Francesca, Domenico Veneziano, Uccello and Raphael as soon as we crossed the Italian border; she gave me to understand that I was boring her – she'd been to Italy before and read the guidebooks and that was that. In France, she had been very much the organiser; speaking French more fluently, she had arranged our hotels and ordered our meals, and I was happy for her to do so. But her Italian was not good, and the tasks fell to me. She seemed to resent my ability – at least until we reached Florence. There, she suddenly relaxed and allowed me to introduce her to the paintings I knew so well. We returned to our hotel that evening with sore feet but abuzz with excitement.

'I'm sorry, Henry. I thought you were showing off at first, you know, the way men do. But this is something you really know about, isn't it? Italy. You speak so differently, in Italian. Your whole personality changes.'

'How do you mean?'

'Well, you shout, for a start.'

'Only to make myself heard.'

'But you'd never dream of shouting, in England. Even at 4B.'

'Oh, you'd be surprised. The trouble with 4B is, they make so much noise themselves, they wouldn't hear you even if you did shout.'

'And you gesticulate, when you're speaking Italian.'

'Oh, a little, I suppose...'

'Not a little - all the time! I swear, if I tied your hands behind your back, you wouldn't be able to say a thing!'

'Well, Italian needs gestures. They're part of the language.'

'And English doesn't need them?'

'Not in the same way, no. It's not so expressive.'

'You know what I think? I think you must have been Italian in a past life. Come to think of it, the way you put that waiter in his place, this morning, you could practically pass for one in this life!'

'No, no, no!' I shook my head, 'I'm told by the *cognoscenti*, my accent leaves much to be desired.'

'False modesty!' she wasn't letting me off the hook. 'I just wish the rest of the staff room could see you going native like this! They'd have the shock of their lives!'

'Thank you very much!'

'When you speak Italian, I can see what you must have been like when you were a student.'

'How do you mean?' I rather hoped she could not.

'A bit showy! Flamboyant, even! You had a bit of dash and style about you, in those days, didn't you, Henry? Where did it all go?' She smiled at me to show she didn't mean the slight. But she did.

'I really can't imagine. In my youth, I was practically young Lochinvar, riding out of the West.' Dorothy often mistook my irony, in the early days. I didn't recognise my own rather repressed undergraduate personality in any of her character sketches, but if dash and style were considered desirable accoutrements, I would willingly plead guilty to both.

'In the last century, you'd probably have gone out to India, to be a colonial administrator. You'd have liked that. It would have suited you better than running the English Department at Effingham School. You could have let the Italian side of your personality have full rein.'

Privately, I thought it much more likely, had I the misfortune to live in that century, that I should have been a clergyman disputing the minutiae of dogma. But if colonial administration carried a higher social cachet with the young lady, so be it!

'When did you first come to Italy?' she demanded.

'From Cambridge, in my second Long Vac. I spent the first summer boning up for the Oldham Shakespeare Prizes. The second was considerably more entertaining!'

'Did you come on your own?'

'No, with a friend from college, Chris Fanshawe.'

'I can picture it. I suppose you motored down in his E Type Jaguar…'

'As a matter of fact, we came by train. It was raining. And very hot, being July. Rather like being a steamed vegetable, I imagine.' I could remember it vividly, feel the humidity on the backs of my hands.

We wanted to see as much as possible of the work of Piero della Francesca. The Legend of the True Cross in Arezzo is like a series of crystal windows into the fifteenth century; for us, it was like a time machine. By drenching ourselves in both the writings and the pictures of the period, we felt we could taste the authentic flavour of the age: in our imagination, we were living in the Renaissance.

That was pure joy, that trip, with Fanshawe, such good fellowship. And the added excitement of discovering the treasures of the Renaissance for ourselves, with fresh eyes, as every generation should. The first encounter with the Renaissance is one of the most important events in a young person's education. If you are ever going to understand the current state of human progress, you have to appreciate the significance of the Renaissance.

What gave this particular artistic movement such importance? Ostensibly, it was nothing more than a rebirth of interest in classical art and fashion, in the Papal States and their neighbours, around the middle of the fifteenth century. We are fond, in our own century, of revivals of past decades: this revival looked further and deeper. But then, it had Plato and Aristotle to re- discover.

To me, it was an advance of the human spirit. The Renaissance was not merely a cultural development, but almost a visceral change in the nature of the species, a stage of evolution, like standing up, instead of going on all fours. The Renaissance told ordinary people they could stand on their own two feet: it said individuals were worth something; it changed all our values. It set artists beside princes. It stood for freedom. An idealised freedom of artistic and political expression, unattainable in reality. But a powerful dream. And one that rightly continues to inspire, generation after generation.

As I recall them, the visits to Renaissance shrines with Fanshawe and with Dorothy seem strangely intertwined, separated by 27 years but equally present to me now. We stood many times in front of the same paintings. I saw myself between these two people, my friends. I felt sorry they had never met. I saw myself sharing some of Fanshawe's spirit and love of life with Dorothy.

She needed something to believe in. She professed herself an agnostic. Once I had confessed my Christianity, she exacted a promise from me not to evangelise. I kept my promise, as always. I wondered if she would find the Renaissance easier to believe in than God: those paintings are one of many roads to God, as well as to understanding.

*   *   *

Fanshawe was in high good humour. He had been chortling to himself since an incident at the border post had reminded him of Oscar Wilde's arrival in America. He was still savouring the moment, as we jostled our way out of the bus station in Florence with our suitcases.

'I have nothing to declare but my genius!' He repeated it at full volume to the passing crowds, '"Nothing to declare but my genius"!' – Henry, imagine the joy of thinking up that remark! And the even greater joy of delivering it at Passport Control! Dear old Oscar – he really was very close to being a genius, you know.'

'He wrote some pretty mundane stuff, for a genius.'

'He wrote comedy. Why not? Shakespeare wrote comedy, too.'

'You're not seriously comparing Wilde with Shakespeare, are you?'

'Only in one respect. They both had enough of the common touch to know what would make the great British public laugh. Both old theatricals, come to think of it. You mustn't think of Shakespeare as a god. He didn't have supernatural powers, you know. He just wrote about human beings as he saw them.'

'But how did he manage to see them so clearly?' I had been puzzling over this for some time. 'Such remarkable insights. His psychology is impeccable - and his language so simple. How did he know? Where did it come from, that incredible grasp of what makes human beings tick? Why did it happen? Why should we have one towering genius, and then no-one worth comparing with him for four hundred years?'

'I suppose you're going to tell me God's responsible.'

'I'm sure He is. And He will doubtless unfold His mysterious plan to us in the fullness of time. But I'm not asking God; I'm asking you. Go on, explain the phenomenon of Shakespeare. I challenge you.' I had found from experience that the best way of dealing with Fanshawe was to set him difficult questions I'd been pondering myself. Coming fresh to a problem, he often came up with highly original solutions.

'I suppose Shakespeare was Shakespeare because we needed him. You know, cometh the hour, cometh the man. You could see him as a sort of spokesman, the voice of the age. He just happened to be the person who most adroitly put the ideas of the time into words. So, what we get from Shakespeare is the distilled wisdom of a very powerful civilisation, Elizabethan England.'

'Do you find any of that remotely convincing?' I demanded, 'Because it sounds like a load of old tosh to me. You'll end up giving the state supremacy over the individual artist, if you're not careful.'

'Oh, Henry, don't spoil the game! One doesn't have to be convinced by an idea in order to put it forward. How limiting that would be. I enjoy putting up notions, to see if they'll float or sink. Mostly the latter, of course, with you around.'

'Glad to be of service', I said, smugly.

'But, typically of you, Henry, there's one vitally important point that you don't seem to have noticed, at all!'

'What's that?'

'We're in Florence, my dear chap! The eye of the storm! Epicentre of the Renaissance!'

'So we are, and if I'm not much mistaken, that grubby-looking pile across the road is our hotel.'

His jaw sagged a little, but only for a moment.

'Can it be? Never mind. We'll need an extra bottle of wine! The main thing is, we're in Florence!' Pausing only long enough to hand me his suitcase to carry, Fanshawe re-addressed himself to the passers-by in the street. *'Bongiorno, Firenze, bongiorno! Come sta?* I 'ave nozzing to declare – but my genius! What's the Italian for genius, Henry?'

By the time we reached the rather dingy entrance to the hotel, Fanshawe had gathered a small but select crowd of interested parties and hangers-on. When I looked up from signing the register, he was having his shoes polished while he tried to sign an autograph. I clicked my tongue in disapproval and raised my eyes heavenwards for the sake of the receptionist, but in my heart, I just wished I had Fanshawe's share of charm and vivacity, rather than my own rather meagre supply. As usual, he was right: the main thing was that we were in Florence.

Dorothy had studied the Renaissance only superficially. This was her first full immersion in the experience, and I was delighted to be the one to open her eyes to such wonders. Like accepting Christ as the central figure in the spiritual universe, accepting the Renaissance as the central factor in European development demands a certain amount of re-adjustment of previously-held values.

Fanshawe and I had discussed the matter at some length. Our conclusion was that the Renaissance was surely the high point of Judaeo-Christian civilisation. Ultimately, it failed, but it was so noble an endeavour, that it lived on; its influence reverberates down the centuries. Humanity was not yet ready for liberty, equality and fraternity, but it had learned at least that there was a better way of life, to which one might aspire.

We were dreadfully pompous, as undergraduates. We thought we knew it all. We'd lived a sheltered life of academic application; we were by no means as mature and worldly as we thought. We imagined ourselves going formally to pay court to the Renaissance, a pair of precocious young delegates from one European civilisation to another.

We were there, we thought, to learn and compare, to weigh in the balance their cultural achievements, but also to plunder their ideas and their energy for our own poor civilisation. In a sense, we were like tomb-robbers, (archaeologists, to employ the euphemism). Every treasure we saw, we examined, catalogued and valued. And, like Howard Carter at the tomb of Tutankhamun, what wonderful things we found!

The painting Fanshawe was keenest to see was in Milan. He insisted on a special day trip to the *Pinacoteca di Brera* to see it. We were not disappointed. Piero della Francesca's Montefeltro Altarpiece is an unforgettable sight. It's a masterpiece of perspective and composition, in which a rudely healthy and robust baby Jesus floats serenely in front of his iconic mother, surrounded by a throng of dignitaries, biblical, historical and contemporary.

'Isn't that the chap who commissioned the painting?' I asked, 'dressed in armour, kneeling in front of Mary?'

'Yes, Federico da Montefeltro. Frisky-looking cove, don't you think?'

'I think he looks quite distinguished. But then, I imagine you expect to look distinguished, if you're paying the artist, don't you?'

'Do you know what I like most about this painting?' Fanshawe looked suspiciously pleased with himself as he asked the question.

'What?'

'That helmet, just in front of old Federico.'

'Why? What's the significance of it?'

'It's a monument to Federico's roving eye. Look at it closely.'

'It's damaged. There's a big dent, over the right eye.'

'Exactly! What happened, you see, was this: Federico had made love with this beautiful woman in an oak tree. Doesn't sound the most comfortable place to do it, but that's the story. Well, afterwards, instead of falling at Federico's feet with gratitude, like all the rest, this lady wouldn't have anything more to do with him.

'So, when Federico saw her at a jousting tournament in 1450, he hopped off the judge's stand and joined the lists. Now, to make sure she'd recognise him, he wedged the visor of his helmet open with an oak twig. Big mistake! He got whacked with a lance and nearly died. It broke his nose, as you can just about see. And he lost the sight of his right eye, which you can't see, because Piero painted him from the other side.'

'I'm surprised he didn't have the helmet melted down.'

'Quite the opposite!' Fanshawe's excitement was attracting a number of curious listeners, to whom he was all but oblivious. 'He kept it on display ever afterwards, to show his remorse. Because he realised that if he'd been killed, he'd have thrown his life away for nothing, let down his family and left his people without a leader.'

'Extraordinary. I can't see Harold Wilson doing that, can you?'

'I can't see Harold Wilson commissioning a painting of any kind. Unless it was on the wall of a block of flats.'

'All right, less of the high tory, if you don't mind.'

I tried to quieten him down before he decided to climb on some favourite hobbyhorse or regale the casual onlookers with an embarrassing anecdote. 'You're in Italy now. Right-wingers get lynched.'

'You mean Mussolini? Wasn't a mistress the cause of his downfall, too, just like old Montefeltro, here?'

'It's obviously a well-established tradition in these parts.'

'I blame the rampant heterosexuality, you know.' Fanshawe shot me a challenging look. This was a subject he always loved to debate with me.

'Oh, don't start all that again.' I had no intention of joining Fanshawe's double-act. 'Some of these people probably understand English!'

'Of course. Why not? English is an easy language. I've spoken it myself since I was knee-high to a bicycle. I picked it up just like that...'

And he was off again, like a butterfly looking for the next flower on which to alight. He had told me his story, and told it with panache. That done, he had exhausted the interest of the painting and started inspecting the young Italian men passing by, or so he boasted to me, since he knew how offensive I found him in that vein.

Fanshawe clung to his homosexuality as though it were the membership of an exclusive club. At that stage of his life it was more of a Greek ideal for him than an active practice. At heart, he was a hopeless romantic, fantasising about an unattainable perfect love. I mistakenly saw my role, his friend, as bringing him back to earth, once in a while.

When I went with Dorothy to see the very same paintings, the holiday with Fanshawe was eerily present. I heard myself saying to Dorothy the same words I had used to Fanshawe, or, to be frank, more often appropriating some of the insights he had given me.

In a way, I went back in time; I experienced a minor renaissance of my younger self, and recaptured some of that 'first, fine careless rapture'. And I was teaching a willing pupil, which always makes me happy. For Dorothy's first true encounter with the Renaissance, I made sure she saw the finest works and heard the same clarion call I had heard, with Fanshawe, all those years ago.

We went to Arezzo, to see Piero della Francesca's series of paintings of *The Legend of the True Cross*, and to the great man's home town of Sansepolcro, in Florence. Perhaps this is some trick of memory, but it amazed me how often Fanshawe's and Dorothy's views on the paintings coincided. I am not a believer in any of this astrology nonsense, but at one point I almost caught myself enquiring about Dorothy's birthday, to see if she shared a sun sign or whatever it is with Fanshawe. Perhaps my own prejudices about the paintings influenced their reactions; perhaps my way of introducing the paintings evokes a given response from my listeners. But I suspect the answer is more complex than that.

We made a point of seeing as many of Piero's rare self-portraits as we could. Dorothy felt she could understand an artist's work better if she knew what he looked like.

'He's so much older. I can't get over it. I can still see the pious young innocent from the *Madonna della Misericordia*, but only just.' We were in the *Museo Civico* in *Sansepolcro*, standing in front of the magnificent *Resurrection of Christ*.

'He doesn't look too old to me' I protested, 'He was probably over fifty when he painted this, you know. He doesn't look it.'

'"Maybe not, but he looks as if he's lived through a lot of pain and disappointments, doesn't he?' Dorothy looked at the figure of Piero as one of four Roman soldiers guarding Christ's tomb. 'He's still a handsome man, but so tired. Life didn't turn out as well as he hoped, for all his success.'

'I'm sorry' I interrupted rather curtly, 'but you're still seeing it as a secular painting. It's not, it's religious; its only purpose is to reassert vividly Christ's return from the dead. He's just about to step up on the tomb. Look at those guards. Do you think they're just asleep?'

'Well, I presume so, yes.'

'I think they're dreaming about the Resurrection. They're so close to the one redeeming event in the whole universe, they're all seeing it, in visions. He's absorbing the revolutionary idea of a life after death. That's why he looks so – so smitten. It's Alberti's classic proof of the divine power of painting: he believed friendship could make absent people seem close by. That painting could almost bring the dead back to life.'

We left Italy at speed, invigorated, drove through Monte Carlo with barely an envious thought and raced along the coast road towards Cannes. Musician friends of Dorothy's had offered weekend accommodation at a borrowed villa in the hills outside the town and we were hoping to arrive in decent time for dinner.

We need not have hurried. The villa was one of fifty, built just after the War on the slopes of a little hill covered with olive trees. We stopped at the concierge's sentry-box as we drove in and Dorothy was handed a crumpled envelope of keys and an apologetic note from her friends, who had been called away to play in an orchestral concert in Vienna.

We found the house and let ourselves in. It was built in typical Provencal style, with vaulted ceilings and hand-moulded, irregular archways between rooms, and there was a central fireplace and chimney. I felt at once that I had been there before.

'Well, don't you think it's a brilliant place, Henry?' Dorothy was gallantly determined to look on the bright side of our hosts' desertion and the consequent disappearance of dinner.

'Yes, I'm sure it'll be home from home, as soon as I can find the teapot. I suppose they do have a teapot, do they?' I was trying to find my way in the musicians' kitchen.

'Of course. Christine is English, Henry.'

'So you say. The tea, regrettably, is not. Jasmine-scented, at a wild guess. *Très éxotique*, I'm sure'.

'We could light a fire, later on. It's a wonderful fireplace, and it's just cold enough for it.'

'Does that involve chopping any firewood?' I enquired sagely.

'No, there's a huge woodpile at the end of the terrace.'

'Splendid. In that case, I'll volunteer to set the fire and keep it going.'

'All right. But don't burn the place down, whatever you do.'

'I was a Boy Scout, you know.'

'I know.'

'How did you know?'

'I'm afraid it's obvious, Henry. Baden-Powell would be proud of you. You're a credit to the troop.'

'You're too kind, my dear!'

Frankly, I was enjoying myself. I don't mean to evoke self-pity when I say that was a rare occurrence: we are all responsible for our own happiness or unhappiness – at some level or other we choose it for ourselves. I learned long ago how to be alone, how to survive as a little floating island brushing against others but never involving with them. But I had been more deeply alone and for longer at Effingham School.

At my previous school, I had left friends behind and lost touch with them and not made other friends since. Not real friends, the friends of your heart, like the men from university days, some of whom still keep in contact from time to time. I had many associates and acquaintances at Effingham, but no-one I would have cared to confide in. And then, when Mother died, and I sold the house, I had no reason to go back to the village...

Until Dorothy Pargeter opened my eyes and took me by the hand and led me into the sunlight. And left me there.

The Provençal villa followed the contours of the hillside. Magnificent fifty or sixty-year-old olive trees had balconies and spiral staircases simply built around them. Rather than clearing the trees, the architects had built the villas to accommodate them. I spoke to one of the neighbours about it. He told me they harvest the olives, every year, and give each resident several litres of olive oil, as their share of the crop.

It was a lovely place to wake up, with the first clear rays of the sun lighting the distant Mediterranean, with Cezanne's mountains still dark blue on the other side of the horizon. By the time Dorothy finished her shower, I had made a foray to the nearest shops. I had croissants, *pains au chocolat* and large breakfast cups of coffee with hot milk, ready on the terrace.

She wore a white towelling bathrobe she had found in her friends' bedroom, and brushed her long hair to dry it in the sunshine.

'How clever of you to find the *boulangerie!*'

'I thought you'd be pleased. I must say, they were very friendly.'

'We're just far enough from Cannes to avoid the rich and precious.'

'We'll go in and look at some of them this morning, shall we?'

'I thought we might, yes. A little stroll along the *Croisette*. I'm afraid we're about a month early to see naked starlets posing for publicity photographs on the beach. I'm sorry.'

'Don't apologise. Naked starlets always put me off my lunch.'

'Really? I wonder why that is. Most men seem to like them.'

'I tend to agree with Malcolm Muggeridge' I said, sliding another rich and buttery croissant on to my plate, 'on the subject of strip tease.'

'What did he say?'

'He saw little purpose in arousing desire when there was no real prospect of satisfying it. If you'll pardon the indelicacy.'

'Mister Barraclough! I'm not at all sure that I will!' Dorothy rocked back on her chair in mock horror. 'Have you shared these views with 4B, by any chance?'

'I may well have done, yes' I admitted, 'They raised the subject in a class discussion, as I recall.'

'I wondered where they'd got it from' she mused, 'This explains a lot.'

'I'm sorry if I've caused you any embarrassment. I do encourage free speech, as far as possible. If I'm going to teach them anything useful, I've got to know how they think!'

Dorothy was silent for a moment. 'Yes' she said, 'You're right, of course. You're full of surprises, Henry. So many hidden talents.'

'Not hidden depths?'

'Oh yes, those, too. Hidden everything. A hidden man, altogether, that's you. You've hidden away for years, haven't you? How long is it since your mother died? Seven years! And, from what you say, you haven't let anyone get close to you in all that time. You need people, Henry. You need to share things with others; you need to be gregarious and involved, like you were in Italy.'

'Oh, Italy's different' I protested, 'Italy's hardly real, once you've left it.'

'It's very real while you're there, though, isn't it? I felt incredibly alive.'

'Ah, that's the spirit of the Renaissance!'

'I wonder.' She moved to a deckchair and slipped the bathrobe from her thin, white shoulders, to bask in the early sunshine. She might have been a cat. Long, dark hair, freshly washed, formed a floating frame for her face. Lazily, she brushed it aside to allow the rays of sunlight to caress her pale flesh. She sensed me watching her. I probed a little deeper.

'I'm glad you invited me to come on holiday. I just wish I knew why.'

'You'd be surprised!' she tried to suppress a smile, 'It's actually because you're so aloof, so detached from everything that's going on.'

'That's not much of a recommendation.'

'I thought you were so self-contained, we could probably have a very nice holiday without getting in each other's way.' she said seriously, 'And it's not healthy to be alone too much.'

'Well, there's a certain pleasure in being able to follow one's own channels of thought to their natural conclusions. That's not generally possible if you live with a lot of people.'

'Other people's thoughts might be more interesting.'

'They probably would, but how can I be sure of that if I don't develop my own thoughts first?'

'That's all very well, but time is short!' She seemed unaccountably emotional on this point. 'We all have very difficult decisions to make. Who to trust? That's a question none of us can afford to get wrong.'

'Who did you trust? And how did it go wrong?' I didn't mean to pry, but I wanted her to be able to tell me if she wanted.

'It doesn't matter who!' She looked up sharply, as if I had caught her unawares. 'I'm sorry. It was the man I told you about. I sometimes miss him, that's all.' She touched my knee lightly and smiled. 'It's not your fault.'

'They say it's better to have loved and lost than never to have loved at all.' I suggested, but Dorothy looked away, clearly not consoled by the thought. 'Of course, it takes a long time to reach that perspective.'

'Have you loved and lost, Henry?'

'Oh yes. I wouldn't presume to speak of it, otherwise.'

'Strange. I always thought of you as being sort of protected by all your books, living so much in a world of ideas.'

'I'm afraid the pain-killing properties of literature have been woefully overestimated. When someone dies – or leaves us, which can be worse, we need time to grieve, then time to re-adjust, to a world landscape that no longer contains that person. It can take a while. Time is the only healer.'

A cloud blocked the sunlight from her face, She squinted up, to see how large it was, decided it would not clear soon, and stood up abruptly.

'Quite. And we'd better not waste it, by sitting here all day. We could have lunch at the Casino. Would you like that, Henry?'

Peremptorily brushing aside my murmured protestations at this possible extravagance, Dorothy decided we both needed smarter clothes for the occasion and was kind enough to iron my shirt and tie. She put a new roll of film into her camera before leaving the villa.

A large plate of *fruits de mer* at the Casino's excellent restaurant, together with a dry white burgundy, put us both in a convivial frame of mind, but Dorothy was disappointed to find photography was not allowed.

'I can't see what harm a few photos would do,' she grumbled.

'I suppose they're afraid they might be used to plan a robbery.'

I was fascinated by the elaborate security, having never visited a casino before. 'I wouldn't fancy their chances. It's like Fort Knox, in here.'

'There is one way of getting money out of them.'

'Eh? What's that?'

'Winning it!' Dorothy examined the contents of her purse.

'You're not going to gamble!'

'Why ever not?'

'On an assistant teacher's wage?'

'I'm not going to bet high.'

'So I should hope!'

'I'll play for half an hour' she said, checking her watch and standing up from the table. 'Are you going to come and watch, or would you rather stay here and drink the rest of the coffee?'

'I'll finish the coffee and catch up with you later.' I poured myself another cup and settled down cheerfully to observe the goings on. The restaurant was beginning to empty, but there was a constant buzz of activity in the gaming halls. People were surprisingly restrained, I thought, self-contained. I expected an occasional whoop of delight or groan of disappointment, but such expressions are apparently bad form.

It was perfectly obvious from their faces who was winning and who was losing, but everyone made a token effort to disguise it. No money changed hands, only coloured plastic chips, which to my un-tutored eye gave the whole transaction an air of unreality. Perhaps it is more serious in the evening; I may have misunderstood. French sophistication. My theory, for what it is worth, is that the plastic chips enable the losing gambler to deceive himself about the value of his losses. Which is, I take it, essential to the success of any gaming establishment, however grand.

Dorothy was playing Blackjack with two other players and a dap-per young male croupier. She was winning. Three stacks of chips stood in front of her and she had more in her hand. I stood behind her chair while she explained the essentials of the game. She said she had won £200.

'Good heavens! Shouldn't we go before you give it back?'

'No! That's no fun!' She frowned as the croupier uncovered a King and Ace for himself and removed chips and cards from the table. 'Are you ready to go, Henry? I'll have one last bet.'

I watched to see if she would risk all her winnings on this last bet. She did not. She put half of it on – a large bet for the table. She received smiles and nods from the croupier and the other players when she won, threw back a couple of chips in accordance with tra-dition as a pourboire for the croupier, and walked with me towards the cash office.

'Why did you only bet half of your winnings?' I asked.

'It was the only sensible thing to do,' she smiled.

'Well, as it turned out, maybe. But you could have lost a hundred pounds on the turn of a card!'

'That was a perfectly safe bet!' she insisted, 'A certain winner. They're the only kind of bets I like.'

'I thought there was no such thing as a safe bet?'

'That one was,' she explained, 'because either way I would have been pleased with the outcome. Either I was going to leave, winning a hundred pounds, or I was going to leave, winning three hundred pounds. So I couldn't really lose. That's the sort of bet I like!'

'How extraordinary!' It was my turn to he surprised. 'Clever of you to work that out, in the heat of the moment. You know that saying about there being no such thing as a free lunch? You seem to have disproved it!'

The cashier changed Dorothy's chips into a pile of Francs, which she scooped into her purse.

Turning to me, she firmly placed a chaste kiss on my cheek. 'You're an angel, Henry. But I promise not to tell 4B.'

I was rooted to the spot. I caught a faint waft of her perfume. I felt her hair on my face. It was a long time since I had been so close to anyone. I felt her hand caress my neck and shoulders for a moment, then withdraw. A small enough gesture, but it was the first time she had done it since the presentation at school after *Oh, What A Lovely War!*

Since then, we had spent nearly two weeks travelling together; we were beginning to know each other, to be at ease in each other's company. But this small touch, for me at least, marked a change. I think it was at that precise moment that I began to love her.

In the afternoon, we walked miles along the beach. I have an idea I did most of the talking, for once. Dorothy was asking about Mother. Since she died, I have always felt a shadow of disappointment, when meeting new people or new experiences, in that Mother will not be able to share them. Not that she shared a great deal of my life, but I always tried to involve her in what interested me, and she made a valiant effort to keep up with my concerns – a little too closely, at times. I tried to conjure up Mother's spirit, for Dorothy to get to know her, on that beach. I wanted her to know what Mother was truly like. People who did not understand us thought our closeness was un-healthy.

Mother had no-one in the world but me. She did not imprison me, or hold me back. I chose freely to put her first. Was I wrong? Should I have chosen instead to create the next generation, and set about finding myself a wife? Rightly or wrongly, I felt, in my 20s and 30s, that I was already giving enough of my time to fostering the next generation, on a daily basis.

I cannot honestly say I resented the time I spent looking after Mother. Other people look after their children for as many years, without expecting to be thanked for it. Mother needed care and I needed someone to care for. It was what the Americans call 'a sweetheart deal', where both parties benefit. I enjoyed her company, her kindness and gentleness.

Dorothy found it hard to sympathise with Mother, feeling she should have found herself a place in a community of like-minded old dears and left me free to – well, to what? Would my life have been so very different if I had not looked after Mother? It has not been any more exciting since she left me, just a little lonelier. I fear I am set in my ways. We stopped for *crêpes* on the way back to the villa and I retired early, feeling the effects of so much sea air and exercise. It must have been about eleven when I woke with a raging thirst and went to the kitchen for a glass of water.

I was surprised to find Dorothy still awake, sitting in the kitchen. As I came in, she casually spread a newspaper to cover some things on the table, but I had already seen what was underneath. I took a glass from the draining-board and poured myself some iced water from the fridge.

'Would you like some?'

'Oh, yes. Thank you.'

'It helps to ease the throat. When you cough.'

Dorothy looked rather nervous and cleared her throat. She feared I wasn't going to let her off the hook. And she was right.

'You seemed to be having difficulty.'

'Difficulty?' Dorothy was a wary study of vagueness.

'In rolling it, I mean. Wouldn't the papers stick together?'

'No! I – well, I don't know very much about it, I'm afraid. Christine left it for me. For old times' sake, she said. We were students together.'

'Let me try.' I lifted the newspaper and uncovered the cigarette papers, matches and a small polythene bag of dried marijuana, as well as several spoiled cigarette papers with marijuana spilling out of them. I took the papers and a small piece of card, with which I scooped up the loose marijuana. I sensed Dorothy looking rather nonplussed and decided to allow myself to show off.

'Shall I do it for you?'

'Do you know how?' She sounded quite surprised.

'I did go to university in the nineteen-sixties, you know. You couldn't do that without learning how to roll a joint, somewhere along the way.'

'Go on, then. I'll watch.'

She pulled her chair closer to the table and leaned on her elbows. She was wearing the white towelling bathrobe over a white night-dress, her hair caught up in a towel. I thought she looked enchant-ing, which may have accounted for my bravado.

I took three fresh cigarette papers from the packet and joined two of them so that one sticky edge remained on the outside. Then I stuck the third piece at right angles to the first two, so that a small piece of its sticky edge protruded beside the first, both face up. I poured the little heap of dried leaves and flowerets from my piece of card into the centre of the papers, crumbled them a little, and spread the fine mixture into a tidy line.'

'You have done this before, haven't you?' said Dorothy.

'Once or twice' I admitted, 'but not for twenty years or so.'

It took my fingers a moment or two to recall the particular twist re-quired to roll the whole concoction into a neat cylinder without spilling the contents at either end, but I finally succeeded, licked the sticky edge and held it firmly in place while the gum set. Then I twisted one end to seal it and tore a long rectangle off the piece of card, which I rolled into a small cylinder slightly tighter than the main one. This I inserted in the open end and let it unroll a little to form a tight little filter or holder. When I had folded in the tiny scraps of overlapping paper, it looked a masterpiece of craftsmanship, which I presented to Dorothy with a flourish.

'You'd better light it as well, Henry.'

'No, I don't really care for it.'

'How do you know? If you haven't tried it for twenty years.'

Well, it didn't agree with me then. I doubt if it's changed very much.'

'No, but you have.'

'I suppose you're right.'

'And the only way of finding out is by trying it.' Dorothy struck a match for me and set light to the closed end of the joint. Cautiously, I breathed in at the filter end and was relieved to find the smoke not as harsh on the throat as I had feared. She watched me, smiling. I took another puff, inhaled deeply and held it, passing the brightly glowing joint across to Dorothy, who followed suit.

I never went overboard for marijuana and cannabis in the way that so many of my contemporaries did. I acknowledged its powers, certainly, to enhance an aesthetic experience, or any other experience, but I always regretted losing contact with the base line of reality. I enjoy the crisp and accurate functioning of my mind: instant euphoria, however delightful, is perhaps too rich for my taste.

But then, one does not have to drink wine every day to appreciate a fine bottle once in a while.

We laughed, of course, at notions we might not otherwise have found funny. We were carried away by our own earnestness: marijuana gives one a sense of perceiving things with unusual clarity; sometimes this is indeed the case, but at the time it is hard to tell fantasy from reality. We went for a walk and followed the moon through the olive grove where the villas were built. We seemed to be the only people awake; we felt like naughty children on a midnight feast.

'Well?' demanded Dorothy, when we had returned from our walk and made a cup of coffee, now that the effects of the marijuana were receding, 'Did it agree with you this time?'

'Oh yes, it was very agreeable. It makes any form of coherent thought impossible for a time, but that's no bad thing, once in a while. If only one could separate the stimulation from the increasing desire for more of the same, I'd be wholeheartedly in favour.'

'But you're not?'

'Oh, I'm in favour of legalising it, of course, that's just a matter of common sense. We didn't have the moral right to make it illegal in the first place, in my opinion. It has to be up to the individual to choose. It's a personal matter. The State has no business interfering.'

'So why does it?'

'Because it can't control it. It's dangerously liberating. Next time we have a revolution, you can be sure, some substance that makes people feel happy will be at the bottom of it. The danger is that it's still a drug: i.e. the more you have, the more you want. I'm not saying it's addictive, like heroin and so on, but there's an understandable tendency to go on raising the dose, and eventually that does put people under. The stimulating effect is lost, and it just puts you to sleep.'

'Would you like to roll another one, or will it put you to sleep?

'I'll roll one for you, gladly, but I'm quite sleepy enough already.'

She watched from the sofa as I repeated the ritual and carried over the completed joint.

'You're can't have learned that without a lot of practice, Henry. I'm beginning to think you've led a more exciting life than you've let on!'

'If only that were true!' I lit the joint for her, passed it over and leaned back on the sofa to watch her smoke it.

A great stillness descended on us. She gave me the joint to hold. On impulse, I took a deep draught of sweet, heavy smoke and held it until my lungs begged to exhale. I was in control, very concentrated. I knew what I was doing. I was going against all the careful, conservative instincts of a lifetime. I was living dangerously. Mother would have said I had had my head turned by some girl. I puffed again, two or three times.

'You haven't lost the knack, then!' Dorothy was laughing. I must have looked rather odd. I felt quite light-headed. I gave her the joint and she took several deep breaths and offered it back to me. I waved it aside. I sat back and stretched my neck and shoulders. The room seemed rather hazy, as I had taken off my glasses, but I knew it would have looked hazy, even through the correct lenses. I felt relaxed, at peace with the world. Time seemed to pass very, very slowly.

Dorothy was moving languidly. She curled her feet up beneath her on the sofa and rested her head lightly on my chest. She took my hand and pressed it against her face. I remember the incredible softness of her cheek. I placed my palm on her forehead and felt how warm she was. I ran my fingers through her hair, stroked and massaged her shoulders.

I remember it vividly, but I am sure I did not make a conscious decision to do any of those things. Essentially, it was a genetic response: my body reacted to the situation before my mind could work out what was happening. I know this is the normal order of things for most people, but I am in the habit of thinking first and acting (if at all) afterwards. I am not used to such surprises from my body.

Dorothy responded to my wooing, sliding herself further up my chest until her hair pressed against my cheek. I breathed in the perfume of her and held her to me with both arms. I felt an immense longing for her, but also a sort of relief at coming home at last. She seemed so warm and reassuring – and so unbelievably close to me.

She kissed me first through her hair. I was intoxicated by the scent of her, the softness of her hair and her cheek. She inserted a cool hand and stroked my face, smoothing her hair so that it was no longer between us. And then I felt her lips, full and ripe, I tasted them and felt her tongue flicking against mine, shyly at first, then bolder, firmer. I lost myself in her kiss, for how long I have no idea. We paused to take breath, but would not meet each other's eyes before both subsiding again into the primitive ecstasy, the mutual suckling that exerts so powerful a sense of comfort, well-being and love.

Eventually, we had to meet each other's gaze. A person you have kissed is never again the person you knew before the kiss. We were both tentative, feeling we had leaped over the abyss with no promise of a safe landing. She looked very vulnerable.

'Henry, this is the last thing I intended to happen.' She kissed me again, to soften the reproach, but I still felt the sting. This time, I did not respond to her kiss as before. She was right. We were behaving absurdly, in a way that would undoubtedly cause us both embarrassment later on. How could I possibly think a vibrant young woman like that might be sexually attracted to me? She had obviously taken pity on me, she was trying misguidedly to ease what she perceived, perhaps rightly, as my chronic loneliness.

'I'm sorry, Dorothy, do forgive me. I can't think what came over me.'

'It's all right. It doesn't matter.'

'You're very kind. But really – it was the last thing I intended. The grass was obviously much too strong. I should have mixed some parsley leaves or tobacco with it; I'm sure that's what they used to do at college.'

'It was a bit overwhelming, I must admit.' She moved back a little from me, the better to focus.

'We mustn't let this spoil our wonderful holiday. Much as I'd love to continue, I wouldn't want to take advantage of you like this. It wouldn't be fair.' We disentangled further. 'I know how deceptive marijuana can be'.

'You're quite right.' she hugged the bathrobe tightly around her. I had a strong impulse to enfold her in my arms and press her tightly against me, but somehow the moment had already passed. 'I'm sorry. I got carried away as well. You're a very attractive man, you know! And it is rather stronger than I expected, I must say. We shouldn't be so childish.'

She offered her cheek to me for a dry kiss and stood up.

'Thank you for being so sensible, Henry. You're a real joy to go on holiday with. It's been perfect. Now I'm going to bed before I really embarrass myself!'

She stood in the doorway with her head on one side, smiling at me.

I wanted to stop her but I could not find the words. I wanted to take back my cold cowardice, say it was not the marijuana, it was real. I wanted her in my arms again. But I said nothing. I knew I did not deserve her.

It must have been a couple of hours later when I woke to find Dorothy sliding gently under my duvet. I froze for a moment, then relaxed and took her in my arms.

'It's all right, Henry, I'm completely sober now. Your virtue is safe with me. I just wanted to tell you something, before we tactfully blot this evening from our memory banks. It was very sweet of you to make excuses for me, very thoughtful. But I didn't kiss you because I was stoned. I kissed you because I wanted to.'

I said nothing, but I could feel a broad, irresistible smile spreading over my face. For answer, I turned to face her on the pillow and looked deep into her eyes.

'I'm sorry. I couldn't believe it was possible. I couldn't believe a woman like you could possibly want to kiss a man like me!'

Then we kissed again and I felt myself beginning to drift away, floating away to some dreamlike place I scarcely believed in any more. I tried to explain this to Dorothy but she laughed and shook her head.

'Words, words, words, Henry! You rely on them too much. There are times in life when words are not enough, when they don't have the power to express our feelings.'

'I know what you mean, I just want to tell you…'

I had to stop as she put her finger against my lips to silence me.

'Not another word. Do you promise?' I promised. And what followed was beyond any words I can find to describe it. Dorothy was a much more practised lover than I: she gave me no further chance to doubt or hesitate or delay. Her body rippled against me like a wave and mine responded. I clung to her like a drowning sailor to a broken mast. Unerringly, she drew the pain out of me, all the disappointment and discarded dreams. I wept with tears of joy and shook with laughter or sobs, I knew not.

And always, when I opened my eyes she was there with me, yielding, absorbing, enveloping, fusing. She became a part of me, and I of her; we scarcely knew where one body ended and the other began; we flowed in and out of each other seamlessly, in tune, in time, in rhythm, until an incredible, convulsive crescendo swept over us and we tumbled through loving euphoria into a blissful oblivion.

Name: *H Barraclough Esq, CBE*

Form: *-ica*

Book 3: For a Letter

Effingham School
Effingham, Glos.

It was a letter that summoned me to Cambridge. And indirectly, to the delights of Susannah. It was in a letter that Celia unfolded to me the touching tale of the keen young salesman in her father's company who had stolen her heart. And it was a letter that shattered my ecstatic idyll in the South of France with Dorothy Pargeter. Another letter brought me the greatest sadness of my life. I have no reason to love letters.

For three days and nights we basked in the warm glow of mutual approbation. In passion, we looked at each other with the eyes of tigers at a kill. The third night, I lay awake after lovemaking and feasted my eyes on her body. I looked at her – as if for the first time. Moonlight filtered through the olive leaves outside a small arched window high in the handmade wall and made patterns on her back. A gust of wind and they were gone. But her shoulder was there still, gleaming as the moonlight re-established itself, hunched up in sleep, but strong, dependable. Capable, I dared to hope, of sharing a load I had so far carried alone...

As soon as I allowed myself the thought, I brushed it aside as a hopeless dream. To save myself pain, I suppose. And yet I did hope, nevertheless. Who can live without hope? I tried, in a circuitous way, to broach the subject with her.

Dorothy brushed aside all talk of love. 'It's the most overworked and misunderstood word in the English language,' she insisted. 'If a person can't think of a more specific word than 'love' to express what they feel, they must have a pretty limited vocabulary.'

'I think love can be very specific.'

'It's just sloppy use of language, Henry. It's what you and I are paid to try and prevent. Sloppy thinking. The trouble is, we're not a match for Rupert Murdoch and co.'

The red herring was too bright and fishy to ignore. It was clear she did not welcome my clumsy attempts at putting this new and strange emotion into words. For my part, I was prepared to throw caution to the winds and declare my longing for her...

But already I cared so much for her that, if it would embarrass her to hear of my love, I would not impose it on her.

'People won't settle for what Murdoch purveys,' I slipped into a familiar gear, instead. 'Not in the long run. They'll just demand more, like Oliver Twist. More brainwork, for a start. More impartiality. More openness to new ideas.'

She smiled and snuggled her face into the pillow beside me. I have no idea how much of my familiar dissertation on the future of British journalism she was able to catch – precious little, I daresay, but by now her magic was beginning to work on me and I had glimpses of a blissful land that I could only visit with her, through her eyes, inside her...

I pushed the sheet back, so the moonlight could make free with her. I felt a little disloyal, for a moment, but then the rich contours of her body seduced me. Still I lay propped on the pillows gazing at her, devouring her, flying away with her, scaling mountains, and rocking gently with her afterwards in peace and satiety.

'Come with me, and be my love' I whispered, 'And we will ev'ry pleasure prove...'

'Promises, promises, Henry,' came a sleepy voice from deep in the pillow. You'll just have to make do with the pleasures you can find in this bed. Anyway, I thought you were tired.' She rolled over and fixed me with a quizzical stare, shading her eyes against the moonlight.

'Not in the least!' I protested. 'I've had more sleep here than anywhere.'

'Yes, but you've had more exercise here, too. That's if I'm to believe what you're telling me.'

'It's true.'

'You haven't made love with anyone for ten years?'

'That's right.'

'It's just such a terrible waste, when you're so good at it. So caring and considerate. And patient.'

'That's not patience, it's self-indulgence. I'd like it to go on and on.'

'So I noticed!'

As we spoke, she unwound herself from what little remained of the sheet and insinuated herself beside me, around me, beneath me, on top of me. And there she sat back and looked at me with cool, laughing eyes. I never noticed her freckles by day, but I swear I saw them in that moonlight, a sweet scattering across the bridge of her nose and cheeks. To me, she was divine. Misty brown eyes bore down on me, wide eyes, bewitching eyes full of warmth and life, promising, teasing, with yet some mystery yet unsolved. I felt my blood surge to meet her as she sat astride me, rocking back and forth, exploring, settling. Her moistness brushed against my penis and the sensation was electric.

A wave of desire poured through me, urged my body against hers. The next wave would have carried me deep inside her, but she diverted me with her hand. She moistened the tip of my penis at the mouth of her vagina and then pressed it slithering against her clitoris. We played a delicious hide-and-seek after that, pressed together, sliding, touching, always moving. I was neither inside her nor outside her, but suspended, tingling, between the two: sensation piled on sensation, as if our skin had dissolved and the flesh between us joined.

Other parts of my body became highly sensitive: when she raked her teeth across my shoulder and breathed on my neck, it was like an electric current shooting down my spine. I longed to push inside her and complete the ecstasy, but still she held me at bay. And still the sensations mounted. I felt I was falling very slowly, spinning through endless cloud...

Her breath in my ear came more harshly and her spine stiffened. She drew back a little to look into my eyes and said the word 'Now' three or four times, very slowly, very softly. And this time when I pressed my penis against the mouth of her vagina there was no resistance and I surged on inside her, on into the depths of her mystery, on into the heart of her femininity.

She caught her breath. Her eyes closed, as if involuntarily. I had never known such a sensation: she allowed me to possess her completely and consumed me totally; she overwhelmed and empowered me at one and the same time.

For a moment, she lay still and held me close. Her body began to tremble. Her eyes opened again and found mine, and this time there was a helplessness, a vulnerability about her that spoke straight to my heart. The rhythmic movement began again, with each thrust taking me deeper inside. Her vagina tightened sharply and squeezed me for a moment, then released me, then squeezed again more powerfully, and again, and again, and our bodies took on this new rhythm, moving as one.

I wrapped my arms around her tightly to embrace the trembling as it built to a crescendo. She pressed her forehead against mine and breathed into my mouth, gasped a few half-words as her body throbbed convulsively against me. She gave herself over to me completely. I was astonished by the ferocity of this passion. No woman in my life had opened so much of her innermost self to me. It was the most precious gift I have ever received.

We could smile at each other now, hardly moving, wonder-struck at the perfection of the moment. She lay her head on my chest, started nibbling at me, kissing me lightly, stroking my stomach with her hair, running her tongue around my belly button. I protested that I was no longer twenty-one, but she was already teasing me with her tongue and my response was evident. Deliberately, almost lasciviously, she pulled her long, dark hair away from her face and fixed me with her lovely eyes. Her tongue flicked provocatively at my genitals. The rest of my body had ceased to exist, or at least had ceased to matter. Every nerve ending, every atom of sensation was focused there.

Pouting a little with her lips, she pressed them against the very top of my penis, watching me all the while, making sure I could see exactly what she was doing. Then very slowly, she enveloped me with her mouth, squeezing me, sucking me, setting me on fire with desire to pour into her, teasing me out of my lair of loneliness, daring me to fly with her, effortlessly shattering all the protective walls I had built around myself, all those years. I was not so foolish as to resist.

My seeds were on the brink of exploding into her mouth when she paused and took me into her body again and kissed me with her mouth all salt and sticky. I could not believe how perfectly our bodies fitted together; I could not believe the longing she had awoken in me. I felt utterly at one with her; I wanted to break myself down and exist only inside her.

When I closed my eyes and sniffed the morning air, I felt I had never before savored that experience so deeply. All my senses had quickened at once; what I felt for you, my love, enhanced every aspect of my being. With you at my side, I felt like a god. Or at least a man.

The sensation lasted precisely until I walked back through the main gateway to the little complex of villas. The concierge enquired my name in a rather superior manner, then that of 'Madame', which he knew quite well already, although he affected to have forgotten it. With a flourish befitting a member of the race that gave us the guillotine, he produced a blue envelope addressed to Miss Dorothy Pargeter, c/o her musician friends.

I promised to deliver it, but I knew at once that I was the Hanged Man, carrying his own death-warrant. She was out on the balcony when I got back, wearing her friend's dressing-gown with her hair in a towel.

'Coffee's on, Henry!' Then her face dropped a little when she noticed my expression. 'What's the matter?'

'Nothing at all!' I replied, rather too breezily, 'Letter for you. No escape from your creditors, eh?'

The smile faded from her face as she took the envelope. She held it as if trying to postpone the moment, but then ripped it open, took out the contents and abruptly turned her back on me. I tasted neither the coffee nor the croissants. Something precious had been taken from me and there was no redress. Dorothy was gone. Oh, her body was still there, hunched over a large breakfast cup of milky coffee and a couple of handwritten pages. But the woman I had left asleep in bed, languorous, relaxed, easy to be with – she had gone and been replaced by the nervous, nail-biting young woman I had seen in the staff room from time to time in her first few weeks at the school.

'I shouldn't have brought you that letter, should I?'

'Of course! Don't be silly! It's from – from some friends of mine. They're going to be in Kent about the time we get back. They want me to call in and see them. Don't mind, do you?'

'Not in the least! I can easily get a train from Dover.'

'Yes, probably be better than hanging about for me. I might stay there overnight, if we're back in time.'

The rest of our holiday turned into a race against the clock. Dorothy lost all enthusiasm for the little Provençal villa that had been the scene of such ecstatic moments and decided she wanted to drive part of the way back to Dover that night, to be sure of getting a mid-day ferry, the next day.

She tried so hard to conceal the evident change in her feelings that I joined in the pretence, and we both aped a gaiety that neither of us believed for a moment. What farcical pretences we English go in for, to avoid confronting our own emotions.

I am more to blame than most. I wrapped myself up, early in life, to insulate myself against a domineering grandmother and a mother who did not, I believe, truly want to smother me but knew no other way of protecting me from a world she so deeply mistrusted.

So, I cut myself off from the rawness of being. I took no risks and little exercise, apart from some walking. I buried myself in books and set myself reading targets that swallowed all my time. There was none left over for learning about feelings or getting used to being with people. Reading books circumscribed my whole existence. I lived in a world of other people's imaginations. No wonder I have never successfully passed myself off as a normal human being!

I tried to fit in, tried hard, sacrificed much. But everywhere they scented the pariah dog, the outcast in me. When I set out on this journey, literature was a high calling, arguably the greatest of all the arts. Now, it has been marginalised, devalued by its younger, brasher, media cousins. A book is praised if someone makes a TV series from it; symphonic music succeeds, only if it provides a suitable accompaniment to a film. Creativity is not encouraged and excellence is not appreciated. These are the ramblings of a bitter old pedagogue: I comfort myself with the promise to destroy these exercise books once I have bled my secrets into them. Then, at least, no unfortunate readers will ever have to unravel them. Although if Dorothy were to ask to see them, one day... I dismiss the thought as soon as it is born. Such sentimentality has been my downfall.

And yet... much of my life and work has been posited on the basis of such an ideal universe, even if existing only in the shared experience of like-minded scholars. Hesse's idea of a community linked by admiration of Eastern philosophy, scattered across the globe, but knowing one another when they meet, is a very attractive one: it offers a shred of hope for the future.

I would like to think the best lessons I gave at school helped to conjure up that perfect universe. It is essential for young minds to have some ideal to which they can aspire; otherwise, it becomes too easy to settle for second best, in everything.

The Lower Sixth, that summer, took a great dislike to Gerard Manley Hopkins, a Papist, indeed, a Jesuit, but a particular favorite of mine.

'He was out of touch, Sir,' offered Beefy Thomas, one of the sporting bloods of the school, 'living like a monk. What could he know about life? He chickened out of living his own life. He probably didn't have a clue about the real world!' Beefy's praetorian guard rumbled its approval.

'What is the real world?' I protested. 'Are you sure you know? Some people choose to live in a world of their own imagining. Who is to say that is less real? Eh? Besides, Hopkins chose to live a life of prayer and contemplation! You can't have a spiritual vocation and keep up with world affairs as well, you know, Thomas: it does involve some sacrifice.'

From the murmurs and smirks, I gathered most of them felt that missing out on sex was the greatest sacrifice they could imagine. This was a view I had recently come to share - but I was not about to share that opinion with the Lower Sixth.

'Don't you see, Thomas,' I tried an appeal to the more sensitive soul that I was sure lurked within the burly rugby player's bosom, 'Giving up so many sensory pleasures must have heightened his other senses. That's why he was so aware of aspects of the landscape: because he lived so simply, he could focus clearly on very simple things – and appreciate them.'

'Doesn't make sense, Sir.' Beefy was resolute in defense, loth to concede any ground. 'Why give things up when you might like them? Seems to me there's enough rules in the world already, without making fresh ones for yourself – don't you agree, Sir?'

Beefy knew his audience. The Lower Sixth disliked discipline of all kinds and Beefy made Hopkins' self-discipline sound particularly perverse. I needed to regain the initiative:

'You're a lot of Philistines, not prepared to listen to reason! You're so busy criticising Hopkins' life, as you imagine it, that you've none of you found time to hear his poetry.'

A dry voice cut through from the back row: 'Do we have to hear it, Sir? Can't we just read it to ourselves?' McLeish was a scientist, taking English 'A' level, I felt, for the sole purpose of annoying me. He was heading for a redbrick university to read Mechanical Engineering. Most of his interjections were utilitarian, geared towards efficient processing of data. Today, he was the catalyst for one of my tirades.

'Poetry is music, McLeish!' I snapped, 'It's intended to be spoken, or sung, or chanted. The words are not arbitrary algebraic signs; they deserve to ring out, to have the beauty of their sound appreciated. Poetry must have a voice!'

I could have sworn I saw Beefy Thomas give a brief flicker of understanding. It was one of those moments that renew one's faith in teaching. Most of our seed falls on stony ground, but sooner or later, if we persevere, some of it must take root.

'Beefy,' I said. Several of the less mature members of the Lower Sixth tittered. 'Thomas, I mean. Would you be kind enough to read something for us? I believe it's on page 27.'

The rest of the class began to shuffle open their books. 'No, there's no need for the rest of you to follow it. Just listen to the words. Try and hear the music: never mind the meaning, for once.'

'God's Grandeur, sir?' inquired Thomas, gruffly.

I nodded. 'Read it as slowly as you like. Just savour the words.' A few of the boys licked their lips and gave an exaggerated mimicry of eating, but most watched Beefy scanning the poem, wondering if he'd buy the dummy, to use their parlance.

'Go on!' I urged, 'You've got a powerful voice: let's hear it.'

Flattery is an invaluable tool for a teacher: if applied at the right time, it builds confidence. Sarcasm has the opposite effect, undermining and eating at the soul, like rust. Besides, I have a temperamental preference for the carrot, rather than the stick.

Beefy did his best to rise to the occasion. He was used to charging into a scrum and carrying his opponents several yards up the pitch with him: surely he could shoulder the burden of God's grandeur?

'"The world - is charged with the grandeur of God!"' he declared pugnaciously, glaring around at his audience, daring anyone to contradict him. He glanced again at the book and continued:

'"It will flame out, like shining from shook foil;
It gathers to a greatness, like the ooze of oil
Crushed. Why do men then now not reck his rod?"'

I caught a glimpse of growing panic in Beefy's eyes, as he coped with the long string of monosyllables. I tried to give him a nod of encouragement, but he'd lost the thread.

'Wreck his rod, sir? Wreck his rod?' The scorn was withering. The Lower Sixth wondered how I would tackle their ferocious standard bearer.

'You know what it means, don't you?' said I, momentarily forgetting that I'd told them not to bother with meanings. 'No? – Anyone? – Yes, Lander...'

'Watch out for the punishment, sir.'

That's the idea, Lander, yes. Fear the judgment of the Lord. If we appreciate God's grandeur, we'll show him a proper respect.

'A sort of Headmaster of the Hereafter, sir?'

I must confess, I laughed. I rather pride myself that the boys don't often succeed in putting me in place, but young Lander was a bright spark, and he'd managed it once or twice.

'I take your point, yes,' I admitted, 'I suppose there has always been an element of the Heavenly Headmaster about my vision of the Almighty. Must be an occupational hazard, don't you think? And now, Lander, if you'd be good enough to continue entertaining us, by reading the rest of the poem...'

I had not really noticed Jonathan Lander till that moment. Well, I mean, I had taught him and marked him out as one of the smarter members of the form, but I had not really appreciated his potential. He read that poem as if he was part of it, quietly, but in a tone commanding attention. The pain of it rang clear, like a bell.

"Generations have trod, have trod, have trod;
And all is seared with trade; bleared, smeared with toil;
And wears man's smudge and shares man's smell;
The soil Is bare now, nor can foot feel, being shod..."'

Memory plays tricks, insidiously blending the wisdom of hindsight with our recollections, but somehow the boy's voice evoked not just the meaning but the spirit behind the words. Proof of the presence of God, as Hopkins might have insisted. It was quite hypnotic. He took us right down to the despair, the terrible loneliness of earthly decay, at the end of the octet, and managed the transition to the more upbeat sextet with consummate ease. In a trice, we were away from the factories and the dark streets, out in the open air at dawn, in the warmth of God's presence again...

"And for all this, nature is never spent;
There lives the dearest freshness, deep down things;
And though the last lights off the black West went,
Oh, morning, at the brown brink eastward, springs.

Because the Holy Ghost over the bent
World broods with warm breast and with ah! bright wings!'''

There was a long silence at the end of the poem.

'Poetry, gentlemen!' I said, rather grandly, 'I can offer you no finer example. Like Yeats, I lay my treasures at your feet. Tread softly. Feel the power of the words.' The bell rang and I let them go.

'Read some more Hopkins tonight. I'll set the essay questions tomorrow.'

And in a moment, normality had overtaken them, they were scratching themselves, stretching, pushing the chairs out of their way. A dozen different conversations all began at once. But they had felt the poem. I knew that. They had gained something from the lesson, then, some fragment of greater understanding, that they would carry away with them. Could I really aspire to anything higher?

The problem was that I thought I could. I believed, when Fate presented me with a talent like Jonathan Lander's, I was under an obligation to nurture it. Why be a teacher if not to open people's eyes? Lander had a flair for literature, indeed, but more excitingly, I now knew he could act.

I was on my way to the staff room for what I considered a well-earned cup of tea when the inspiration struck me. I knew exactly what to do: Jonathan would play Othello for me that winter: if he was half as good as I expected, I'd make damned sure he got into RADA.

*   *   *

We had two favourite walks, at Cambridge. Both followed the river, but in character they could hardly have been less alike. If we wanted to meet friends or just watch strangers, we made for the Backs, where the River Cam rolls sedately through the back-gardens of the colleges, where tourists gawp at the public face of the University. But if long-dead writers were to be our only companions, as so often they were, we took the somewhat muddier path that leads beside the River Granta to Grantchester.

'You've got to expose yourself, Henry!' Fanshawe lollopped along the towpath, taking twice as many paces as my measured tread, so that he could face me and gesticulate as we walked.

He always preferred to see the person he was talking to: he loved to shock, and his greatest fun was watching people's reactions. Given my sheltered background, I imagine he found me rather an easy target.

'I'm not in the habit of exposing myself' I observed calmly.

'That's exactly my point!' Fanshawe seized it like a well-bred terrier. 'You've got to take more risks, or you'll miss out on the feast of life!'

'I'm not sure I've been invited to it.'

'Nonsense, Henry! Of course you are. You're here, aren't you? And it is a feast. Spread out in front of us. The whole of the world's literature – we can pick and choose. It's a huge privilege. And it's no good just skimming the surface: we've got to be prepared to leave our preconceptions and our conditioning behind and experience each writer's work as fully and openly as we can. Ours to judge, the art and the artifice.'

'I do read with an open mind!' I protested. 'I try very hard to make out what each writer wants to tell me...'

'It's not enough, my dear chap!' Fanshawe was in full flow now and brushed aside my comments with a languid wave of the hand.

'We've got to read with open hearts, not just open minds! Come to that, we've got to live with open hearts! God knows, we're not here for long: we may as well make the most of the time we've got! You've got to throw off that old tweed sports jacket, Henry, with the leather patches on the elbows. And the corduroy trousers, and the sensible brogues. You've got to feel the wind on your skin and the earth between your toes. Otherwise, how do you know you're alive?'

He paused to gauge the effect. I, knowing him, jumped in: 'Cogito, ergo sum, I suppose. I think, therefore I am.'

'Too much thinking and not enough sex! That's what's wrong with Cambridge: it's brain-heavy. It's forgotten its balls. Don't ever fall into that trap, Henry. Don't forget where your balls are.'

He looked so earnest, I burst out laughing and at once he joined in. That was one of many engaging characteristics: Fanshawe switched moods so swiftly, I could hardly keep up with him. He was mercurial; he flowed so easily from one thought to the next. I knew he was so much more alive than I was. I wanted to share his life-force.

Mother and grandmother aside, I had never been so much in thrall to another person. I had not formed the traditional close attachments at school: I found no kindred spirits there. Many of the boys had been superior to me in sporting achievements, but I did not admire them for it. True, they had strength and coordination above the ordinary. But to what purpose?

I had to admire Fanshawe, because he was the first man I knew who was truly himself, without reference to others. He went through life like a man on horseback, looking down benignly, exchanging a friendly word, but always from on high. He was set apart from the rest of us; he made no apology for it; that was simply who he was; it was his birthright.

His self-confidence alone would not have commanded my admiration. There were a hundred empty-headed young men at Magdalene as stylish and well-mannered as Fanshawe. But he was so bright: his mind sparkled with ideas; it was intoxicating to try and follow the flow of his thoughts.

At school, I had always come first in English. I suppose I expected to excel – but in the supervisions we shared, at college, Fanshawe always outshone me. I found myself competing, like a sportsman, keen to win the praise of our Director of Studies. So I was always going to respect Fanshawe. But then the respect grew into admiration and the admiration into a kind of love. I can put my hand on my heart and say I have known no-one to compare with him.

We paused at a landing-stage on a bend of the river, to quote Yeats and Hopkins at each other. A girl with long dark hair and a lace shawl walked along the towpath half a field away and Fanshawe quoted Hopkins' *Spring and Fall*, under his breath, so as not to spoil her reverie:

"Margaret, are you grieving,
Over Goldengrove unleaving?
Leaves, like the things of man, you,
With your fresh thoughts care for, can you?
Ah, as the heart grows older
It will come to such sights colder
By and by, nor spare a sigh
Though worlds of wanwood leafmeal lie;
And yet you will weep and know why.
Now, no matter, child, the name:
Sorrow's springs are the same.
Nor mouth had, no nor mind, expressed
What heart heard of, ghost guessed:
It is the blight man was born for,
It is Margaret you mourn for."

He turned away from me, at the end, and the last few words were muffled. I sought out his face and saw tears rolling down his cheeks. I put my arms around his shoulders for a moment, while he regained his composure.

'Thanks,' he said at last, 'Afraid I got a bit carried away. I started off addressing the poem to that girl, and then I found I was speaking to myself. I felt the passage of time. I felt a little piece of my life break off and go floating down the river towards the sea.'

'Well, we can none of us stay eighteen forever. Even you.'

'I know, but nor do we have to pretend we're sixty-six and retired before we really are!' Fanshawe had this idea that I was pre-empting my whole career, just because I'd once mentioned my dream of re-tiring to a cottage in the Lake District. 'You're a good friend, Henry.' he said, smiling, 'and a very good influence, what's more. You help to keep my feet on the ground. I sometimes think, but for you, I'd just float off into some other plane of existence: there's not much to keep me here.'

'Don't talk rubbish! You've got the world at your feet. You'll be able to do anything you want.'

'Do you know, the Buddha sat under the bodhi tree for eight years before attaining enlightenment. What if that's what I want to do? Do you think our masters would let me do that?'

'There's no need. The Buddha's done it already. Surely one perfect oblation is sufficient for the universe.'

'Maybe it is, in Christianity. But Buddhism's different, you see, they have thousands of bodhisattvas.'

'Do they, indeed? And what's a bodhisattva, when it's at home?'

'Well, I'm a little bit hazy about it, but as far as I can make out, they're people who've reached the very edge of enlightenment and are now holding back from the final step into the Light, until everyone else can join them, and all reach enlightenment altogether.'

'What if some don't want to reach enlightenment, thank you very much?'

'Well, they may think they don't want to, but when they get there, they'll realise it was just what they needed. I mean, it must be, mustn't it? By definition. You're not going to say 'Oh, by the way, I reached enlightenment last night. Wasn't much good. Seen better on the telly. I don't reckon this enlightenment's all it's cracked up to be, you know...'

'It all sounds very fascist, to me. I think everyone should have a choice as to whether they attain enlightenment or not.'

'Do you know what this place used to be, Henry?' Fanshawe was off on another tack, as usual.

'Used to be, when?'

'It's here somewhere.' Fanshawe was rummaging in the undergrowth on the bank. He ripped out a couple of handfuls of long grass to reveal an old wooden sign with pale blue paint almost washed off. But you could still make out a couple of words: 'MEN ONLY'. Fanshawe was triumphant. 'There you are! It's the old nude bathing spot.'

'Don't be disgusting.'

'It's not disgusting, it's a tradition! Very popular in Rupert Brooke's time, I believe. They've got one at Oxford, too. Don't you know the story about - who was it? Maurice Bowra, I think. Anyway, it doesn't matter who it was: Bowra or whoever had been swimming with three or four other dons, and they were sunbathing on the bank, when some ladies came along. Well, all the others grabbed hold of towels or whatever and covered their private parts.'

'So what did Bowra do?'

'He just took his hat and covered up his face with it. And lay there, naked. Well, when the ladies had covered their confusion and moved on, the others asked him why. And Bowra said: "I don't know about you, gentlemen, but I am more frequently recognised by my face than my genitals!"'

*   *   *

In the reading competition, early in that summer term, after my European misadventure with Dorothy, I had cause to remember Fanshawe's rendition of *Spring and Fall*. None other than Beefy Thomas chose it for his voluntary piece. Not a good choice, I felt, given Beefy's style of delivery, but Dorothy, who was also judging the competition, was quite taken with it.

'Frankly, Headmaster, I wouldn't have believed Thomas had it in him to read that piece with such sensitivity,' she insisted, then throwing a cursory bone in my direction, 'Mr Barraclough's done wonders with him.'

'Indeed, Miss Pargeter,' the Headmaster harumphed in his usual all-knowing way. 'Does you credit, Henry. Well, you two are the experts: if you want to give the prize to Thomas, I shan't stand in your way.'

'Aren't we being a little premature?' I admonished them firmly but politely. Dorothy sank back into her chair, trying not to look too resentful at having her colours perfunctorily lowered. 'There is one more entrant waiting to read his voluntary piece.'

'Yes, I thought we hadn't seen them all.' The Headmaster mentally patted himself on the back for being right again, replaced the spectacles he had removed to speak to Miss Pargeter, and consulted his list. 'Wheel him in, then, Henry. Who is it?'

'Jonathan Lander. Curiously enough, he's reading something from Hopkins, too, something rather more demanding, as I'm sure you'll notice.'

Lander had done well enough in the two compulsory readings to reach the final group of six, but now he excelled himself. *The Leaden Echo and the Golden Echo* is one of the great tests, for a reader of Hopkins. It only makes sense if you get the very complex speech rhythms exactly right. But Lander was magnificent. I shall remember to my dying day the way he made the change from Leaden Echo to Golden Echo. First there was the tumbling down through decay to death and worse:

'So be beginning, be beginning to despair,
O there's none; no no no there's none:
Be beginning to despair, to despair,
Despair, despair, despair, despair.'

The pause was audacious. It went on ... and on ...while the last baritone reverberations faded into the farthest corners of the Chapel. Then came the answering echo, as if from those very corners, an emanation of hope...

'...'Spare!
There is one, yes I have one (Hush there!);
Only not within seeing of the sun,
Not within the singeing of the strong sun,
Tall sun's tingeing, or treacherous the tainting of the earth's air,
Somewhere elsewhere there is ah well where! One
One. Yes I can tell such a key, I do know such a place..."

Dorothy would not be moved. I don't think she can have listened to Lander at all. She merely spent the time cooking up fresh reasons to give the prize to Beefy Thomas. She liked the contained strength of his reading. She found his gentleness appealing. I tried to tell her that *Spring and Fall* needs much more than gentleness, it needs understanding, maturity; it is, after all, an adult speaking to a child. Beefy, for all his physical development, was still too much the child, for the poem to ring true.

Perhaps I was being unfair to him. He was competing with a distant, treasured memory: I could hear Fanshawe's voice...

"And yet you will weep and know why.
Now no matter, child, the name:
Sorrow's springs are the same."

And when he spoke them, the lines were not false, because he had the authority, the gravitas, above all, the wisdom to say it and mean it. I suppose it was an unfair comparison. But what upset me most was the injustice to young Lander, who had tackled an exceptionally difficult piece and shown a remarkable command of the internal rhythms.

'It's like comparing a symphony with a song!' I protested, 'Thomas' piece is a single melody, a single mood. Lander's is orchestral, there are movements, changes...'

'It was certainly a lot longer, Henry,' pointed out the Headmaster, who had shuffled his feet a little at the end of *The Leaden Echo*, I fear thinking it the end of the poem. 'I wonder if you shouldn't give them a limit, next year. Fourteen lines, or so. Quite enough to judge...'

'I'll bear that in mind, Headmaster. I'm very grateful to you both for coming to help with the judging this year.'

'Not at all, Henry. I like to be involved. And it's good for you to know you've got such an able assistant as Miss Pargeter. I've told you before, Henry, you do too much for the school. Delegation, that's the key! If you learn to delegate, you can lighten the load a little.'

'That's all very well in theory, Headmaster...'

'I'm afraid Mr Barraclough finds our opinions unwelcome, Headmaster. He'd rather make the award himself, as usual.'

'Not at all! I'm as keen as anyone to open up the judging process, as long as it makes sure that the best man wins. But in this case, it seems about to lead to a gross miscarriage of justice. Jonathan Lander's reading was the best I've heard in twenty years. If you really couldn't hear it, Miss Pargeter, I can only suggest that for some reason you didn't listen.'

'Come, come, there's no need for all this!' puffed the Headmaster, enjoying himself immensely. 'I take Miss Pargeter's point, about the delicacy of Thomas' reading: it's not normally a quality I would have associated with him, but a very commendable effort. I like to see the school's sportsmen taking a part in the artistic extravaganzas, you know – goes down well with the parents.'

'No doubt, Headmaster, but with respect, we should still make the award on the basis of excellence. In past years, I have sometimes shared the prize, but on this occasion, I really can't see any justification...

'On this occasion, Mr Barraclough...' Dorothy's cheeks had reddened and her nostrils flared for battle.

But the Headmaster had tired of the game. 'Think I'd better guillotine the debate, don't you? Clearly, it falls to me to exercise the casting vote, which I do in favour of Thomas, with a judges' special commendation for Lander. Damned fine opening bat, Thomas, you know. Did you see his fifty the other day?'

I shook my head. Dorothy inclined hers, nodding sympathetically.

'The thing about sportsmen, Henry, is that they've got the will to win. That's what you need, to succeed in the arts, or any other field of endeavour – the will to win! Determination, do you see? Can't beat it!'

Fired by his own eloquence, the Headmaster went on to make the announcement. Lander was not so much shocked as puzzled. I followed him out of the Chapel and assured him that his reading had been quite exceptional, in my view. He smiled and thanked me, said he didn't really care much about prizes, shook my hand and left.

To my surprise, Dorothy was waiting alone in the Chapel when I went to clear up my papers.

'I wanted to apologise,' she said.

'Not at all. You made your point and carried the day.'

'Not just about that. About the way I've behaved for the first two or three weeks of term.'

'You've been perfectly civil...'

'Exactly,' she said, nodding vigorously, 'Civil. That's what I've been. I'm sorry. I just felt very awkward, about how to behave with you. I mean, I didn't want to pretend the holiday didn't happen, but I didn't want to put you under an obligation – I thought maybe it would be best if our professional relationship went on just as before. And then, when you were so correct and polite and cold and so English I thought that was how you wanted it, too. It was only when you got angry, just now, about the reading competition, that I realised how angry you still are, about what happened. So – I'm sorry. I really am. Upsetting you like that was the last thing I wanted to do, after you'd been so gentle and considerate...'

Once again, she had overwhelmed me. I saw myself as I must have seemed to her – stiff, priggish, ungrateful, inflexible... Why had I gone in for this ridiculous pretence of not caring, when we met again at school? Was it merely to protect myself? Or did I, more sinisterly, have some wish to hurt her? I suppose I reasoned that if she cared about me, she would make the first approach; if she did not, we both had a job to do, and we should get on with it, in the interests of the young people in our care.

Stuff and self-justification! How we delude ourselves! There was no reasoning about it. I was afraid. Afraid of my own emotions? No, but afraid of rejection. Afraid of becoming the laughing-stock of the school again. Afraid of being again that odd, thin, ginger, bespectacled boy cowering in a corner of the playground as the chase for the football sweeps past and leaves him in the dust.

I would have chased footballs, if it would have made them accept me; but when I did try to chase footballs, it was worse: instead of ignoring me, the other boys noticed my inadequacies, and blamed me for them. On the whole, it was preferable to be ignored. I usually took a book into the playground, in case further defence should be required.

The scent of Dorothy, close to me, awoke my senses from the moment of reverie. Blindly, I went to her, enfolded her gently in my arms. I told her it was not her fault, but mine. She bowed her head and I felt the softness of her hair on my cheek.

What I did not hear was the Headmaster coming back into the Chapel. Dorothy backed away from me as if scalded.

'What's the matter? Don't back away, please. I need you…' A nervous jerk of Dorothy's head alerted me to the danger.

'I need you to – ah, help me sort out these books, Miss Pargeter, if you'd he so kind.'

'Certainly, Mr Barraclough.' Dorothy went to the two rows of contestants' seats and began collecting books and papers.

The Headmaster pounced. 'Ah! Spectacles. I thought I'd left them there! Not still arguing about the reading competition, I hope, Henry, Miss Pargeter?'

'Not at all, sir,' as Dorothy turned, a few steep rays of reddish sunlight from the high Chapel windows caught her face. I stepped forward. 'We were discussing how to implement your instructions on delegation, Headmaster.'

'Delegation! Yes! It's the life-blood of any management system, you know. Of course, you have to maintain a strong core of command. Control. But the great advantage of delegation is it gets things done!'

The Headmaster gazed wistfully around the Chapel, as if feeling that such a peroration demanded an audience of two or three hundred, rather than two. But being a realist and a practical man, he gave a small shrug of his shoulders and made for the exit, advising us in passing to 'carry on'. As the heavy door closed behind him, Dorothy laughed and threw herself back into a chair. 'Henry, you were brilliant! Have you done this before?'

'Certainly not.'

'Anyway, I'm sorry. I didn't mean to embarrass you. I just wanted us to be able to speak to each other like human beings again. I don't know what went wrong, at the beginning of term. It doesn't matter whose fault it was.'

'Thank you,' I said, 'thank you for breaking the ice again. I'm afraid I have this terrible habit of closing myself off and getting on with my own life.'

'So you should. It's the only one you've got, so you may as well enjoy it. But don't forget, there are a lot of other people in the world: you'll have a much more interesting time with us than without us.'

'I'm sure I shall. Thanks for the reminder.' I wanted to be beside her again, but my legs remained obstinately rooted to the spot. There was a gap between us that I could not bridge. She was smiling at me, and I at her; we had swept away three weeks of awkwardness, laughed it off in a moment. We were together again, not loving, perhaps, but affectionate. And yet there was still something unspoken, a half-heard note of warning, that kept me from going to her again with open arms. If Dorothy felt any such reservation, she gave no trace of it. She quickly gathered the few remaining books and papers and took my arm as we went down the steps from the Chapel to the car park. I was rather flattered: I wondered what the Lower Sixth would make of this spectacle; I rather liked the idea of the Lower Sixth seeing me with Miss Pargeter on my arm, and I must confess, I daydreamed a little about that, while Dorothy gave me her critique of a production she had seen in London, at the end of the Easter holiday. She asked if I was going away for the May Day weekend. To tell the truth, I had forgotten all about the Bank Holiday, but I invented plans to tidy the garden and mentioned a long-awaited library book that had just arrived.

'You know what I've never shown you?' She was unlocking the door of her car. 'The photographs of our trip!'

'Oh yes, I'd forgotten about them! Did they turn out all right?' I hadn't forgotten about them at all, but I'd been too proud to ask to see them before and I was still too proud to admit to that, so I felt the white lie was forgivable. More importantly, we were rapidly approaching her car and my bicycle. I wanted desperately to arrange to see her again, but couldn't find the right words.

'Why don't you come round and see them now?' she said, before I could speak, 'I'll even cook dinner, if you're feeling really brave.'

'I'd love to, thank you.' I was still adjusting my bicycle clips but she revved the engine and opened the passenger door, so I jumped in with as much dash as I could muster, and we were off through the school gates at thirty miles an hour!

I know now just how meticulously Dorothy plans her moves on the chess-board of life, but at the time I was convinced she did everything on the spur of the moment. It seemed a wonderfully romantic approach. I tried to think when I had last met anyone so anarchic. Who else would change direction like that at the last moment, on a whim? Of course, it was Fanshawe.

Quite by chance, Dorothy happened to have a couple of tickets for the Saturday matinee of *Coriolanus* at the Royal Shakespeare Company, in London. A cousin who was going with her had been taken ill. In the interval, I was surprised to find she knew several people in the audience. She explained that the tickets had come from a theatre club run by the PTA at her previous school. But then she declined their invitations to join them after the performance, saying we had a dinner engagement.

She introduced me to one or two of them, but there was hardly time to exchange a word before we were moving on again, through the busy throng around the bar. At one point, she was very affectionate, almost flirtatious, whispering in my ear and touching my cheek as she spoke, but the moment passed.

I did have a sense that I might be just a minor character in Dorothy's drama; now I feel I was more of a prop than a character, merely a device to achieve an intended effect.

At the time I was beguiled again, swept along in her wake, happy enough but a little dazzled at finding favour again so abruptly, so unexpectedly.

Ah, Dorothy, you always had such a power over me. I should have been warned. If Mother had still been with us, she would have taken delight in warning me. She would have seen how unsuitable you were; she would have seen through all your tricks. But would I have taken any notice? I am afraid, to be honest, as I am still trying to be, not wishing to deceive myself, that I would have delighted in contradicting Mother and would probably have suspected her of unworthy motives into the bargain. I might have accused her of interfering in my life, of not wanting me to be happy. My behaviour would have been quite adolescent: that is one of the effects parents have on us: to them, we are always children.

And then Dorothy would have betrayed me and Mother would have been proved right. She would never have let me forget it. Not that there is any danger of my forgetting. Or should I say any hope?

*   *   *

What am I doing with these grubby exercise books? This is drivel, an old man's sentimental, self-pitying drivel. I thank the Lord I did not have twelve of the damned things left over, or twenty. Seven is bad enough. I wonder about losing a couple. But I have never been a shirker, and I do not intend to start now. Let the truth be told, even though it is never to be heard by any other ears. This book is mine. For all the millions of pages on my bookshelves, for all the weight of paper and cardboard and printers' ink, for all the assiduous collection of carefully chosen if eclectic masterpieces made of other people's words, in whose service and at whose altars I have worshipped - for all that, this slim booklet, that I press flat with my left hand and feverishly scribble in with my right – this book is the very first and only book that has ever been truly mine.

That is why I am going to destroy it. Because it comes too close. Because it holds a mirror up to me. I do not want people looking on my nakedness when I am dead. What will be the significance then of my brief spurts and spasms? Stains on a sheet, long since washed away. What of my love, that occasional flower that has bloomed so rarely and been returned more rarely still? What of my love?

I mentioned at the start my tendency to over-dramatise in the hope of finding some excitement in the dreary parade of safe bets and conservative choices that has been my chosen lot. Ironically, in the end I found more drama than I might have wished.

It is the schoolmaster in me. We have captive audiences, you see. We start sentences without knowing how they are going to finish. We burble on. And on. And on. We repeat ourselves. It amuses the boys. We rework our best lines, year after year, like tired old music-hall comics.

Teachers should continue to grow, not stay frozen in time, stuck in the tastes and habits of our university days. Too often, we fail to find the time to read new books or to grow new ideas. We, of all people, should still be learning, actively acquiring new knowledge and skills. How else can we presume to teach others to make the most of their abilities?

*　　*　　*

There was a sharp clack at the front door. The letterbox flap snapped back. The sound reverberated round the empty hall, But beneath it, insidiously, my practised ear could make out the rustling, fluttering sound of a letter settling on the mat.

For a moment I tried to pretend it was nothing important. The electricity bill. A circular. I would go and pick it up later. I am busy, writing. But I was not. I was still crouched over this exercise book. Pretending to be a man hard at work...

But I was no longer writing. I hunched my shoulders, gathering my strength, to receive the next lash from Fate's whip hand. A grenade of reality had just been popped through my front door.

I am not saying I knew the letter was from Dorothy. I am not telepathic. It could have been from anyone. But it was not. It was from her. Eventually, without writing another word, I went to pick it up. The envelope is yellow, lightly scented. She always loved to smell flowers. I can see her now, snuffing the air to savour the night-scented stock on one of our walks.

I am not going to open it. Who does she think she is, writing letters to me, after all this time? After what she did to me? Or rather, failed to do for me, when she had the chance. I have suffered enough from knowing that young woman – I am damned if I will call her a lady!

'And for all this, nature is never spent;
There lives the dearest freshness deep down things.'

Was Hopkins wrong? Is there really only a baseness and bitterness at the heart of it all? I will not believe it. And I have more reason to believe it than most.

'I am a man more sinned against than sinning.'

And I have no right to complain. That is the bargain. There must inevitably be as many sinned against as sinners. Who carries the greater burden?

Christ's example is clear:

'Follow me.'

'We follow, Lord, we follow.'

Like sheep. We queue (like English sheep) for the butcher's knife. And even when we are split and quartered, torn limb from limb and cut through the bone, chopped, filleted, turned to scraps and sausagemeat and boiled away in a slightly greasy vapour, even as the last disintegrating atoms of us float away to merge with the atmosphere... Even then, we are thinking, as we pat ourselves on our little atomic backs:

'All shall be well... And all manner of things shall be well...'

For after all, as Doctor Pangloss so sagely observed, in Voltaire's Candide:

'All is for the best, in this best of all possible worlds.'

Incontrovertible. A complete lie. And absolutely true. A marvellous paradox. For those who care for paradoxes.

It boils down to a question of how we want to live our lives. It is a matter of choice. Do we want to go dancing and skipping, eyes aglow, seeing only the goodness and beauty in the world? Or do we want to face reality with open eyes? Shoulder the burden, carry the Cross. Why do we choose the burden? Why do we look on the cloud, and not the silver lining?

Because experience is our teacher. There may well be a silver lining, but we know in our hearts that the dark cloud will prevail. Despair. There is no spare, no hope, of course. And yet...

Here, to clinch the argument, is the envelope. Its yellowness and its scent seem to have faded a little, in the sunlight. It is almost innocuous, lying there on the desk. I shall ignore it and make myself a cup of tea.

*   *   *

So. The rest of the page is still blank, the teacup half empty. These are the views habitually adopted by the English. Our national myopia. When will we learn that the page is partly completed, the teacup half full?

Why do we adopt so bleak an outlook? I think it goes back to armour. Medieval habits die hard. We fear the worst and clothe our hopes accordingly. We venture out in daily expectation of the modern equivalent of a warlike Pict or Visigoth bearing down on us with a great two-handed cleaver...

Enough butchery. I interrupted myself describing that May weekend in London. That was another time I dared to hope...

We got to Liverpool Street Station far too late. I warned her, but she would not listen. She insisted on dashing up and down escalators in Tube stations, all to no avail.

'Oh well, we'll catch the milk train!' she suggested, brightly.

'I'm afraid not,' I said, scanning the timetable 'The next train is at 5.45 in the morning.'

'You're joking! Three's always one about half past midnight, isn't there? Stops everywhere. I've caught it.'

'Monday to Friday only, I'm afraid. You see the footnote in the timetable?'

'Oh Henry, I'm so sorry! You were right! I should have hurried when you told me. It's my fault entirely...'

'Not at all. We'll cope. What was that film with Humphrey Bogart in it? I miss the steam trains, don't you? These new stations don't have quite the same charisma as the old. Remember the smells? What's that? Before your time? Well, you missed something, then. Steam trains! They were a direct link with Stephenson's Rocket. Imagine what the London stations would have been like in Victorian times: they were the wonders of the age! Cathedrals to people's new mobility...'

She got her own back, in the end: 'What were the stage coaches really like, Papa? Were they as uncomfortable as everyone said?

'Oh, worse, my dear. After a journey from London to York, you couldn't sit down for a week!'

She laughed: 'You are a brick, Henry.'

'You mean something thick, heavy and solid?'

'I mean for taking this... this disaster so well! Most men would have been storming up and down the platform, berating porters. Or me.'

'I will, if you like. If it'll make you feel any better. But it'd be more to the point if we booked into the Dorchester.'

She laughed again and then looked at me quizzically:

'You're not serious?'

'Why not? Single rooms, of course.'

'Just as you like. But don't you think that's a bit out of our price range?'

'Possibly, but I've got a very good friend called Mr Barclaycard, who's offered to pay the bill for us. So you needn't worry about that. Come on. We can phone from here.'

Dorothy liked me being decisive. I should have done it more often. I dialled 192 for the hotel number and got through to the receptionist almost immediately. They only had one room left. I looked enquiringly at Dorothy and she nodded.

The taxidriver who took us across London was obviously keen to get to his next job. She was thrown against me in the back seat as we rounded Marble Arch and set off down Park Lane. She apologised. I assured her it didn't matter, and kept my arm around her shoulders. She sighed and rested her head against my chest. For a moment I felt almost heroic.

I remembered Fanshawe talking about doing everything with 'style'. I always found it a rather evanescent concept, style, but in that taxi I felt I knew just what he was driving at. As if in a dream, we were whisked across the city, received by flunkeys and admitted to a plushly furnished room with two double beds and a refrigerator full of alcohol.

'Well, this is wonderful, Henry' she purred, seating herself on one of the beds, 'Would you like a drink? A nightcap?'

'You mean like cocoa?'

'That's not exactly what I had in mind, no.'

'Champagne, then. I'll phone Room Service.' I suppose it was rather naughty of me: I'd noticed how easily Dorothy was impressed by such tricks, and I was teasing her, but she took me seriously every time. I had never stayed at the Dorchester in my life, but Fanshawe had told a long story about visiting a friend's father's suite there, and stray details of it kept coming back to me. This time, Dorothy was ahead of me.

'There's no need. Look, there are some quarter bottles in the fridge.'

'So there are! Splendid.'

I seized two of the tiny bottles and removed the caps with a flourish while she found some glasses. We drank each other's health.

She savoured the aftertaste of the champagne and looked at me speculatively.

'Do you wish you'd never met me?' she asked, out of the blue.

'No, I could never wish that. You enriched my life. Shook me out of my lethargy. I was beginning to get a bit set in my ways you came along... Didn't do me any harm.'

'I hope not. The last thing in the world I wanted was to hurt you.'

I smiled. 'I'm tougher than I look.'

'Maybe.' She coiled a lock of her hair round her finger and looked thoughtful. 'But you're also very vulnerable. That's what worries me. And now I'm afraid of hurting you more.'

'Nonsense. I'm made of brick, as you just pointed out. Solid.'

'Not made of brick. You know what I meant.'

She started patrolling the room, idly looking in all the drawers and cupboards, taking possession of it, the way women do. I watched her. I remembered her doing just the same in the Provençal villa. It was becoming a familiar ritual. I felt myself warm to the sight of it. I hardly dared to hope. And yet...'

'I always feel so comfortable with you, Henry.'

'Comfortable? You make me sound like a battered old armchair!'

'I don't feel pressured, with you. It's like being with a very close friend. I can relax, be myself.'

'So why don't we agree to stop worrying about the past and the future, and concentrate on enjoying the present? It's all we've got, when you come to brass tacks. I sometimes think the sin against the Holy Ghost, the one unforgivable sin, is not making the most of the present, while we've got it.'

'Which, by definition, is all the time.'

'Precisely.'

And I took her in my arms, looked, as I had longed to look, deep into her eyes, and kissed her. Her mouth was soft. Instantly, I was in a state of bliss. All the wasted years fell away from me.

*　*　*

But now, back in the present, the real present, I mean, there is the yellow letter, on the desk. It mocks me for my pretence, the sham of writing about living in the present while indulging a memory from the past.

What on earth has happened to the young Lochinvar in me? Afraid of a letter! Afraid of words, on a piece of paper? I should be able to deal with words, if nothing else; that may be the only skill I possess.

In that new mood, I ripped open the letter. She did not have much to say. As usual, she was terse and to the point.

'Dear Henry,

Forgive me for writing but I thought if I phoned you might hang up on me. And you'd have every right to do so. I don't know if you want to see me. I rather imagine not. But I would like to see you. I don't want to put you to any trouble, so I'll come at six o'clock this evening, if it's all right with you. You can leave a message on my answering machine if it's not convenient.

with love, Dorothy.'

Not convenient? Not convenient? It's about as convenient as a coffee morning with Genghis Khan and the marauding hordes. Alas, my tranquil heart! I'm damned if I'll open my front door to that... that trollop! It's just what she did before. She came bursting back into my life without a care for the mayhem she was about to inflict on me. Yes, she did! Oh, very well, I cannot say without a care. She did warn me, that night, in London. And, naturally, I ignored the warning. Because I wanted her. And I wanted to be the sort of man who could think like that, live like that. It made me feel more of a *Mensch*.

I do not want her here this evening. I am just coming to terms with her NOT being here. It would set me back weeks - months! But now I am thinking like a patient, recovering from a sickness. I am not ill. I have to stand up to her, that is all, and make it quite clear that she is not wanted.

And yet, the truth is I that want her more than I want my own life. Most of all, I want to breathe the scent of her next to me, for just one more time. I want to look into those eyes again, the eyes that lured me to love her, the eyes that later executed me in cold blood, unblinking, unpitying.

What will she expect, at six o'clock? Tea? No. Too late. Sherry? Too old-fashioned. Perhaps a gin and tonic. Six o'clock – it's too late for business and too early for funny business. She will not expect a meal at that time... or will she? What if we just hit it off as we did before, and she stayed longer than she intended? Well, it would be a considerate gesture on my part to have something ready, just in case. Nothing too complicated.

It's long time since I last cooked a proper meal. Fish, I think, with a crisp, dry white wine. Some *paté*, to start, and a dessert of some kind. Coffee. I seem to remember she had a taste for some ghastly liqueurs…

What am I thinking of? Cooking dinner for her, after the way she has treated me? I would rather poison her. No, I would not. I do not hate her. I cannot. I have tried. I have every justification for doing so, but I am still in love with her, in spite of everything. Some say love and hate are opposite sides of the same coin, but not for me. My love does not turn to hate. It merely withers on the vine, unharvested. And on that cheery note, I shall stop writing and go to the shops.

*   *   *

Which I did. Sniffing round the fish market, I found two very nice pieces of skate. I shall make a cream sauce with prawns. I have cleaned Mother's fish knives and forks. I really cannot remember the last time I entertained. What an anti-social old bastard I have become, of late. Not surprising, with my reputation, some might say. As Iago points out, reputation is easier lost than won:

'Good name in man and woman, dear my lord,
Is the immediate jewel of their souls.
Who steals my purse steals trash; 'tis something, nothing;
'Twas mine, 'tis his, and has been slave to thousands;
But he that filches from me my good name
Robs me of that which not enriches him,
And makes me poor indeed.'

Do I care so much about my reputation? Should I care? If so, then Dorothy is very much to blame, since she took it from me – or failed to restore it. But perhaps I am better off without it. Perhaps it is one of those possessions that we allow to weigh us down. I have an idea that in the East, people carry their burdens more lightly, or shed them earlier. They are therefore freer to concentrate on the essence of the Now. Not a good plan, if it should taste bitter, but otherwise unimpeachable.

And here I am, now, in the middle way, waiting for a woman almost young enough to be my daughter. Waiting for the woman I still love, in spite of everything. Who is late. Of course.

It is six-fifteen. I begin to worry. She is a very skilful driver, certainly, but others may be less so... I must banish such thoughts. At last the doorbell rings. Wish me luck.

*   *   *

I brushed my hair, straightened my jacket and opened the door. She seemed shorter than I remembered: maybe she was wearing shoes with lower heels. She apologised for being late and I said it did not matter. She did not offer her cheek to be kissed when she arrived and I did not volunteer. I may have bowed slightly, from the waist, as she passed me, and closed the door. I may have looked a little ridiculous, but I do not think she noticed.

'I've made a jug of Pimms. Would you like some?' I said, fetching it from the fridge. I started to fill two tumblers.

'No, thank you, Henry, I won't. I'm not really drinking at the moment. A glass of mineral water would be fine.'

'Fizzy?'

'Or still. It really doesn't matter.'

'I wondered if your tastes would have changed.'

'I've always liked fizzy mineral water.'

'Strange. I don't recall... You liked Pimms, I do know..'

'I just couldn't face any at the moment. Sorry.'

She grimaced and sat down, rather heavily, in my armchair. She seemed solider, somehow, slower in her movements.

'I expect you can guess what I've come to tell you.'

'I have no idea' And then I realised.

She is with child.

Name: *Rt. Hon. Henry Barraclough, MP*

Form: *-ic Acid*

Book 4 : For a Boy

Effingham School
Effingham, Glos.

This changes things completely. I had very specific plans for this fourth fresh exercise book, the fourth chapter of my saga. But for once, the present has seized me by the throat. I am to be put to the torch again. So be it. I am content.

I am afraid I did not conduct the remainder of the meeting with Dorothy very coherently. My jaw sagged at the news. It was like a dream. Or a nightmare. I remembered Job and all the tricks God played on him to test his faith. Could this be a test for me? If so, I am afraid I have failed it already.

It seemed such a gratuitous twist of the knife. To see again the woman I love was a gift from God, pure and perfect, like a fine day or a glorious sunset. But to see her fecund and fulfilled, carrying another man's child in her womb, now that was an exquisitely fashioned thumb-screw that I had not foreseen in my blackest imaginings.

It is all over. There is no point in pretending any more. She is gone, and my wild dreams of ever achieving domestic bliss – or even normality – are gone with her, like the wind.

I did not really listen to her, at first. My system could not absorb any more information. It was still too busy processing the bombshell that had followed the hand grenade through my front door.

'The baby's due at the end of July,' she said, 'so I thought I'd start my maternity leave at half-term. They always tend to come early, in my family...' She could have been having a natter with a neighbour over the back fence, while hanging out the washing. It was all so matter of fact.

I wondered angrily whether she had any idea of the pain her news would cause me. Then I reflected, she had no need to come. Her presence alone was some indication that she cared about my feelings. Briefly, I wondered whether she meant to cause me pain, but that, I recognised as paranoia. Besides, I could not believe she hated me. Her behaviour when I left the school had been entirely selfish, but not vindictive.

I smiled and nodded, tried to share her pleasure in the forthcoming event. But my own disappointment swept away all other feelings, pounding away in my brain like a headache that no painkillers could ever relieve.

It had cost her some effort to come to see me, she explained, but she had not wanted me to hear the news from anyone else. I did not trouble to explain that I meet no-one from the school since my debacle. So she came for my sake. I should be grateful. I tried to appear so. I offered her tea, which she accepted. As I filled the kettle, I quietly poured the full jug of Pimms down the sink.

She was very happy, she said, and hoped I was, too.

She recommended making the most of my early retirement.

I said I was finding plenty to occupy myself. I tried to pretend I recalled our time together only occasionally, but I do not think she was deceived. I affected that brittle, pent-up casualness English people use when they are seething inside. There was one moment, one peculiarly crass remark she let fall, that made me want to strangle her, but I poured her another cup of tea instead, and the impulse passed.

Conversation was hard. I wanted to ask about the baby, its father, her feelings for him. She wanted (I think) to tell me. But by the unwritten rules of our class and country, we were obliged to impart this information in code, via a series of platitudes and mundane observations. The emotions were to be kept firmly caged, chained and out of sight. Towards the end of her visit, she ventured gingerly on to more personal ground.

'You're a good man, Henry' she said, 'Too good for me.'

'Strangely enough, I don't find that much of a consolation.'

'Well, you should. I'd have bossed you around unmercifully. You know I would. I'd have made your life hell.'

'You've done that, in any case.'

'No, I haven't!'

'I should know.'

'Don't be so melodramatic. You've got your health, your pension, your freedom, your books, your interests... You've got everything you had before. And something more...'

'Really? What?'

'You know you're capable of loving someone. I think you'd forgotten that, when we met, or stopped believing it.'

'You thought I should be reminded of how agonising life can be.'

'And how wonderful. Or so you said at the time.'

She was right. I had said exactly that, and more. It is easy to be brave in the arms of someone you love. I knew I was not helping my cause by carping. I tried to change tack.

'It's not loving that's the problem.' I said. 'I chose to do that, in a way. It's not being able to see you that hurts.'

She came and sat beside me and took my hands in hers.

'I'm sorry, Henry, there's nothing I can do about that. I'm an expectant mother. I can't very well hang out with my ex-lover.'

'Do you think it's so obvious? People would jump to that conclusion, would they, if they saw us together?'

'That's not the point. You don't want to drag things out: you've got to look to the future, not the past.'

'And you're part of my past and not my future.'

'Exactly.'

'It's all very neat. You move us all around like chess-pieces. Those you no longer need are discarded. And occasionally recalled to active service. If needed, to serve a purpose.'

'You're getting very cynical, Henry. You know, I don't think it's good for you, spending so much of your time alone. You should get out more, make an effort to meet people.'

Suddenly I was tired of the combat. 'I suppose you're right. I just don't feel I have much to offer anyone at the moment.'

'You have a great deal to offer. Don't put yourself down, all the time.'

'I'm a forty-nine-year-old academic with no job, no prospects and a thoroughly jaundiced view of the world. Cynical, as you observed. Not a very lively companion. Not good company.'

'That's because you're thinking about yourself, all the time. Just what you blame Mrs Thatcher for - unbridled selfishness. It's bound to lead to unhappiness.'

'It doesn't seem to have done, for the "Iron Lady". Unfortunately, they don't give schoolteachers baronies when we retire.'

'I mean, you've got to make the effort. You've got to show an interest in people. Otherwise you cut yourself off. If you stop taking an interest in other people, naturally, they're going to stop being interested in you. What's happened to all your quaint, old-fashioned ideas about socialism? And cutting yourself off from people isn't very Christian, is it?'

That, I thought, was below the belt, using religion as well as politics to reproach me. But both charges were true. I had allowed my self-pity to compromise my principles, and I was suffering for it. Dorothy construed my silence as obstinacy.

'Anyway, I'm sure you won't take any notice of what I say. Thank you for the tea. I'd better be on my way...'

And she was gone. She walked, or rather waddled, to the door and I could think of nothing to say that would detain her. As she went down the path, I wanted to call after her:

'Don't go! I didn't mean it! I do want to talk. I do want to hear what you say.... I do care...'

But of course, I said nothing of the sort. Because one does not let one's emotions show like that in leafy suburbia. Whatever would the neighbours think? I held the door open long after she gave me a perfunctory wave and drove off into the sunset.

So this was to be the summer of Dorothy's baby.

*   *   *

I counted back 28 years to my second summer at Cambridge. From Easter on, I was buried in my books. Fanshawe came round, pestering me to join him for a drink or a walk, but I knew he could catch up the lost study-time more easily than I, and I was loth to allow him any advantage in our private battle.

It was also a communal battle, of course, between ourselves and the examiners, or between ourselves and the twenty-odd students from other colleges who might be in the running for Firsts in Part I of the English Tripos. But I think for both of us it was the competition with each other that kept us up to the mark, or in my case up to midnight, revising.

After the last paper of the exam, we bought a large bag of cherries in the Market Square and walked along the river towards Grantchester, dissecting our answers to the questions. Fanshawe amused himself, spitting cherry stones at passing ducks. I declined his pressing invitations to join in. Even then, I found it impossible to be completely childish and irresponsible. Although I enjoyed the child in Fanshawe.

He would caper about the meadow, acting out all the parts in some story, while I proceeded with measured tread along the narrow, partly paved footpath. Then he would resume his post, marching beside me, and would probably change the subject again, entirely on a whim.

To say someone has a butterfly mind is normally something of an insult: it implies lightness of thought, lack of deliberation. Fanshawe had a butterfly mind, but an extremely powerful one, capable of fierce concentration, sharp analysis and cogent expression. He could embrace and compare more ideas in a short space of time than anyone else I have known. Now he flitted back to the exam:

'You used Prufrock in the Eliot question, I suppose?'

'Why should you suppose that?'

'Well, I tend to think of you and Prufrock as sort of soulmates.'

'Thanks very much! I'd rather you thought of me as a young Lochinvar, if it's all the same to you.'

Fanshawe threw his head back and laughed, as I had hoped. His hair was longer now, in the fashion of the times. It fell over his shoulders. The dark, intelligent eyes shone as he chortled at the idea of me on a white charger, scooping my bride-to-be up in my arms and riding off into the sunset. I liked to see him laugh. And it was a wonderful way of shaking off the tension of the exams. He wiped his eyes as his laughter subsided.

'I'm sorry, Henry, you're too much of a grown-up for young Lochinvar. And much better organised. You wouldn't have left things till the last minute, like that: you'd have spirited the bride away the night before, without anyone knowing. Personally, I'd rather have spirited the groom away, but there's no accounting for taste, is there? Or lack of it.'

'You're obsessed, aren't you?'

'Not at all! I haven't thought about sex for days, with all this revision. – Well, not very often.'

'I'm sure. So you actually did some revision, did you? As well as the *Times* crossword?'

'I did both. Although, some days, I must admit, I did devote more time to the crossword than revision. As a matter of fact, I think I found the crosswords more helpful than the lecture notes, when it came to the exam.'

'What on earth do you mean?'

'The mental discipline. The agility. Crosswords make you think, look for the unexpected.'

'If I've got to write four essays about four different writers or literary movements in three hours, I'd rather do without anything unexpected, if it's all the same to you.'

'You didn't just re-write all your old essays, did you?'

'Largely, yes. There's no time to be original in the middle of an exam.'

'I can't agree with you there.' Fanshawe pounced. 'I think it's the best time of all, to try and be original. Show the examiners how your mind works, under pressure. Since you've got all that adrenalin flowing, you may as well use it. You'd probably come up with your best ideas of the whole year. It's good for you, being put on the spot, forced to use your brain instead of your memory – that's what exams are all about – testing you!'

'Is it, indeed?' I got a word in at last. 'It sounds to me like a fine excuse for not revising.'

'It is fine, isn't it? Particularly fine. Like a vintage port. Or, indeed, any port. In a storm. Do you imagine they sell port at the Orchard?'

'Not a chance! Tea, if you're lucky.'

'I feel like a drink. Let's go to the pub, instead. Angus and Tim were driving up for lunch. They might still be there.'

My face fell at the mention of their names. I couldn't help it. 'They haven't still got that car, have they? They'll catch it if anyone finds out.'

I had been hoping to have Fanshawe's company to myself, that afternoon of our blessed release, though I would never have admitted as much to him. His old school friends brought out a shallow, waspish side to him, that I thought of as quite foreign to his true self. Perhaps the truth is that he was ever the diplomat, capable of being all things to all men. He enjoyed playing roles; I suppose he played a role for me.

The rule for undergraduates at Cambridge, for the sake of the horribly congested little streets, was that we were not allowed to keep a car within 25 miles of Great St Mary's Church. For the most part, our poverty enforced a grudging acceptance of this rule, but students with rich parents would occasionally flaunt their good fortune in the time-honoured way.

Every so often, one of them was caught by the Bulldogs and reported to the Proctor and given a dressing down. Then they were fined in multiples of six shillings and eightpence. This amount fascinated me. It was one third of a pound, convenient enough for the accounts. But why six and eightpence? I wondered where it had come from, which monetary unit of the past had been worth a third of a pound. I never found out. Fanshawe's friends had many six-and-eightpences. They spent their fathers' money with gay abandon. And I do mean gay, although it is not a word I care to use in that context. On the redefinition of that particular word, I stand shoulder to shoulder with all those elderly ladies who write to the Telegraph, complaining that a favourite adjective of their youth has been hijacked and perverted. And I disliked Fanshawe's friends, at the best of times.

We were very lucky to go up to Cambridge when we did. A couple of years earlier, discipline had been much stricter. Gowns, which we were obliged to wear only for dinner in College, had been compulsory on the streets of the town after 6.30 at night. The Proctors used to patrol the city centre at closing time with their Bulldogs (not the canine variety – College Porters in bowler hats) ready to give chase to miscreants if required.

There had been a lot of running street-battles between 'town' and 'gown'. Not surprisingly, the fighting petered out very quickly when 'gown' stopped wearing uniform in public. I always felt there was a lesson for Northern Ireland in that. Uniformed British soldiers patrolling the streets was bound to be a provocation – and yet, I suppose spies in 'civvies' would have been worse.

By the time we went up, the 'sixties were beginning to swing, even in quiet Cambridge. Later that summer, when Fanshawe and I walked by the river, French students would 'sit in' to occupy their campuses; American students were already demonstrating against the Vietnam War; while we acquired a taste for fine Port and Stilton and 'rediscovered' the Pre-Raphaelites. Gentlemanly pursuits? Or fiddling while Rome burned?

Traditions were breaking down, even here. Women were about to be admitted to the men's colleges. In my day, there were said to be ten male undergraduates to every female one. I did get to know some young women, generally clones of myself, earnest, with thick glasses and pale, indoor skin, who came to Christian Fellowship meetings.

The enveloping maleness of it all was unhealthy. It fostered and encouraged little cliques like Fanshawe's friends, who were deliberately outrageous. They actually enjoyed giving offence. They were quite open, almost aggressively so, about their homosexuality.

I could not understand what Fanshawe saw in them, He had been at boarding school with them. They were a year older than we were. He never explained in so many words, but I rather presumed they had adopted and corrupted him. They had been a beleaguered minority at school, but at Cambridge they had found others of like mind and become emboldened. They had vague theatrical leanings which they boasted about for all they were worth - not much, in my humble opinion, but Fanshawe found them amusing. They were the jesters of his court, trivial, insignificant, but also *politic, deferential, glad to be of use.'* And conniving. Dangerous.

He always took a strangely uncritical view of them, to my way of thinking. They were his friends and that was that. His loyalty may have been misplaced, but it was total. I presumed he would be as loyal to me. Just as I presumed on Dorothy's loyalty, all these years later.

*   *   *

The trouble was, she took against young Jonathan Lander from the start, just as I had taken against Fanshawe's friends. Blind prejudice is a potent force. The reading competition was only the beginning of it.

I tried to get her to look at his essays, but she showed no interest whatsoever. She said she was happier dealing with the GCSE classes. Although she said she thought she might like to take some of them through to 'A' levels, once she'd established a 'relationship' with them. Women teachers get away with saying things like that. If I were to say such a thing, it would be grossly misunderstood. But I saw the boy's potential and I knew where my duty lay. I entered him for my old college at Cambridge.

The Oxbridge interviews come at the end of the Autumn term. In my day, we got 'A' levels out of the way first, and then sat Scholarship exams in late November, just before going up for the interviews, but they scrapped those exams as being elitist or competitive, or some such nonsense.

Nowadays, pupils tend to apply a year earlier and receive offers contingent on their 'A' level grades. Most colleges give candidates a subject-specific interview, as well as a general one. If they can show a keen interest in their intended subject of study, or a knowledge of it, over and above what they would be expected to acquire through a normal 'A' level course, naturally, they stand a better chance of getting in.

I established a regular practice of inviting candidates hoping to read English at Cambridge or Oxford to attend a special, ten-week course with me, on the Thursday evenings leading up to the interviews. I modelled the sessions on a Cambridge supervision, and worked through the whole panorama of English literature, with extra sessions devoted to Tragedy and the Novel (both optional papers in Part Two of the Tripos).

It was, of course, a considerable extra workload, both for the boys and for me, but the better candidates managed it without too much trouble. It was one way of sorting out the wheat from the chaff. As some sort of recognition for the additional workload, I treated them, not as schoolboys, but as the bright, young adults they were about to become. Countless old boys, over the years, have come back from university and thanked me for it, saying it helped to ease them into a more independent way of working.

Each week, the boys would read the essays they had written, we would discuss and assess them together, and I would introduce the reading matter for the next week and set an essay question on it. This gave them a sense of achieving something each week, and also the pleasure of embarking on something fresh, a new endeavour. Thursday was ideal, because they could get the books they needed from the library on Friday and do the bulk of their reading over the weekend.

Numbers varied from year to year: once I had five in my Oxbridge study group, but generally only two or three. Last autumn's contingent consisted only of Lander and Beefy Thomas, who was trying for an Oxford college which, by strange coincidence, had provided no less than eight members of the previous year's Rugby XV for the annual Varsity Match.

I felt the reference the Headmaster wrote for Thomas was quite unscrupulous, and wished I had the courage to challenge him on it. He cruised over the academic side almost in passing, while describing Beefy's sporting achievements in terms that I, for one, found ludicrously mock-heroic. But apparently, it did the trick.

I was pleased to find that Thomas himself seemed to be taking the whole business more seriously. I asked him before we started if he was prepared to work harder than he had ever worked before, and he promised he was. He was under strong family pressure to settle for Sandhurst and a commission in his father's old regiment. Oxford represented an escape from that tradition.

I told Colonel Thomas to his face that I believed the boy should be allowed to make his own decision. Family habits are all very well, but it is the happiness of the individual that counts. Or such is the creed of my generation. It is hardly my fault if the boy happens to draw that inference from anything I may have said in class. It is my job to lay life's possibilities in front of him. It is then up to him to seize whatever opportunities he will. Colonel Thomas had no right to accuse me of setting his son against the army. The boy was just applying his intelligence. 'If you'd prefer them not to question your values, don't educate them in the first place.' That's what I said to him. It's not, of course: it's what I wish I had said.

We started with the Metaphysical poets of the seventeenth century. I warned them that they would need to allow thinking time as well as reading time, to get to grips with the subject. Lander took the hint; Thomas did not. It was the beginning of term and he had been busy with training sessions and trials for the Rugby team.

'Sorry, sir, I'll catch up in the week.'

'You will not! Then you won't have enough time to do next week's reading, and so it will go on. It's a vicious circle. No, no, after tonight, you'd better put the Metaphysicals off to your Christmas holiday.

'But for your future reference, Mister Thomas, I'd like you to note that I expect you to come here having done the reading and having at least applied your mind to the essay question, even if you have to speak from notes. Attendance is entirely voluntary: it's a privilege. I only want you here, if you're going to participate fully in the discussions. Clear?'

'Crystal, sir. I did most of the reading. I just ran out of time.'

'Not much good saying that in an exam, is it?' I demanded acerbically. 'Sorry, I ran out of time! I could have answered four questions, but I only managed two and a half! You'd make it impossible to get a decent grade, no matter how good the two and a half answers were! Do you see? You make it very hard for yourself if you don't do what the examiner requires. Mismanagement of resources is what they'd call it. And if you are serious about going to Oxford, one of the very first things you'd better learn is how to organise your time.'

'Yes, sir. Sorry, sir.'

I paused to let the admonition sink in. Dictatorial instruction is the least interesting aspect of teaching, as far as I am concerned, but sometimes there is no other way of getting over a fundamental point. Especially with a certain type of boy. I reminded myself that Beefy was probably used to taking orders at home. Perhaps it would do the trick. We moved to defining metaphysical conceits, where Beefy's lack of background reading was beginning to show.

'I know what it is, sir. I don't understand why they call it a conceit.'

'Because it has been conceived - cleverly conceived, with any luck. It's a contrivance. A *tour de force*.'

'So it's nothing to do with being conceited?'

'Not at all, no! Not in the sense of being pompous and self-important.'

'Don't you think, sir' Lander cut in, 'They might have become conceited if they were very good at making up conceits?'

'I suppose they might, Mister Lander,' I laughed, 'But I'm afraid you're adding to Mister Thomas' confusion.'

'No, he's not' growled Beefy, 'I get it all right. I just thought it was a weird word to use, that's all.'

I caught Lander's eye and we tacitly agreed not to pursue the matter. Looking back, I can see I should have given Thomas more encouragement. He was far from unintelligent, but he thought in a logical, linear way. If he failed to find a satisfactory answer to a question, he niggled at it until he worked it out. He would probably make a good scientist – or soldier, though I'm reluctant to admit it. He lacked that quicksilver brightness, the ability to relate apparently disparate ideas in a unified pattern, to see easily where an individual work of art fits into the grand design.

I am not putting this very well. I suppose the truth is, I did not really see Beefy Thomas as scholarship material, whereas I knew Jonathan Lander could do it, given eight weeks of solid work before the interviews. However, as I kept reminding myself, that decision was not mine to make.

It was not for me to judge: my task was to help each of them, as individuals, to realise their highest potential. But when you have been jumping through the same old hoops, year after year, for more years than you can count on your fingers and toes, you cannot help it. You know. You just know who is going to succeed and who is not.

If Beefy felt left out, in our supervisions, I am sorry. In another year, he might have fared much better. But Jonathan Lander needed to work at his own pace; we could not wait to explain everything three times over to Beefy. We had a lot of ground to cover. I wanted Jonathan to feel he had a real grasp of the whole sweep of English literature, some sense of the underlying pattern, not just an insight into a selection of isolated writers or literary movements, but an appreciation of great literature as the highest art known to man. If Beefy could not keep up, we could not afford to wait for him. If that is the favouritism of which I have been accused, so be it.

*　　*　　*

I modelled these sessions very deliberately on my own experience at Cambridge. Dr Rice, our Director of Studies in English, was, I think, probably the only truly great man I have ever known. Yet even he, in his wonderfully bullish and robust way, had a hint of the Prufrock about him, 'an attendant lord' to his illustrious friends – WB Yeats, TS Eliot, WH Auden – somehow, Dr Rice had contrived to be on genial terms with most of the great poets of our century.

He had known them all, discussed their poetry with them practically as it came off the printing presses and stalked those same Grantchester Meadows with them, deliberating the issues of the day. He had chosen not to earn his living by writing, but to share his wisdom through teaching, and he had an extraordinary gift for opening students' eyes. He had more books dedicated to him than any man alive: they were spread out on his table, each September, the last season's crop of perfectly phrased and heartfelt dedications, thanking him for laying the foundations for so many brilliant careers.

Everyone who was fortunate enough to read English under Dr Rice carried away a vision of the arts as the soul and salvation of the world. He showed us where we might fit, in the great scheme of things, if only we dared to believe in ourselves. He left us all with a greater zest for the struggle and a keener appreciation of the whole moral universe.

There are many men and women in Oxford and Cambridge who claim to be Masters of Arts. Few deserve the title. But Dr Rice was the genuine article – as my erstwhile pupils would put it, he was 'the business'.

Dr Rice was fond of shocking his students, whom he found generally too conservative by half. Fanshawe liked to relate the story of his interview, when Dr Rice had asked if he had ever made love with a woman. Fanshawe, fearing, as he claimed, that the next question would be very much closer to the mark, nervously replied that he had not. Dr Rice suggested he should remedy this omission at the earliest opportunity, since 'an understanding of the art of love-making is essential to an appreciation of literature – and, indeed, of life!

It may be true or it may be absolute gibberish, but it made us realise that we had irreversibly left the sixth form behind. This was for real.

Rice was a man of immense humanity, loth to hurt. But he was Irish enough to enjoy taking his young charges down a peg or two when necessary. I received my comeuppance when I read aloud my essay on TS Eliot, which concluded with a fine peroration:

'And I wonder what Mr Eliot himself would say about such an interpretation of his work, if he were here today.'

There was an uncomfortable silence after I finished reading. Fanshawe was silent, deferring to the great man, waiting for his opinion. Dr Rice shifted in his chair, adjusted his stiff leg to a more comfortable position, fixed me for a moment with a beady eye and murmured: 'The last time Eliot visited my rooms, he sat in Mr Fanshawe's chair.'

I was justly rebuked and I knew it. I remember nothing else that was said in that supervision, but the critical judgment of my egotism had been delivered. Cleanly and concisely, Dr Rice had burst the bubble of my pomposity.

It shook my confidence, a little. In future I adjusted my academic style accordingly and tried to avoid the jaunty perorations of the popular press. I still find it hard to write in anything less than complete sentences, even in this private journal, which I alone shall ever read.

I would no more split an infinitive than commit pack rape. Why can I not bring myself to use a preposition to end a sentence with? Why am I so hidebound by convention? There is no need for it. I am an outcast now, allowed, even expected, to break the rules. I can do as I please.

I kid myself that I have not always been an outcast. I wore the uniform of the middle classes, but few were fooled. Inside, I am like Hesse's *Steppenwolf*, the lonely hunter. That is why I had to practice so assiduously the art of seeming to be an ordinary English gentleman.

I longed for Dr Rice to enquire if I had ever made love to a woman, so that I could stake my claim to manliness, but he never did. After my blissful but incomplete encounter with Susannah, I felt I had some idea of the importance of love and desire, how the experience could take over our whole being. How little we know, and how slowly we learn. I am still learning. How far will the rack stretch? Dorothy is carrying a child. My Dorothy. But not my child.

Or could it be? The idea is so fantastic, it frightens me. The last time we made love was at the beginning of the Autumn term. If she was to give birth at the end of July, the child could not be mine. But what if it were due to be born earlier than that? What if she came here, yesterday, with an elaborate pack of lies, simply to throw me off the scent? She is more than capable of such deception, if it suited her purpose.

Yes. But what could that purpose be? Even if the child were biologically mine, I could hardly go and claim it from its mother and putative step-father. Given my reputation. This is fruitless, bootless speculation, thoughts that arise unbidden at midnight, one of many voices of the Devil, come to tempt us. How could Dorothy be carrying my child, and I be unaware of it? Am I so insensitive? I will not believe it.

Did she come to tempt me? Or to torture me? Was there, in some part of her, an inclination to come to me and confess everything – to be with me at last, to be mine? Would she have opened her heart to me then, if only I had behaved in such and such a way? Could I have won her back, after all? Could I yet win her?

Do I dare to hope, like Hopkins? Do I dare to eat a peach, like Prufrock? I have heard the mermaids singing, each to each. I have lost hope that they will ever sing to me. And I know the song of this particular mermaid, this enticing Siren. I know the sweetness of her. I know enough to block my ears.

But I cannot block my imagination, which runs wild, unchecked by reason. I see myself with Dorothy. After all that has passed, I would throw away my pride and go to her and kneel. My love is pure. I have suffered like a dog. And I have suffered in silence, for her sake. Does that not entitle me to some consideration? In my heart I know it is a weakness, this undemanding, all-giving love. Worse, it is unappealing. I call to mind Yeats' warning:

'Never give all the heart, to passionate women.'

It is ironic. Yeats himself gave all his heart, time and again. It is what fires his poetry. He turned suffering into art. That is true alchemy, turning pain into gold. Most of us just turn our pain into pain for others.

Why did she come? Why scrape open the wound, just as the first cicatrice was forming? Not for nothing. Please. Let there be more to it, than that. She would come to tell me about his child. A letter would have sufficed. But she would come in person if she wanted to tell me that my child was his. Oh, yes. That would appeal to her sense of theatre.

'There are many events in the womb of time, which will be delivered.' And one in Dorothy's, it seems. A bun in the oven. A son for

me, at last? Am I Job, and this another twist of the torturer's knife? Or old Abraham, blessed at last, beyond my deserts...

I must keep my feet on the ground. I must not be carried away with absurd flights of fancy. May I not allow myself to hope? No, no hope, for that way lies more agony.

And yet... I have endured so much already, shall I be afraid of a little more? There is nothing I can do. I must wait and see when the child is born. It is the sensible thing.

If he or she arrives in July, I will abandon my fantasy. Even if the birth were to be in May, that would be no proof that the child is mine. I remember Solomon's solution to such a problem... cut it in half!

'Goats and monkeys!' I hate the furious speculation this forces me to undertake. For the first time, I will not record my thoughts: they are unworthy. I will not defile these pages with my wild visions of their traitorous coupling. But if the babe is born in May, I shall want to know the truth, no matter what the cost.

Until then, there is only pain to be had from hoping.

I must dismiss it from my mind. There is no other remedy.

*   *   *

I am trying to conjure up a time that is gone, lost in the mists, and yet it is fresher to me than today – or than today was, before the bombshell hit. The years at Cambridge were my halcyon days, had I but known it. I had more kindred spirits there than ever I found in the world of my later life. The old Steppenwolf was almost accepted, for a while.

Cambridge was neatly divided into cliques, a dozen or more main ones, with all sorts of sub-cliques springing off them. There were the Rugger Buggers and the Rowing Bores, but I had never shown the slightest aptitude for any sport and had no intention of doing so as an undergraduate.

There was the God Squad, of which I suppose I was a member, while distancing myself from the tub-thumping evangelical tendency that tended to make the most noise. I liked to go to Compline, a fifteen-minute service at 9.30 in the evening. I found it very soothing to speak to God about the day, to bring Him my problems and my achievements, however humble.

There were the Student Activists of the Left and the Young Fogeys of the Right. The latter, with whom I appeared to have more in common, tended to congregate at the Cambridge Union, where I heard some truly magnificent speakers. I once saw Enoch Powell savage Richard Crossman brutally in a debate. He took poor Crossman's arguments, one by one, and tore them limb from limb, scattering the debris round the hall.

There were the Luvvies, although not known by that appendage at the time. There were Footlights Luvvies polishing sketches, Marlowe Society Luvvies practising serious Shakespeare, while dreaming of the RSC, and ADC Luvvies practising the more Machiavellian arts of theatre politics, always jockeying for position.

Fanshawe disapproved of the ADC clique, probably because he would secretly have liked to be a member, but feared failure.

'I'm told they can pull each other off and slit each other's throats at the same time,' he informed me, 'Ambidextrous, you see? Damned clever!'

The Beer-and-Darts Brigade were convivial enough, but I felt I had little in common with them. I couldn't throw darts and beer made me sick. And then there were the Swots. I suppose I was Chief Swot. But being Swots, we never stopped working for long enough to get to know one another, so we remained isolated in our little cells.

I wondered, at one time, whether Cambridge was not just a gigantic asylum, dedicated to the treatment of that well-known mental disorder, intellectual over-development. If the treatment was successful, inmates would be released in three years. If the condition seemed to resist the initial treatment, they would be invited to stay on as Fellows.

The other significant clique, I suppose, was the Velvet Mafia, the homosexual network, with whom I had more contact than I might have chosen, thanks to my friendship with Fanshawe.

The event I recall most vividly took place on a crowded lawn beside the river, that glorious June of our second year. Fanshawe had invited me to lunch in a pub, the Plough at Fen Ditton, thereafter to sit and drink Pimms on the lawn, cheering madly as any of the Eights from our own College rowed past. It was a Cambridge tradition I had never witnessed before, so I was pleased to be invited to participate. Unfortunately, several of Fanshawe's old school-chums were in attendance.

'Do you know anybody who's going to the Jesus Ball?' enquired Angus from Magdalene, a tall, vain, viperous young man. 'Apparently, it's turned out the most awful fiasco!'

'Wouldn't be seen dead at it. It's so kitsch!' chipped in Angus' sometime lover, Tim, 'Prancing about like village idiots, all night, and then punting up to Grantchester for breakfast, and paying a small fortune for the privilege!'

Fanshawe had been watching my reaction through half-closed eyes.

'What do you think, Henry? Are you a bit of a Ball-fancier on the quiet, so to speak?'

Angus and Tim sniggered together.

'I think you know the answer to that,' I said, with some dignity, 'I've nothing against perfectly normal couples enjoying themselves. The mating rituals of spring are a long-established tradition. Those able to take part should be allowed to do so without being derided for it.'

Ooooh!' howled Tim and Angus, like the pair of old queens they were fast becoming, 'What a bitch! Mind her claws!'

'Henry's absolutely right!' pronounced Fanshawe, silencing them. 'We are bitching about it, and we're bitching because it doesn't cater for us. I'll tell you what! We should have our own May Ball! Let's organise one for the Long Vac Term. Shall we? We could hold it at Queens, and call it the Queens' Queens' Ball! It'd be a scream!'

'Yes, and guess who will be doing the screaming!' I cut in. 'Promoting illegal sexual practices? They'd send you down for that!'

'No, they won't.' He was smugly convinced. 'They'll give me a bit of a wigging. Oh, and fine me a few shillings, I suppose. But they wouldn't want to sacrifice my First. The College doesn't get enough of them. It can't afford to waste any!'

'So you are going to get a First. You're confident of it.'

'Frankly, I am. So are you. Why won't you admit it?'

'I wish I was! But I'm afraid I can't read the examiners' minds, the way you can.'

'Don't be so touchy! You know you deserve a First. Not like this idle pair of good-for-nothings: they'll be allowed Pass degrees, if they're lucky!' Fanshawe rode over Angus and Tim's protests with relish. 'It all goes to show there's more than one way of skinning a cat!' And he paused for a deep draught from his umpteenth mug of Pimms.

'What on earth are you babbling about?' I enquired, from my habitual vantage point as the outsider.

'More than one way of passing exams, I mean.'

'Oh yes, and what are they?'

'Well, genius in my case and honest hard work in yours!'

Fanshawe tried to make a joke of it, but there was truth in what he said. And the presence of his friends, sniggering away, gave the remark a harder edge than was perhaps intended. I snapped back at him, genuinely angry for once, but my words were drowned by someone firing a pistol, up the river, at the start of the races.

'My God, they've got Edward Kennedy!' exclaimed Tim, clutching his forehead theatrically.

'Oh, you're so sick!' bleated Angus, in delight.

Over lunch we had heard the news that Robert Kennedy, campaigning for the Democratic nomination, had been shot in a California hotel kitchen. Another of the voices of freedom, silenced by the gun. For all of us, it awoke sad memories of his brother's assassination, the first cataclysmic shock of our young lives. Where would it end?

'It's all in Nostradamus.' Tim was chattering away to anyone who would listen. 'Three brothers would come to power, he said, and they'd all be destroyed, one after another.'

From a hundred yards or so up the river, the sound of cheering was getting louder as the leading Eights in the line reached the first groups of spectators. Fanshawe ignored Nostradamus. He was looking at me, with his head on one side.

'Please don't take offence, Henry, my dear chap,' he said, coming to the side of my chair and putting his hand on my shoulder, 'You know I adore you. I just can't find an acceptable way of expressing my love and affection for you, that's all.' And he bent down and kissed me on the lips, in full view of everyone. I was stunned. I pushed him away and wiped my mouth with my pocket handkerchief. I felt myself blushing. I thought everyone was looking at me.

Fortunately, I was wrong. Everyone was looking at the leading two boats in the Division, battling their way down the Reach. Three times the prow of the second boat came level with the stern of the leading boat, but then those oarsmen strained a fraction harder and their boat inched ahead again before contact could be made and a bump claimed. The inebriated audience at the Plough cheered itself hoarse and the boats disappeared around the bend in the river in a haze of spray, with their battle still unresolved.

The next few boats in the division had apparently bumped each other earlier in the race, because there was a lull, now, and the spectators' interest returned at once from cheering to drinking.

Fanshawe squatted on his haunches in front of me, forcing me to meet his eyes. I did so reluctantly. I told him I found his behaviour outrageous, unacceptable. But even then, furious as I was, I could not feel mortally offended. He looked so innocent.

'I'm awfully sorry, Henry. Do forgive me. I can't think what came over me. Good heavens, this stuff is stronger than you think, isn't it? I was just overcome by a sudden impulse, that's all. No harm done, I hope? I wouldn't ruin our friendship, for the world.' And he offered me his hand.

'Platonic friends, if you don't mind!' I insisted, shaking hands briefly.

'Do you have so many offers of love and affection, that you can afford to reject them without a thought?'

'From some people, yes!' I said, grimly.

'In fact, if it was any concern of mine, which of course it isn't, I'd say you might well have a pretty lonely life, if you never let anyone who really cares about you get close to you!'

'It is, as you say, no concern of yours. Just try that mallarkey again and I'll punch you on the bloody nose!'

I'm sure I had never in my life said anything like that before, but Fanshawe moved back, as if taking it seriously. Tim and Angus cheered ironically, mocking me.

'There's no need to descend to the gutter, Henry,' Fanshawe was mildly reproving.

'You're the one who belongs in the gutter. Or a public toilet. But I'll assume, with good reason, that you're drunk, and say no more about it.'

'I love it when you're masterful,' said Fanshawe, with a wicked gleam in his eye. 'It's all right, I'm only teasing you, Henry. But didn't you rise to the bait?'

I didn't know what to say. I supposed I had over-reacted, rather. I felt a bit ashamed. And very uncomfortable. Fortunately, two boats from the bottom of the division had made a bump just upriver of the Plough's lawn. The cox of the victorious boat had allowed the prow of his craft to beach on a soft part of the river-bank, while one of his crew nipped ashore for long enough to break off a branch of green leaves from a tree or bush. This was the traditional victory symbol. A fresh bough was placed in the bows of every boat that succeeded in gaining a bump. That boat would then move one step up the ladder for the next day's race.

'Look at the cox in that boat, Tim,' said Angus, giving him a nudge and a leer.

'I am looking at them. What a mouthful! And they don't even seem to be tired, some of them. Must be all the excitement!'

'I'll say! Sliding up and down like that, all in perfect rhythm. In, out; in, out; in, out...'

'But no orgasm.'

'I expect they come when they make a bump, don't you? The one at the front looks as if he has.'

'Ooh! I see what you mean... Yuck! And what about that monstrous chap with a long beard? He looks as if he's put his shirt on and left the coat-hanger in. Talk about muscles: he's got muscles in places where I haven't even got places!'

I made my excuses as quickly as I could and left them to egg each other on to further excesses of vulgarity.

*   *   *

The Long Vac Term was a joy. People who begrudged their Summer Vacations and never stayed for a Long Vac Term missed living in an altogether more relaxed University. With no formal lectures or weekly supervisions, it was Cambridge with all of the joy and none of the stress.

We were nominally studying for the Oldham Shakespeare Prizes, but as it turned out, we spent roughly half of our time reading and half chatting. Fanshawe and I shared a set of rooms on Main Court, opposite the Chapel. We had a study-bedroom apiece and a spacious, wood-panelled sitting room, comfortably furnished with a Chesterfield, well-worn armchairs, bookcases and a large table with half a dozen chairs around it.

My way of preparing for the Oldham exam was to identify three or four important areas of study which gave rise to the liveliest debates among Shakespearean scholars. I would then read and make notes on their major differences of opinion, with frequent references to the Shakespeare texts in question. Finally, I would formulate a view of my own that would generally act as a sage mediation between the combatants. Thus, I hoped to be armed with a mass of potential essay material for the exam.

Fanshawe's preparation consisted of reading or re-reading Shakespeare's entire canon and committing vast chunks of it to memory. He regretted that the task would not afford him the time to consider the views of any critics, but said he bore the prospect with signal equanimity. I half-expected him to abandon the enterprise after half a dozen plays, but he persisted, as only Fanshawe could, once he had his teeth into a project.

He was capable of working incredibly hard, almost obsessively, if a subject interested and inspired him. He had a way of focusing all his energy, bringing extra force of concentration to bear. Pirate radio stations blaring pop music did not seem to distract him in the slightest. In a way, I think they helped to isolate him from the world. They set up a barrier, behind which his brain was free to work at full power.

'I like sonnets!' he proclaimed, one afternoon, as we made tea and toasted crumpets. 'Don't you, Henry? Pithy. To the point. You know where you stand, with a sonnet. I think I might leave behind a slim volume of my sonnets.'

'Really? Written some, have you?'

'Not yet, no.' Fanshawe brushed aside this minor inconvenience with a wave of his hand. 'But I will, you'll see. Meanwhile, time spent in reconnaissance is never wasted, is it?'

'That depends. It has been argued that time spent in reconnaissance is always wasted, by definition.'

'That's a rather radical view for you, isn't it, Henry?'

'I didn't say I held the view. I merely propounded it. Whence this sudden affection for the sonnet?'

'Dear old Bill!' announced Fanshawe through a mouthful of buttered crumpet. 'He was the master. He lays his soul bare, in those sonnets. Tells you everything you could wish to know.'

'Including how to answer exam questions?'

'Of course. And some much more important things, too,'

'Jan Kott thinks Shakespeare was a communist. Does that come through in the sonnets, do you think?' I had heard Professor LC Knights pour civilised scorn on this radical suggestion: I wondered if Fanshawe would take the same line.

'Communist? You might as well say he was a Jehovah's Witness: you'd find as much evidence. It's fundamentally wrong to take dramatic writing and infer political or any other kind of opinions from it. These are words made for other mouths to speak: you can't draw conclusions about the personal opinions of any writer on that basis. Now, the sonnets show you the real man.'

'The real man?' I echoed mockingly. 'And who was that, pray?'

'Well, he was certainly homosexual. No doubt about that:
"Oh thou, my lovely boy, who in thy power
Dost hold Time's fickle glass..."'

'What about the Dark Lady?'

'Mere camouflage, my dear chap. Just a homage to literary convention.'

'That's rubbish, and you know it. You're not thinking of using that sort of nonsense in the exam, are you?'

'If the spirit moves me, I might. I haven't a clue what I'm going to write in the exam. It's a matter of supreme unimportance. What I'm talking about is an insight into Shakespeare. The sonnets make him so much more accessible, so much more contemporary.'

'Jan Kott's point, entirely. I suppose the Shakespearean canon is rather like the Bible, in that it's open to all sorts of different slants and interpretations. You pays your money and you takes your choice. I imagine Angus and Tim are pretty thrilled about your new theory, are they?'

'You really don't like queers, do you, Henry?'

'I wouldn't say that, for a moment. It's none of my business. I take people as I find them. Their sexual preference is only one facet of their personalities.'

'As a matter of fact, I think Shakespeare may well have been bi-sexual, rather than just homosexual. Lots of people are, you know, sometimes without even knowing about it. You know yourself...'

'Don't start all that again, for heaven's sake!'

'It's no good hiding from your real self, Henry. I know, you've told me all about the beauteous Susannah *ad nauseam*. But life doesn't stop; sexual energy's like electricity – you can't store it, you just have to channel it, use it... That's the only way to make it grow.'

'And why should I want to do that?' I demanded.

Fanshawe smiled and gave a huge, two-handed Jewish shrug.

'Because it's there?' he said enigmatically. 'Because you're alive, and not dead? 'Cause you're still capable of choosing to be happy instead of miserable? How many reasons do you need?'

'So, are you saying I'd be happy if I was like you and Tim and Angus? You don't seem outstandingly happy to me, any of you. Now, you're pretty boys. Later on, you'll be a bunch of sad old queens. Why should I want to join your club, even if it were possible to do so by choice?'

'Because you're one of us already, my dear. You're just pretending not to be, for some reason. Don't miss the party altogether, will you?'

'Look here. For what I very much hope will be the last time, I do not find erotic what you find erotic.'

'How do you know what I find erotic?' Fanshawe was all agog, entranced at the prospect of discussing his favourite subject once again.

'Because you insist on spelling it out to me in nauseating detail, that's how. You leave absolutely nothing to the imagination.'

'Ah, the imagination! The most important erogenous zone of all! *"He that robs me of my imagination takes that which not enriches him, yet makes me poor indeed!"'* Waving aside my murmured correction *'Reputation!'* he continued:

'How do I love thee, Henry? Let me count the ways: I love your well-worn suits, your total disregard of fashion; I love your spectacles, which declare your earnestness; I love your ginger hair, your Brylcreemed locks; most of all, I love the way you insist on impersonating an elderly gentleman of sedate, fixed habits, full forty or fifty years too early! You must have adopted this personality years and years ago, and now you've forgotten how to be anyone else – let alone yourself – whoever that may be!'

Ninety per cent of what Fanshawe said was entertaining nonsense – which left ten per cent to probe my soul, demanding truthful answers. Often those answers came later, in the dark of night, when I lay awake, gazing at the moon through the one small stained-glass pane in my window, which bore the college crest. Fanshawe's rebuke, on the lawn at the Plough, cost me some sleepless hours. Who was I to refuse an offer of love and affection, indeed?

It was true that I was now more alone than I had ever been. I still wrote to Mother and Grandmother once a week, but no longer a letter each, with the news carefully apportioned. Now I wrote to them both at once, as befitted our changed situation. I had broken free, and they knew it. It forced them to sweep aside their differences and unite as never before. Susannah had gone to Birmingham University and taken up with a trumpeter. I had several friends at college, but only one friend of the heart, and that was Fanshawe. Why should I deny him?

One reason, which I think I sensed even then, was that I was still in awe of him. There was never any real equality between us, Tripos Firsts aside. I never understood what a man like him, every inch a winner of glittering prizes, saw in someone as mundane as myself. I was grateful for his interest: but I did not for a moment think myself worthy of it. I was always expecting him to take up with people more brilliant than I. Above all, I enjoyed his company so much. Life had more zest when we were together. Mine did, at least. He showed me a new way of looking at the world. Why should I deny him?

There was truth in what he said, about me choosing my own personality. I had had to grow up and be the man of the house. So I chose to emulate my dead father, a stooping sixty-year-old of precise habits and a cripplingly withdrawn nature. I filled the vacuum in the house by becoming my father. I loved my mother. Not physically, of course. There is no need for any kind of physicality, if you are sufficiently English.

So there I was, at 21, with the persona of a sixty-year-old. It was true that I could visualise my retirement more easily than my incipient career. The cottage in the Lake District, where at the last I would catch up with a lifetime's reading and writing and put my papers in order – that was real to me, even though the exact location of the cottage changed every time I went walking in the Lakes, as I did, most summers.

I had, of course, planned my future, in the precocious manner of undergraduates: Head of English by 30, I thought, Deputy Head by 40, Head at 50, with time for a move to one of the very best schools before hanging up my cap and gown. Maybe a Ph.D on the way, just for vanity's sake. As a career path, it seemed logical, inviting and achievable, from the lofty heights of confident Cambridge. What I failed to take account of is the part of our destiny that lies in the hands of others.

Fanshawe was right: the stiff personality I took to Cambridge was an old shell I had long outgrown. I knew the shell no longer fitted me, but it was the only shelter I had. At Cambridge, for the most part, I gathered it around me, pretending I knew exactly who I was and where I was going, even if no-one else did.

If I discarded that shell, who would I be? How different from my own invented self? I hardly saw myself as a rebel, after inhabiting such a conservative mould for so long, but presumably anything was possible.

Or was it? Could I truly change myself from a lonely person to an impassioned lover? Could I take the risk of failing? If he wanted me, how could I deny him?

Did he want me? He said so, but it had become something of a running joke, a pose we adopted in relation to each other. I lay in bed and wondered what it would be like to hold his body naked in my arms, to feel his flesh against mine.

I tried to find some shred of desire in myself. I had never held any-one naked, in all my life. I had wanted desperately to hold Susannah in my arms; I had known desire. Could I feel desire for Fanshawe? At times, late at night, I imagined I might. Then, in the early dawn, the old revulsion returned. Only I was unsure whether it was truly a revulsion at having sex with a man, or just fear of having sex at all. There was nobody I could ask for advice, no reference book to con-sult. The only answer lay within myself.

I told Fanshawe nothing of my private speculations. There were times when we were perfectly happy together, united as friends; I felt instinctively that any physical relationship between us might destroy that friendship, which I valued highly. There were times, when he was playing silly buggers with Angus and Tim, when I found him utterly unappealing. Then we would dine together in Hall and I would be seduced again by the wonderful flow of his stories and observations. I loved him. There is no denying it. And I could not find an acceptable way of expressing that love.

I do not think it is a unique problem, among 21-year-olds, even today. Night after night, that Long Vac Term, I lay in bed, trying to overcome any barriers in my mind. I was always acutely conscious of Fanshawe sleeping in the room next door.

I visualised myself going to his room, lifting the single sheet that covered him and lying beside as he woke. His body would be beautiful in the moonlight. I would caress him with my hands, relaxing him. He would stretch like a cat, luxuriate in the sensation. And I, would I be beautiful beside him?

Whenever I made the mistake of picturing myself, the bubble burst. I saw this pallid figure, thin and unfit, lying beside a bronzed Adonis. I saw his eyes, dark windows to the soul, and then I saw my own eyes, as he would see them, blinking, caught without spectacles to protect them, fearful, ridiculous. I saw his young skin, firm and burnished, and beside it my own, wrinkled, withering even before its prime. It was repulsive. I was already old, before I had a chance to be young. I did not dare enough. I did not let myself learn by experience. I analysed each situation in advance and avoided the pitfalls. Until recently, at any rate. I foresaw only too clearly the failure of any attempt I might make to love Fanshawe, and so I never took those fateful steps towards his room.

It was the last week of the Long Vac term before I gave him any hint that my feelings for him might be capable of changing. We went on a picnic, up the river towards Grantchester. Tim and Angus had hired one of their college's punts and took turns at showing off their prowess with the pole. After lunch, we sunbathed. I massaged suntan lotion into Fanshawe's back and shoulders, and allowed him to return the compliment.

Later, we moored the punt by a bend in the river, to go swimming. Having no aptitude for water sports, I rarely joined in, preferring to make caustic comments from the safety of the boat, but on this occasion, I swallowed my reservations about the faecal content of the water and took the plunge.

Fanshawe was a natural swimmer; he was in his element in the water, lithe, strong and capable of staying underwater for a prodigious length of time. Once, I became quite alarmed: I thought he must have caught his foot in some underwater reeds. Tim and Angus were out of earshot. I realised he could be drowning as I stood there. I jumped in at once and swam to where I had seen him dive, but I couldn't see him. I tried to swim underwater myself, but breathed in some water by mistake and started to choke. In seconds, I was the one in trouble.

Luckily, Fanshawe surfaced nearby and came to my rescue. As he swam up to where I was floundering, he managed to lift me high enough in the water to get a good breath of air. My head cleared and I lay on my back and floated, so that he could easily raft me back to the safety of the punt. I put an arm round his neck as we floated beside the punt.

'How can I thank you?' I said.

Do you really want to know?'

'If you want me to go to bed with you, I will.'

'When?'

'Tonight.'

'You sure, Henry? You haven't suffered a spot of brain damage from nearly drowning yourself, have you?'

'No, I've been thinking about it. Maybe you're right. Maybe I shouldn't turn down your offer of love and affection. If it still stands...'

'Of course it does, my dear chap. Of course it does.'

Fanshawe threw both arms around me and submerged my head again, unexpectedly.

'Mind out! You've just saved my life: don't drown me again!'

On the way back, we shared one of the seats in the punt, leaning against each other, laughing. Tim, who was punting, started making snide remarks about us to Angus.

'Where did we pick up the honeymoon couple?'

'I think they hopped into the boat after we stopped for that swim. Bit sickening, aren't they?'

'Looks as if Fanshawe's going to win that bet with you, though.'

'What bet?'

'Don't you remember? You bet him twenty quid he couldn't seduce Henry by the end of the summer.'

'Tim!' Angus was genuinely disapproving. Tim gave a rather fussy shrug of his shoulders. Fanshawe glared at him.

I could hardly ignore the barb: it had been aimed at me, and had scored a direct hit.

'He told me about that bet.' I said. 'We're going to split the winnings, aren't we?'

Fanshawe laughed but went very quiet. For a long time after that, I tried to convince myself there never had been a bet, it was just a nasty figment of Tim's diseased imagination.

That night, we had dinner at a rather swish French restaurant on the road to the railway station. We drank white wine and red wine and more white wine and cognacs with our coffee and smoked a joint of marijuana on our way back to our rooms in College. None of it worked. For the first time, we were completely uneasy with one another, like strangers, clumsy.

'Do tell, Henry,' said Fanshawe, lighting a small cigar, 'what on earth has brought you to this momentous decision?'

'You have,' I replied. 'I've never known anyone like you. It's true. I feel privileged to have known you, whatever happens between us. I'd like to demonstrate that in some way, but I'm not particularly good at showing my feelings. If you want me, I mean really want me, if it's not just for a stupid bet, you must show me how you want to be loved, what will give you pleasure.'

'So you've come as a human sacrifice, Henry. You speak of my pleasure, but what about yours? You've got to want to do it too, you know. Otherwise it doesn't work. It's no use just being a victim. I'm not a sadist. I don't want to hurt you.'

'I'm very glad to hear it!'

'It wasn't just the bet: please don't think that. I mean, I really did want to go to bed with you.'

'You did,' I said, dully.

'It's not that I don't fancy you. It's just that I have – it's hard to explain – strange appetites.'

'So I had always gathered.' I waited for further explanation.

'The thing is – I like you, Henry. I like talking to you. I know how your brain works; it's different to mine, but it's interesting. I'm fond of you, really fond. What am I trying to say? – I'm saying don't mess it up for us. I don't want to treat you the way I treat my ex-lovers.'

'I don't really understand...'

'Of course you don't. Why should you? I'm trying to break it to you gently, my old love, that I'm not about to make your girlish dreams come true. I'm touched that you were ready to make the ultimate sacrifice for me, but I think I'll stick to the chaps at the Gents in the Market Square. More anonymous, you know. After all, one doesn't really want to take breakfast with one's indiscretions of the night before, does one? You know who put it rather well? Old Bill, of course.'

And he proceeded to quote the whole of Sonnet 128 from memory:

'Th' expense of spirit in a waste of shame
Is lust in action; and, till action, lust
Is perjured, murd'rous, bloody, full of blame,
Savage, extreme, cruel, not to trust;
Enjoyed no sooner but despised straight;
Past reason hunted, and no sooner had,
Past reason hated as a swallowed bait
On purpose laid to make the taker mad;
Mad in pursuit, and in possession so;
Had, having, and in quest to have, extreme;
A bliss in proof, and proved, a very woe,

Before, a joy proposed; behind, a dream.
All this the world well knows, yet none knows well
To shun the heaven that leads men to this hell.'

*   *   *

So, when the Headmaster asked me the McCarthy question, the 'Are you now or have you ever been?' question, I had no satisfactory answer to give him. Superficially, the interrogation was conducted in a perfectly civilised manner, but it made me feel like a dead fish on a slab, waiting to be filleted and dispatched.

'I've spoken to the lawyers, Henry, and they've asked me to check something with you, of a rather personal nature. You don't object, I hope? Good. They want to know if you'd be prepared to sign a declaration, on oath if necessary.'

"What sort of declaration?' I had always known this question would be asked of me, one day, and still I had no answer.

'Well, it's, er – a declaration that you have never, at any time in your life, been involved in any sort of homosexual relationship.'

'I see.'

'You'll sign it, then.'

'I'll do no such thing. And I regard the suggestion as a flagrant invasion of my privacy.'

'Well, the lawyers seem to feel such a document might well be needed – in your own interest.'

'They can whistle for it. I'm not signing anything.'

'I'm bound to say, Henry, as a friend, that they may construe this against you.'

'Let them. The fact is, I have not now and I never have had a homosexual relationship with Jonathan Lander. If that's what I'm accused of, I'm not guilty.'

And for the first and only time in my career, I walked out of the Headmaster's study and slammed the door.

Book 5: For Silver

Effingham School
Effingham, Glos.

Silver is my element. I've always identified with silver. It has a very special quality. Value without brashness. Understated elegance. Gold is finer, of course: the sun itself is gold. Clouds are silver. Others may see them as grey, but to me they are silver, more precious than they seem. People worship the sun as the source and sustainer of life, but clouds are no less essential. We depend on them. No-one worships clouds, for all their ever-changing beauty. We take them for granted.

If gold comes into your room, or your life, you know about it. If you fall in love, or have a child, or paint a masterpiece, or show or receive great kindness, or sing or make music that lifts people's hearts, you know at the time that these are golden moments, to be cherished and preserved. There is not a great deal of gold in life. What there is deserves to be loved and admired. It is true beauty, tempered in the fire.

Silver moments are subtler. They come when least expected. After my humiliation in front of Fanshawe and his friends, I expected him to discard me, but he did not. He was gentler; he stopped teasing me. We remained friends for the whole of our final year. He said I was his rock. He dived from me into all sorts of scandalous adventures and always returned. We trusted each other and no longer judged. It was a sort of love, and not to be denied.

I talked him through his bad trip when he experimented with LSD. I found him reasons to go on living, when a German dancer he loved was killed in a car crash. I supported him, as a true friend should. And in return, he cared for me. As much as he could.

We enjoyed our final year at college, without too much pain, on my part – but I still felt the sting of being rejected by Fanshawe and, indeed, by Susannah. My sexuality went into cold storage: I was numb, frozen, desensitized. I told myself that if love came again, I would not deny it. But love did not come. And, not wishing to repeat my humiliation, I did not search for it.

I was alone for several years. It is not such a terrible fate. The single person is master of his or her destiny; couples must seek each other's permission to breathe. I diverted my energies elsewhere.

I learned my craft as a teacher. I gave worker education classes, where I learned more than I taught. I learned, for example, that Conservative political views were incompatible with my Christianity. Mother, a lifelong *Daily Telegraph* reader, never forgave me for this betrayal of what she liked to regard as our station in life.

I intended, when I started, to use this book and the next to record the happiest times of my life, the silver and the gold. A final reckoning of the accounts. But Dorothy has spoiled my plans again. Why does her presence always change everything?

When we were together, last summer (was it only last summer?), I believed it was forever. We spoke of growing old in each other's arms. Growing old! I had never felt so young.

I was full of ideas. I remember being brave enough to take Dorothy for a stroll around the boundary at a school cricket match.

'Henry, what about the Headmaster? '

'He's here to watch the cricket, not us.'

'You hope!'

'I'm sure of it. Never mind him. I've had a thought about the holidays. I wondered if you'd like to come to the Lake District with me.'

'I'd love to. You can show me all the places you've spoken about. We can follow in the footsteps of Wordsworth and Coleridge! How exciting!'

"Well, "exciting" could be over-egging the pudding a little, but I think we'll both be able to relax there. Plenty of exercise, fresh air... We can take stock of things there, gather our strength for the onslaught of another academic year.'

'Let's not look too far ahead, Henry, or we'll miss the holiday altogether!'

'Sorry. Nothing wrong with planning for the future, though.'

'No, you're right.' She came over and kissed me on the cheek. 'As long as we can enjoy the present, as well as the future.'

I found myself smiling a broad, broad smile. 'I think you know how much I'm enjoying the present.'

She was smiling too, looking into my eyes, in that hypnotic way she had. 'I have got some idea, yes.' She pressed her body against me quite provocatively.

'Er, the Head has got a pair of binoculars over there...'

'You said he was watching the cricket.'

'Well, yes, he is, actually…

'Then you can give me a kiss.'

'What, here?'

'No, on the lips.'

'I mean, on the cricket-field?'

'All right. Don't kiss me, then, if you don't want to...'

'I do!' but she was off, striding ahead of me and I had to catch up with her. I had missed my chance, for the moment.

Life with Dorothy was never dull. In the last half of the summer term and the first half of the holidays, I felt a deep contentment with my lot, that I had never felt before.

I believed the miracle had happened: after all my failures, against all the odds, I had found the woman who was right for me, and we would devote the rest of our lives to making each other even happier.

I wonder if she ever believed that.

*   *   *

The asterisks represent a pause in writing of several days. Having reached the one vital question on which I fear my life may depend, I needed time to think. And sleep.

I need to acclimatise to this new isolation, after the comparative buzz and excitement of my years as a schoolmaster. I should spend a few days readjusting to my present circumstances, rather than losing myself in wistful remembrance of times past.

But I find I cannot bear to live in this present, for this present holds no Dorothy and no hope of her or, worse, the wrong Dorothy, carrying another man's child.

The child was the clue. It was staring me in the face, only it took me some time to realise the truth. Why had she come to me? Did she fear another outburst? – No, she knew I had been silenced. She would not come for nothing. She would certainly have a purpose. But what was it? Her visit suggests I may still have some power over her destiny. What can it be?

The idea struck me like a revelation. How did I not think of it at once? What if the child she was carrying were mine? In that case, might she want to come back to me? It was an intoxicating thought, that I hardly dared contemplate. In more sombre moments, I wondered if she had ever really wanted to be with me. Perhaps, all along, I was simply a means to an end.

Every line of questioning I pursued led back to that same puzzle: did Dorothy ever love me? And could she love me again?

At times I was sure of it. After coming home from the market one fine morning last summer with a plastic bag full of fruit and vegetables, I remembered how she had given herself to me. She held nothing back, I would stake my life on it. I have, indeed, staked my life on it. As a woman, she gave me everything. She said she had never been so naked with a man.

'Naked inside, as well as outside. I want you so much, Henry. I didn't think I could feel such desire.' She reached out and stroked my face. 'I know you. I know how gentle you can be. And how strong.'

'Whatever I am, you make me so. I look deep in your eyes and I feel myself falling under your spell again. I am yours to command.'

'Then I command you to love me. Now, as only you know how.'

Her hair fell on the pillow as she turned the power of her eyes on me. I breathed her scent as if it were life itself.

'When you look at me like that, all the other times we've made love come flooding back to me. It's as if they still exist, those moments, wonderful moments. The overwhelming moments of ecstasy have a life of their own, that goes on.'

'In a parallel universe, you mean?' All the while, she kept her eyes on me and just kissed my skin with hers. I felt myself at once spiraling down into her eyes, beginning to melt into her body.

'No, in this universe. There are moments when we fuse together, that we almost become another being. Do you feel that? I seem to leave myself behind and melt into you.'

'I love feeling you melt into me. Like this.' With a cool hand, she guided my cock between her thighs and slithered astride me, holding my gaze all the while, like a hypnotist. Indeed, I was entranced. 'Go on, fuck me. I want you to fuck me harder and deeper than you've ever fucked me before.'

My body responded to her command. It was a moment of sublime happiness for me. Of those I have loved, some have loved me in return. No one had ever seemed to desire me as she did. I was complete, a whole human being, for that moment. And then she enveloped me. I remember the incredible smoothness of her cunt. Involuntarily, my cock surged inside her. She caught her breath and her eyes flickered for a moment and then fixed on mine again, but with such a warm and loving gaze. It set me on fire. I pushed deeper and deeper inside her.

Sometimes our love-making was gentle. This time it was fierce. There was an urgency about it, a sort of desperation. The words fell away. We became bodies, writhing together instinctually, answering a need in each other that we had never acknowledged quite so openly.

I have no idea how long we made love. We tasted all the intimacies we had learned over the past few months. We were swept along in a rolling confusion of limbs. The delight of it was not just the physical sensation but the closeness we achieved. We were no longer separate, but had fused into a single being; we seemed to share each other's senses.

At last, before the final ascent, we found ourselves facing each other, wild-eyed and a little breathless. She half-opened her eyes and looked at me, looked deep inside. I realised that I had never been so close to another human being, or so happy, in my entire life. I tried to put my feelings into words, to explain to her how much she meant to me.

'I wish you could feel what I feel.'

'How do you know I don't?' she replied, 'or maybe what I'm feeling is even better.'

'I can't imagine how it could be. You've opened the door to another world, for me. It's like breathing pure oxygen. I feel as if I'm coming to life, for the first time.'

'I wonder if it's possible to feel what some-one else is feeling.' She stroked my cheek. 'Your joy is infectious, Henry. I do share it. We've both been hurt, and we've healed each other.'

'I never dreamed it was possible.'

'You don't hold back anything, do you? You give me so much of yourself. I hope we don't ever hurt each other.'

'There's no reason why we should. For the first time in my life, I don't want to hold anything back. I'm yours, if you want me.'

'Go on, then. Give yourself to me. Just let go of everything.'

'Even myself?'

'Especially yourself. Lose yourself inside me. Merge with me. Melt into me.'

'Yes! I want to pour into you, everything, all of me. I want to burst out of myself and swim deeper and deeper inside you. It's the bliss I was born for.'

'Let me feel what you feel, at that moment. Share it with me. Let me feel you swimming up inside me. Let me suck you up into my womb. And then you can penetrate me all over again: the head of your sperm can burrow into my egg and make new life in me. And then you'll have to stay inside me for a long time, growing in me.' All this she whispered to herself, as much as to me, like a mantra. Dorothy was always very susceptible to words, some might say especially her own.

I must confess, I was hardly impervious to her words, myself. Dorothy had a way of conjuring from us both feats of endurance and heights of passion that I never imagined possible. She was still for a moment, then looked at me again, hiding nothing. I made love with her eyes.

'Now,' she said. 'Now. Now, drive into me, now. Have all of me. I've never been so open to you. I want all of you inside me.' I felt her contract around me quite sharply and soon a series of squeezes began, each one sweeter than the last. It was in response to her fading crescendo that my cock surged up inside her again, my balls tightened. I was about to pour my whole life, my whole existence, into her.

The next three or four seconds lasted a delicious eternity.

I caught her eye and saw that she knew, that she was watching me, with me, a part of me at that most intense point. How I adored her. And what bliss she gave me. It was overwhelming.

The last shreds of resistance in my body dissolved and every nerve focused on the first huge contraction that sent my seeds into her, and then another, and a third, astonishingly, even more cataclysmic than the first two. I felt omnipotent, as if I could be any part of my body at will. I was my cock, plunging inside her. I was her cunt, receiving me. I did not know where my body stopped and hers began. All the darkness of my life fell aside and pure joy flowed into me and out of me.

I tried to focus all of my consciousness into a single seed. I was with it, in it, when the third contraction propelled me into the lovely place where I longed to be. In my imagination (was it imagination or true perception?) I swam inside her womb. Fighting off rivals, I pressed inside her again, I made love with her all over again, deep inside her. She opened to me again. I possessed her, and was possessed, as never before.

If you make love with someone in that way, it is very hard to bear when they leave you. It is difficult to disentangle emotions that have begun to grow around each other like vines, for support. Naïvely, I took it to mean that we would stay together, now that we had found each other, after so many lonely years of searching, almost giving up hope...

It was a day or two before we went back to school in September. Remembering that time, I cannot doubt that she loved me. She gave herself to me completely. And I, to her.

And yet... What if she knew? What if she knew it might be the last time we would be together? Perhaps it was her farewell gift to me, and I too dull to understand. If so, she was wise not to tell me. If I had known how things really were between us, I would have ruined the precious moment with questions and recriminations. As it was, I saved all my private pain and heartache for later.

Perhaps she did not know, but felt some woman's intuition that our love was coming to an end. Why did I not feel that? Why did I not protect myself? I should have remembered Yeats' warning:

'Never give all the heart, for love
Will hardly seem worth thinking of
To passionate women if it seem
Certain, and they never dream
That it fades out from kiss to kiss…
…He that made this knows all the cost
For he gave all his heart and lost.

I ignored his admonition, to my cost. I tried to extinguish myself in this supremely passionate woman. I fear I may have succeeded.

The dreadful possibility that begins to torment me is that in extinguishing myself, I may have set light to a new life, which Dorothy now carries in her womb. This could change everything. If I do not discover the truth of the matter, I think I will run mad.

I cannot stop thinking about her. The memory of her, struggling out of the low armchair I gave her to sit in – and then going to the door, to see herself out. How boorishly I behaved. How self-centred! No wonder she stopped short of telling me the truth. I did not deserve it. Or her. Or our son, or daughter. Or any of the happiness which could yet be ours. The stakes in this game of life and death could be no higher.

Why did I not have the sense to take her in my arms and kiss her? Since we parted, I have slipped back. I am as stiff and stand-offish as I was, before she taught me how to live, how to give, without counting the cost. That is my defence, poor and pathetic as it is. I don't deserve her. She gave me a chance to change myself, to embrace life, instead of hiding from it, and I failed to take the opportunity. I disappointed her.

I swing between optimism and pessimism. I am sure I could become again the person she loved. Would she love me again, if I did? Each moment of joyous certainty leads inexorably to another moment of fear and anguish. Each flicker of doubt is matched by one of hope. Such is the metronome of my life. I recognise the old rhythm of it, like a familiar heartbeat, but a timid one.

So I vacillate between equal certainties: she loves me; she loves me not. What difference does it make? She is respectable, married to another man. But if she is carrying my child...

Perhaps I am clutching at straws, but I believe she might choose to come back to me. She left me, to go to him. Why should she not leave him and return? She would want the child to know its natural father. The tantalising thought is never far from my mind.

The child, I must get to know the child. But now, I can only wait.

My mind drifts back to last summer term, my last at the school, as it turned out. My life revolved around Dorothy, even when we were apart. For once, there was world enough and time.

We were companions, as well as lovers. We enjoyed the same things, it seemed, theatre, crosswords, walking... and we enjoyed them even more for the other's presence. Is that love? The passion of Provence, so cruelly interrupted by that letter, could never quite be re-kindled in busy term-time, but it was there, for me at least, bubbling away, under the surface. Our friendship, our conspiracy was transformed by having touched the heights of ecstasy together.

Dorothy, I have always been alone, but I never felt lonely, till I lost you. Sensibly, I had come to regard being an only child as a fact of life, unchangeable. I was brought up to be resourceful, self-sufficient.

I needed to experience true companionship, to feel the loss of it. As the glorious release of the summer holidays approached, I felt more like a pupil than a teacher.

You filled my waking hours as well as my dreams.

We had many bright moments together, did we not, my dearest? Remember those long, cool evenings after school, sharing strawberries and white wine, laughing together at the foibles of the rest of the staff. How I loved our complicity in that.

It was wonderful to have a genuine ally, one who understood the frustrations that go with a calling to teach the next generation. For a calling it is, or can be, and you had felt it too, or so I thought.

Was I just a plaything, a bargaining chip in a much more serious game? Did you use me, manipulate me to serve your own ends? I will not believe it. How could any human being play with another's affections like that? Did you? Was it in the cause of love? If so, I could almost forgive you, for I too have suffered in the cause of love. Could I ever think of your love for him without hating it, and you? If I truly loved you, I would love your love, respect your wishes, not seek to change you.

All these words do nothing to replace the touch of your hand on my neck, the explosion of energy when your eyes met mine. I am your creature, whether you wish it or not. My flesh hardens in the sight and presence of you. Our bodies are drawn together. We both feel it.

We went on our pilgrimage to the Lakes. We trod in the footsteps of Wordsworth and Coleridge and enjoyed an animated discussion on the value of de Quincy's contribution to the canon of Romantic literature. Not much, in my opinion, but Dorothy has a special regard for the writers she regards as visionaries – Blake, Yeats, Hesse, Huxley, a few others. She fought a stout rearguard action to justify the inclusion of de Quincy in this elevated company, and I was feeling genial enough to give some ground, in the end. The sheer exhilaration of the mountain air, the vistas, the space, all were having an effect on me. I never take enough exercise; I forget how right it feels, to be physically tired.

We found a tiny patch of grass clinging to a mountain top. Dorothy wanted to make love there,

'What if somebody comes?'

'I hope we're both going to.' She always watched my reaction when she passed a remark of that ilk. She never seemed to tire of that particular *double entendre*.

'I'm not saying I don't want to. It just seems silly to risk a charge of indecent exposure when we've got a perfectly comfortable bed, back at the hotel. We'd both lose our jobs, you know.'

'Oh, Henry, don't be such a pudding. Who's going to see? We'd hear them.'

'Not necessarily. Not if we were...'

'In the throes of passion? Deafened by desire?' There was a hard edge to her mocking, which she softened just in time. 'What's wrong with taking a chance once in a while? Remind ourselves we're alive.'

'I'm keenly aware of that. Thanks to you. I've never felt so alive. Sometimes, I think I was half asleep all my life. Till I met you.'

'Exactly. That's what I'm here for. To wake you up. I'm a human alarm-clock, ringing away on your bedside table, reminding you that there's a glorious day out here, waiting to be lived. And if you don't live it, you lose it.'

'Surely, it's not quite as cut and dried as that. Of course, one wants to make the best use of one's time, however much there might...'

'Henry, what it boils down to is this.' Her tone was getting dangerous. 'Do you want to fuck me in the daylight or not? 'Or would you rather just do it under cover of darkness? Are you ashamed of me?'

'Of course not. I'm unbelievably proud of you. I don't want you risking your reputation for a few moments of pleasure.'

'Oh, it'll be more than a few moments, I promise.' Then she turned the full force of her eyes on me, and I was lost.

My resolve melted away to nothing, and I felt my body stir for her, responding to her, beginning to be in tune again. I did not, I suppose, know very much about love-making, for a man of my age. I am not very experienced. Perhaps what to me was cataclysmic and overwhelming is really quite commonplace. But I do not believe that. I think if men could experience the joy I felt with Dorothy, there would be no more wars. They would see the pointlessness of it, and rush home to their wives.

Of course, she had her way. There was never any doubt of it. Usually, I delighted in Dorothy taking the lead in our love-making, but this time I felt rather exposed. Literally.

Was I really being prudish and unreasonable? Surely, at least, my wishes deserved some consideration. Or was it the first breath of cold air blowing around our passion for each other?

Afterwards, we shivered and huddled together under my overcoat and I felt, not for the first time, as if I was being stage-managed according to some pre-conceived plan of Dorothy's.

'There, that'll give us something to think about in the long winter months at school.'

I had to agree, but I needed to find fault with something, to re-assert myself.

'What happened to living in the present?

'I do live in the present. A far as I can. I savour every moment. But if the present improves the future, what's wrong with that?'

'There's no guarantee that it will'

'Oh, you're in one of those moods, are you? Surprising. A good fuck usually shocks you out of your crustiness.'

'I know. I'm sorry.'

And I was. But there was no taking back the moment of doubt. It hung there, between us. We considered it, wondered if probing it would make it better or worse. She decided to probe.

'Perhaps I'm losing my appeal.'

'I hardly think so. On recent evidence. I'm sorry. I'm not really used to these bucolic romps in the wilderness.'

'But wouldn't you like to be? Don't you feel more alive?'

'Of course I do. You're absolutely right.'

She smiled and nodded: 'Good. That's what I like to hear. Is there any coffee left in the flask?'

I took the thermos from my rucksack and poured two cups.

I produced a small hip-flask and put a measure of whisky in the coffee, instead of milk. We sipped contentedly and watched the steam rise and vanish.

'I'm sorry, darling. I find it hard to keep up with you, sometimes. There are moments when I can't believe my luck.' I confessed. 'Then I have this terrible feeling of impending autumn.'

'But autumn's beautiful. The colours of everything! I love sensing the changing seasons. It reminds us we're part of the earth.'

'I see its beauty. But autumn is all about death. You can't get away from it. Why are the leaves beautiful? – Because they're dying.'

'You're a Christian. You're not supposed to be afraid of death.'

'Anything that's alive is afraid of death. Even Jesus feared death. That's what makes his sacrifice so great. He actually became man; he wasn't God pretending to be man: he became a man, with all our doubts and fears, and suffered as we suffer. And died for what he believed.'

'Yes, I know that's what people say,' she mused, 'but do you believe it, Henry? Do you, really, in your heart?'

'I believe Christ died for me, yes. For all of us. And I believe that, in some mystical way, that one perfect sacrifice was sufficient for all of us. It makes it possible for us all to have eternal life.'

'So we didn't have eternal life before Christ was crucified.'

'No. We were trapped in time. From cradle to grave, we couldn't escape from it. We lived only in the present.'

'Surely, that's the ideal. You remember the talking birds in Huxley's *Island*, who were trained to say "Here and now" all the time, just to remind you?'

'Living in the present is essential, on one level. But it's not as good as living in the all-time, the totality we go back to, when we die, when every moment is equally present.'

'How can it be?'

'It's only possible if you set yourself free from time. Then you can concentrate on, be in, any moment you choose. Look, it's as if you had a vast library, full of books. They're all present, aren't they? They're all accessible. But you're not reading them all at once.'

I thought this an extremely apposite analogy, which had not occurred to me before. So I was somewhat piqued when Dorothy broke into an uncontrollable fit of girlish giggles.

'I'm sorry, Henry' she offered when she had regained some of her self-control, 'I couldn't help it: for a moment, I had this picture of you up there in heaven...' She paused to chuckle afresh at this apparently risible spectacle. 'And you know what it is? – It's not clouds and pearly gates and angels with harps, at all, it's...'

'What is it?'

'It's a library! It's perfect! Wouldn't that be heaven for you? Open all hours, till eternity. With all the books that have ever been written and all the time you need to read them. That'd be pure bliss for you, wouldn't it? Henry's personal heaven. I must say, I'd be a lot more interested in going to heaven if God was going to let us each choose our own.'

'I don't see why not. But mine would not be a library.'

'What would it be?'

'A warm bed, with you in it, of course. And eternity to make love in as many ways as we can imagine.'

'No books?'

'No books.'

'You surprise me. Well, I'm going to have some books in my heaven, so what will you do while I'm reading them?'

'Watch you.'

'Sounds a bit boring.'

'Not at all. If we've spent eternity making love, I'll know every word you're reading, just from looking at you.'

'So you'll be able to read my mind? What a frightening idea!'

'Only when you want me to.'

'We'll still have some privacy, then? We won't be totally subsumed in each other.'

'I don't know.' I looked at her. I loved her eyes, her mouth, the brightness of her. 'Actually, I think being totally subsumed in you might be best. Then I'd never leave you.'

'No.' Suddenly she was gentler, and a little sad. 'I'm sure you wouldn't. But I might leave you, Henry. Then where would you be?'

'What? You're not serious, are you? Is this your way of breaking it to me gently?'

'I don't know if I'll leave you. I hope not. But I still feel as if I'm walking on sand. I don't know how firm the foundations are.'

'I'll carry you.'

'Then we'll both sink: it may be quicksand! No, I love being with you, Henry. I care about you very much. You make me laugh, you make me think, you make me feel alive. But I don't know about the future. That's why I live in the present. Maybe it's because I've loved and lost. It's only natural to be a little – tentative.'

'I understand.' Or I thought I did.

'I don't really understand it myself.' She wrung her hands and looked away. 'But I do sometimes fear what the future may bring. Things may be difficult next term. That's why I wanted us to have this time away together.'

'Don't worry - next term will be fine. With this new Deputy Head to take the administrative load off my shoulders a little, we'll have more time for each other, more theatre; we'll get away more often...'

'It's the Deputy Head I wanted to talk to you about, actually.'

'What about him? Your friend.'

'Well, not exactly.

'He's not your friend?'

'No, well, yes, but more than that. In the past. Much more.'

I felt like a child whose toy has been taken away.

'Much more. You mean...'

'We were lovers. It's all right, we're not any more.

'I see. Why didn't you mention this before?'

'I didn't want to spoil the holiday.'

'Why should your mentioning an old love affair spoil our holiday? We're grown-ups. We've both had lovers before. This one's a little close to home, I grant you, but I'm sure we'll manage to work togeth-er. I'm looking forward to meeting him.'

'The thing is...' She was still quite distraught.

And then the penny dropped. 'You're not telling me he's the mar-ried man, the one who upset you so much?' The tears came now. 'I'm sorry, Henry. I'd rather he wasn't coming, now, but there's noth-ing I can do about it.'

'And you still love him.' She turned her head away, almost imper-ceptibly, but did not deny it. 'Are you still – seeing him?'

'No! No, not for months. It's over.'

'But not for you.'

'It's over, that's all! I wish I hadn't mentioned it. You'd never have known.'

'I'm glad you did. I'd hate to have found out later, once we'd started working together...'

'That's what I thought.'

But I hated finding out then. All my happiness was dashed from my lips. Jealousy took me, and doubt. What was true? Dorothy had never been particularly forthcoming about the details of her previous love affair and I had respected her right to be silent. If she did not wish to tell me, clearly it was no concern of mine. I have never been of a possessive nature, but now I combed my memory for information about Stephen Green.

She had been out for a drink with him when he came for the interview for the job. She invited me, but I did not go.

Why the devil not? All the cats of Hell gnawed at my belly to know what was said at that meeting – what was done... Oh, was I cuckolded then? Why does it hurt so much, to know that another man has taken your woman? Or to suspect, and not know – that is so much worse.

I think it is because love is about continuance. It is not just a thwarted desire to possess another person exclusively. It is the genes that are hurt, for they have lost a chance to live on, to regenerate. And so my wandering mind finds its way back to the present, to the baby growing in her womb. How shall I know if it is mine?

Stephen Green will have no such doubts. He will accept the congratulations of his colleagues. He will hand out cigars. As decisively as he ordered his lawyers to speed his divorce, so he could make a fresh start with his new woman. And my child.

I have no rights. I can hardly claim it from its mother. I am already disgraced. People would laugh, or sneer, or frown, or impute foul motives. It is not yet born, and already I am fenced away from it. Society protects it from the likes of me. It makes me want to harm it, just to spite them... No, that is nonsense. I am carried away by my own venom. Why should I be venomous? If my child is to have the gift of life, surely that is a miracle for which I should thank God. And if it is not my child, it is still a new life, a gift from God. I have spent my own life nurturing young human beings, in my way. No, I wish the babe no harm; but I wish it may know its own father, whomsoever he may be.

I went back to school that Autumn term in a ferment of emotion: Dorothy assured me she had firmly resolved to have nothing more to do with Green, beyond the professional contact required by her position, but still my stomach churned at the thought of the man she had loved working in my school, having won the job that I once thought was mine.

When he arrived, he was hard to hate. I was ready for a monster, but I met a man, like myself, or rather not like myself in any respect, but still a man. I saw at once why they had given him the job: his dynamism appealed to all the members of the staff, even those who, like Colonel Pepper, had sailed in with Noah's Ark and had known the school in its grander days.

He was here to learn, as well as contribute, he told us at our first staff meeting. If we had any grievances, complaints or concerns, we were to spare the Headmaster and take them to him. The Green door, we would find, would always be open. It was let slip that he was a competent football referee, with a license from the FA to prove it. There was general acquiescence to his offer to take on the lion's share of sports coaching. He seemed to be a man's man, and yet, as I alone knew, he could be a woman's man as well. He took us aside, one by one, and flattered us by focusing on what we had to say. He made us feel special; he won our loyalty by paying attention to us. I say 'us': naturally, he didn't command any loyalty from me, but I was offered the same treatment. He caught me in the playground at morning break on the first day of term.

'Mr. Barraclough, I'd be glad of a word, if you can spare a moment.'

'Certainly, Mr Green. In your office?'

'Nicer in the fresh air, don't you think? May I call you Henry, since we're going to be on the same team, so to speak?'

'As you wish, I'm sure, Mr Green.'

'Do call me Stephen. The fact is, Henry, I'm delighted you've decided to stay on. I know how highly the governors value your abilities.'

'Not as highly as they value yours, apparently.'

'I don't think that's true, at all. The way it was put to me, they interviewed two outstanding candidates, one a staff member and one from outside. The only way of keeping the member of staff and bringing in the outsider as well was to give me the job and keep you on the strength. I'm sorry about that, Henry. In an equal contest, you'd have won hands down.'

'I understood, in sporting parlance, it was generally considered to be an advantage to be a member of the home team?'

'Generally, yes, but not on this occasion, I'm afraid. Look at it from the board's point of view: they knew you'd be a splendid Deputy Head, but then they'd have to find another outstanding Head of English to replace you. I certainly couldn't handle your job, even though we both know you could handle mine.'

'Kind of you to say so, I'm sure.' He prowled round me like a cat that has found a mouse in open space, and watches it searching for a bolt-hole before dispatching it. Or so I felt. I let him continue, feeling sure his words would sooner or later reveal his duplicity.

'Your Department is a shining example, especially with regard to Oxford and Cambridge entrants. Frankly, I think a lot of the others could learn from you. How many Oxbridge places are you going for this year?'

'Just a couple, this time. Thomas and Lander.'

Good prospects?'

'If they work at it, yes.'

'I'm sure they will, under your eagle eye. I understand you have your own method of preparation?'

'Hardly my own. It's something that's evolved over the years. Seems to work,'

'Proof of the pudding, eh? You give your Oxbridge candidates extra tuition, don't you?'

'Just for the final year, yes. It prepares them for the way they'll be expected to work at university. It's not cramming. I don't want to force-feed them, to squeeze them through the doors into a place they don't deserve; I just try to encourage them to realise their potential - show what they can do.'

'This involves a fair amount of unsupervised coursework, does it?'

'Yes. The focus of their work is a weekly supervision, such as they'll attend as undergraduates. I ask them to read the essay they've written about their past week's reading, and I introduce the topic for the next week. We manage to cover a lot of ground, if they're bright, so long as they put in the reading. It gives them a fairly comprehensive overview of English literature. Puts things into perspective.'

'I'd be fascinated to sit in on one of your sessions, if you'd allow it. When do they take place?'

'Thursday evenings, generally, But I doubt if you'd find much to interest you.'

'I'm sure I would. Which room do you use?'

'I generally conduct the sessions at home. It's more informal. More grown-up.'

'Yes, I see. Do you know if your premises are covered under the school's insurance policies on these occasions?'

'Well no, I've never thought to enquire...'

'Of course not. No matter. Leave it to me. I'll see to it.'

'We could hold them at the school, if you wish...'

'Wouldn't hear of it, old man. If you don't mind letting these lads turn your house upside down, that's your call. I'll just make sure you're covered in case anything goes wrong.'

'Covered for what?'

'Fire, accidents, the unexpected. Better safe than sorry, eh?'

'Indeed.' I could not put my finger on it. He was polite enough, even deferential, but somehow, he contrived to invade my privacy with every well-intentioned word. I was damned if I'd have him sitting in on one of my supervisions. Think what ammunition that would give him:

'Ideas above his station, that's Barraclough. He thinks he's a Cambridge don, with his little elitist band. I wouldn't mind, but it's not fair on the rest of Upper Sixth English: they're treated as second class citizens; they don't get the special treatment, so naturally, they don't have the same ambitions…'

Oh, no. I'd been dealing with school politics long enough to see that one coming. But was I wrong to treat him with suspicion from the first? Maybe it was an olive branch, and I mistook it for a stick. Could I have made my peace with him? Surely, we were sworn enemies since before we met. So, I chose a cool, distancing manner and tried to keep my powder dry.

'I hope you're settling in all right? Let me know if there's anything I can do, won't you?'

'Thank you, Henry, I will. As a matter of fact, your Miss Pargeter's an old friend of mine. She's filled me a little in on the situation here. We were at Bramley together, you know.'

My Miss Pargeter! I wonder the devil didn't say our Miss Pargeter! But that would have been an act of open warfare, and neither of us was ready for that yet. So, we continued circling round each other, like two wily old stags. Or was it one wily young stag and a silly old fool?

'Dorothy spoke very highly of your work, I must say. It seems you've won quite a convert.'

'Most flattering, I'm sure.'

'She told me about your little trip to Paris and Florence. Showed me the photographs.'

I looked up sharply, but he seemed unconscious of having given any offence. His manner was as bluff and genial, as hail-fellow-well-met as ever. What had she told him?

What commentary accompanied the photographs? Perhaps that was why she had been so keen on taking them. I wondered if there had been any photographs of Provence, but as I recall, Dorothy's love affair with her camera ended at the Franco-Italian border. After that, she had turned her attentions to a more personal affair.

'I think we both appreciate Miss Pargeter's gifts and dedication as a teacher.'

'Absolutely! She's a gem. It's been a pleasure, Henry. I said I'd drop in on the Head before the end of break, so if you'll excuse me...'

He bustled off across the playground, a bulging sheaf of papers tucked under his arm. I wondered on which sheet he would record details of our conversation, for I was sure he would. He seemed a man who paid attention to detail. A man after my own heart, perhaps, in other circumstances.

The weekly supervisions with Lander and Thomas went very smoothly at first. Stephen Green did not make good his threat to join us, and we journeyed from Chaucer to the Romantics without the boys missing too much of the reading, as far as my eagle eye could tell.

The considerable gulf in their abilities was apparent to us all, but I don't believe Jonathan Lander and I made things too uncomfortable for Beefy Thomas. His approach to English literature was down-to-earth and methodical; Lander's was much more in tune and intuitive. He stood back from the works and let them weave their magic. So he was able to come up with a genuinely original response, rather than a précis of the three critics he'd managed to scan in the week.

I'd seen the process many times before: Thomas was heading for a safe pass, while Lander was scholarship material. He was at ease with the work and reading voraciously. He was beginning to make connections between the different areas of study. The bright ones are always good readers. That might sound platitudinous, but I mean they are intelligent readers; they do not read like sponges, but with their brains switched on and their critical senses awake.

I always made Shakespeare the centerpiece of the course. I have no truck with those modernists who seek to dethrone our greatest writer. For me, Shakespeare bestrides English literature like a Colossus; all the rest are led by him, inspired by him and indebted to him. This may be an old-fashioned view; it is certainly a considered one. The focus of our study that term was to be *Othello*. I had my reasons, I confess. Dorothy had agreed that I should direct the main play the following term and *Othello* was once again in the running, despite some dark caveats from her about the difficulty of casting it from the pool of talent available.

I had a shrewd idea that Lander would surprise us all. In this, I was not mistaken.

I gave him some of Othello's great speeches to read aloud, one Thursday evening, and I thought it was a remarkably good first attempt. He caught the vulnerability of the Moor at once. Thomas gave us his Iago with a notable lack of sympathy.

'You're making him too villainous, Beefy.' I complained.

'He was villainous, sir,' protested Beefy, 'he was just about the most villainous character in literature.'

'Yes, but if he'd behaved like it, do you think Othello would have been fooled for a moment? He dissembles, Iago, that's the whole point. He's a master of pretence.'

'I don't see why.'

'How do you mean?'

'Why does he want to destroy Othello?'

'For devilment.' offered Lander. 'Because he can.'

Beefy sniggered and Jonathan began to join in.

'Something amusing?'

'Just a private joke, sir.' said Lander. 'Thomas told it on the way here tonight.'

'Really? If it's sufficiently diverting to distract us all from *Othello*, you'd better regale me with it, Beefy.'

'Oh, no, sir, I couldn't.' Beefy looked very uncomfortable.

'Not like you. I've heard you're the life and soul of the party.'

Lander came to his colleague's rescue. 'It was a riddle, sir. Why do dogs lick their er – testicles?'

'Jonny!' Beefy was reddening visibly.

'And what is the answer to this fascinating riddle?'

'Because they can!' And they both broke into gales of laughter while I shook my head in mock despair. I was glad they felt relaxed enough with me to share their smutty stories, but I did have to maintain some semblance of an air of disapproval.

'I'm delighted to hear your conversation reaches such elevated levels. I was afraid you might waste your time discussing all the reading you've been doing, in the hope of pulling the wool over the my eyes.'

'Oh, we talk about that on the way home, sir.' Lander's eyes were brimful with amusement. Beefy was still trying to work out how they'd got away without being told off for vulgarity, but Lander's mind was already racing ahead. Not for the first time, he reminded me of Fanshawe, with his bubbling enthusiasm.

Of course, he was young for Othello, lacking, according to Dorothy, the gravitas for the part, the dignity, but he was potentially heroic. In his tale of the wooing of Desdemona, it was easy to see how she might fall in love with him.

'She loved me for the dangers I did pass
And I loved her that she did pity them.
This only is the witchcraft I have used.'

It is a lovely picture. Othello is at first unconscious of the admiration he excites in the girl. I wondered if I had ever excited anything like admiration in Dorothy's eyes. But no. All the admiration was on my side. I admired her style, her confidence, the easy grace with which she manipulated the older members of staff. Perhaps I was just another old fogey, to be twisted around her little finger, to her own ends. I returned from my brief reverie, to realise Lander was saying something about the moral universe of the play:

'Don't you think it's a little simplistic, sir, seeing Othello as good and Iago as evil?'

'How else can we see it?'

'Well, if you look at it as a political play, then it's all about power. Othello says he doesn't use witchcraft, but he conjures up power for himself, by speaking, by fighting, by leading his men...'

'That's what he is,' growled Beefy, his military background coming to the fore for once, 'a natural leader.'

'And so a potential despot,' returned Lander, 'like Coriolanus. You could say Iago does everyone a favour, by exposing Othello's ambitions. He brings him down before he does any real damage.'

'You can say anything you like,' returned Beefy. 'You can turn the play on its head, if you want, but I don't think it's what Shakespeare intended. Othello's nothing like Coriolanus. People follow Othello because they admire him. Coriolanus is aloof, he cuts himself off from everyone. That's not leadership.' Beefy paused pugnaciously, as if taken aback by his own eloquence. He and I both turned to Jonathan, expecting a sharp riposte. He seemed lost in thought for a moment, then shrugged and smiled.

'You're absolutely right, Beefy. It wasn't my theory. It came from one of those critics you recommended, sir, Jan Kott. I was convinced when I read it, but when you go back to the play, it doesn't work.'

'Right. Point to Mr Thomas, then,' I observed.

'It's not a political play, at all,' Jonathan continued, 'or, if it is political, it's conservative. The high and mighty deserve their privileges and the low and crawling are as venomous as you could imagine.'

'Does this make it less interesting, or less successful as drama?' I enquired, sensing an essay title emerging from the discussion.

'Maybe Shakespeare chose the wrong hero.' suggested Lander. 'Iago is the most interesting character in the play, but Shakespeare doesn't bother to explore his motivation.'

'I don't think Shakespeare had heard of motivation' I ventured, but Jonathan had embarked on another theory.

'If he'd called the play Iago, he could have shown us how Iago has this terrible tragic flaw in his nature – he just loves destroying people, he can't help it. I mean, it's a bit of a cop-out, the ending, isn't it? *Demand me nothing. What I know, I know. From this time forth, I never will speak word more.*"'

'"A cop-out"? Is that how you'd describe it?'

'Not exactly, sir. I could probably find a more acceptable term for the same idea. Or shouldn't we criticise Shakespeare?'

'No, no, criticise, by all means, if you can discern flaws. But, when you're sitting your "A" level exam, make sure you back it up with solid evidence from the text.'

'Quotations, to prove we've read it, you mean?'

'To prove you've understood it, even if you've formulated some outlandish theory on it. I'm not advising you to avoid being provocative. If you've got something original and interesting to say, that's vastly preferable to re-hashing some published critic's material. Above all, try not to bore the examiners. Imagine what it's like to mark two or three hundred essays on the same subject. Anything original is enormously welcome, as long as it's well argued and backed up with quotations.'

After discussing the topic they'd been working on, I introduced the subject for the following week and gave them a reading list. Tradition dictated that we finished the evening with a small glass of port or Madeira. A very civilised way of rewarding effort, I've always thought.

The new term picked us up and swept us along with it, as new terms do, especially the September ones. The whole school community has to re-adjust and coalesce into a new organism, distinctly different from the creature that dispersed in July. I saw less of Dorothy than I had hoped. I watched, jealous as Othello, but hiding it like Iago, whenever Dorothy and Stephen Green were together, but I saw nothing untoward.

As she said, she maintained a perfectly correct professional distance; she was not unfriendly, she laughed at his jokes and seemed comfortable enough. But my imagination was out of control. *'Goats and monkeys!'* I saw them coupling, writhing together as she and I had writhed, *'knotting and gendering like toads in a cistern.'*

The bitter taste of it is there still. Why did I torture myself in that way? There was no need for it. But...

'Trifles light as air
Are to the jealous confirmation strong
As proof of Holy Writ.'

Was it for that I threw away my hope of happiness? Why could I not have faith?

'For she had eyes and chose me!'

I know that sense of wonder. Othello hardly dares to believe what has happened. Despite his appearance, this lovely young woman has taken him to her heart. It is breathtaking.

There were times, with Dorothy, when I marveled at my own good fortune. And there have been times since, when I have wondered if I could bear the excruciating pain of it. Losing a lover is a more poignant grief than losing a friend, even to death, for there is something almost tangible about the memory, the raw scent of another human body, the closeness, the half-remembered images of bliss, the complex residue of love and loss.

I poured the Madeira for the boys. We smiled and drank to each others' health.

'Sir,' Beefy leaned forward earnestly, the tiny Madeira glass smothered in his paw, 'How do we prepare for the interviews?'

'You don't, really. I suppose you could polish a few *bons mots* that you feel may be appropriate – but it's probably better just to relax and be yourself. Let them know what you think. They won't bite, or not where you expect, anyway. I remember Dr Rice, my old Director of Studies at Cambridge, used to...'

I caught a look of complicity between the two lads. Perhaps I'd told them the story before? Never mind, it was a good one.

'Used to, ah, delight in asking keen young candidates the question (and here I gave a fair parody of the great man's voice): "Have you ever made love with a woman?"'

Thomas and Lander caught each other's eye again and laughed. The young are more easily embarrassed by sexual matters than their elders. Which in part, I suppose, was the point of the question.

'Why did he ask that, sir? Wasn't any of his business, was it?'

'They didn't know what to answer, do you see? They wanted to create the best impression, like yourselves, but they didn't know if

they should pretend to be worldly wise, or confess to being innocents abroad.'

'What was the right answer?' Beefy demanded.

'The truth. It's usually the best answer. Apart from any other consideration, it saves you remembering what lies you may have told.
Whatever answer one gave, Dr Rice was going to take the occasion
to commend the experience of love-making. He said it was the basis
of most literature, and the only way to understand it was to find out
what the poets were talking about, in person.'

'If the candidate was a woman, would he ask about making love
with a man?'

'There weren't any women candidates, in my day. Most of the
colleges were all-male. And three were all-female.'

'Would making love with a man do or did it have to be a woman?'

'Jonny!' Beefy wore an expression of disgust.

This was rather *risqué* for our little *soirées*, but the boys seemed
genuinely interested, and I was not going to be the first to 'cop out'.

'I shouldn't imagine that possibility would have occurred to Dr.
Rice, frankly.'

'I just wondered. With all those all male colleges. It's nothing to
be ashamed of. Is it, sir?'

'Homosexuality? Certainly not. And it's nothing to be proud of,
either. It's simply a fact.'

'Would it open one's eyes to literature in the same way?'

'In a rather different way, I should imagine.'

'But it would work? Would homosexual love work just as well as
heterosexual love, in that respect?'

'I can't really say, Lander. It wasn't discussed, at the time.'

My deliberate use of their surnames was usually enough of a jerk
on the reins to restore order. It took us back to school and reminded
us who we were. But on this occasion, Lander seemed not to notice,
absorbed as he was in pursuing his thought.

'Shakespeare himself is homosexual in the sonnets, isn't he, sir?'

Fanshawe was very fond of the same argument. I knew every twist and turn of it, but I was not about to rehearse the details with Thomas and Lander.

'So it has been suggested, yes. And argued, fairly cogently. But I think if you make some allowance for the different mores of the time, you'll find Shakespeare, at heart, is as heterosexual as we are.'

'Really, sir?' Lander was clearly ready to explore this further, but I decided to open up a safer line of enquiry: 'Look at the evidence in the plays: How well did Shakespeare understood the nature of love? Look at *Romeo and Juliet. Antony and Cleopatra. Othello!* They are all brimful of heterosexual passion.'

'But *Othello* is mainly about the conflict between the two men, isn't it, sir?'

I had to agree that it was. Beefy wasn't so sure: 'I think it's the relationship between Othello and Desdemona. That's what you remember about it. You're hoping it'll work out for them, all through the play.'

Perhaps inadvertently, Beefy had roused a favourite hobbyhorse of mine, and I couldn't help weighing in: 'You know, Beefy, I have a feeling that "relationship" is another of those recently coined English words, like "motivation". Astonishingly, Shakespeare managed to write all of his plays and poems without reference to any of them. But tell me about this "relationship" between Othello and Desdemona. Do you see it as being fully consummated?'

Beefy looked nonplussed. Lander tried to stir the pot for him:
'He means did they...'

'I know! I thought they must have done. They talked enough about it, didn't they? I mean, that's why he kills her, isn't it? Because he can't bear the thought of someone else making love with his wife.'

'I don't think he ever did make love with her.' Lander chimed in firmly, 'If he had, he wouldn't believe Iago's lies for a minute. So now it's clear what the play is actually about: it's a dramatic warning against leaving too long a gap between your wedding and your honeymoon. If Othello hadn't gone off to fight that war against the Turks, they might have lived happily ever after.'

I laughed and Beefy joined in grudgingly and shook his head, as if a fleet-footed winger had just sprinted past his outstretched arms.

'Highly original, Jonathan. Very good. You'd back it up with appropriate quotation from the text, I trust, and then dismiss it stylishly. A reference to Sir Francis Drake, perhaps, a much less peremptory leader, prepared to make the battle wait while he finished his game.'

I passed Lander the decanter of Madeira, which generally circulated only once. This was clearly a special occasion, deserving of some celebration.

'Well who's right, sir?' Beefy still wanted to know the answer. 'Were they actually lovers or just...' He searched for the word,

'Wannabees?' suggested Lander.

'They weren't actually anything, were they? Except words on a page. You have only the text to study, as I have.' I considered giving them a note on post-modernism, but decided to answer the question instead:

'Remember the two time scales in *Othello*. The shorter one heightens the dramatic intensity and gives Othello and Desdemona no time to consummate their marriage. Othello is sent to Cyprus to serve Venice by fighting the Turks, Desdemona follows in another ship, and so the scene of the murder is the marriage bed. Is it an attempt by Shakespeare at meeting the criteria of the Aristotelian unities? Effectively, the action takes place within twenty-four hours. So, according to my reading of the text, and you're free to make your own call, no, Othello never made love with Desdemona.'

'Perhaps he was afraid.' Lander chipped in. 'If it was really the first time. Daunting prospect. That's why he was prepared to listen to Iago. It got him out of a difficult situation. And he knew Iago was in love with him, anyway.'

'What?' Beefy's howl of outrage and my own came almost in unison. 'That's a load of crap! Sorry, sir, but it is, isn't it?'

'Iago's followed Othello for ages.' Jonathan piled up his argument, brick on careful brick:

'He wanted to be Othello's Lieutenant, but then Othello gave Cassio the job, instead. So, Iago was jealous of Cassio, he wanted him dead, out of the way, so he could take his place. And Desdemona, well, Iago must have been incredibly jealous of her. Otherwise, why would he let Othello murder her? Iago's happiest when he goes through that sort of mock marriage scene with Othello, in Act 3, Scene 3, where they kneel, and make solemn vows to each other, and Iago says: *"I am your own forever"* and Othello tells him: *"I greet thy love, Not with vain thanks, but with acceptance bounteous."'*

'Excellent!' I exclaimed. 'A completely specious argument, backed up by appropriate quotation from the text. A perfect example of what I was talking about, earlier.'

I could hardly be impervious to the hints. But I did not know whether Jonathan was genuinely feeling the stirrings of a homosexual tendency in himself, or merely trying to get me to rise to the bait. They left together, after the second Madeira, but Lander was back on the doorstep, five minutes later, for a book he had left under the armchair. He did not explain how he had come to notice its absence while walking home, and I did not enquire.

'I'm glad you've come back, Jonathan. I wanted to have a quiet word with you, without Beefy's ears flapping.'

'Of course, sir.' Lander waited for me to continue.

'I couldn't help noticing that most of your textual analysis, this evening, came from a particular vantage point.'

Lander gave nothing away.

'If, say, like our friend Mr Kott, you had come along and interpreted Othello exclusively from a left-wing socialist point of view, I feel it might have limited your appreciation of the play'

'But I wasn't taking that point of view.'

'The point is, bluntly, that I'm afraid the exclusively homosexual view of literature has similar limitations. It's like going to the theatre wearing blinkers. I'm familiar with the approach. I first came across it at Cambridge, but frankly, I don't think you should rely on it exclusively.'

'I see.' Lander looked thoughtful. 'I take the point, sir, but when you say you came across it at Cambridge...'

'I had a close friend there, a very bright and brilliant friend, who delighted in shocking people by developing that particular theory at every opportunity. But even he didn't think of sending Iago and Othello to bed together!'

'What degree did he get, sir?'

'A first.'

'The same as you?'

'The same. Much more brilliantly than mine, I'm sure. More stylishly, without a doubt. He was a wonderful person. No longer with us, alas…'

'I am sorry.' He reached out and squeezed the back of my hand.

'I too,' I clasped his hand in return for a moment and said 'Well, I mustn't keep you. We've both got school in the morning'.

He stood stock still and looked at me. His eyes were cold, empty. I could almost feel him hating me.

'It took quite bit of courage to come back here.' he observed.

'I'm sorry you need courage. You're always very welcome and it's a great pleasure, working on these texts with you.' And I opened the front door for him to leave. In retrospect, I don't see how I could have handled it any more gently or sympathetically. It is a mistake to be too subtle.

*　*　*

Dorothy threw herself into her duties that term with renewed vigour. She stayed late at school and took a pile of work home with her each night. I wish I could say she took me home with her each night, as well, but it would not be the truth. And the truth, although I am going to burn these books, is what they must contain, as far as I can judge it.

We had succeeded, in the summer term, in keeping our relationship entirely secret, and Dorothy wanted to continue that arrangement, particularly in view of Stephen Green joining the staff. I agreed. How could I do otherwise? The secrecy in the summer term had been my own suggestion. Like a legionnaire, dying of thirst in the desert, seeing an oasis, I wanted to make sure it was real before going public. Now the boot was on the other foot.

As it turned out, we hardly met, outside school, for the first three weeks of term. Then, one Friday night, I cooked a meal at home. She wore a short, black dress that flattered her figure. I said as much and remarked that I had not seen the dress before, but she was in no mood for compliments. She was quiet and irritable. She kept moving round the room and would not settle.

'If you've got something to tell me, you'd better spit it out. Otherwise, you won't taste a mouthful of this food I've been slaving over.'

She gave a very small smile. 'Is it so obvious? I am sorry. I am enjoying the meal, I really am. I just can't quite switch off from work, at the moment.'

'Would you like to talk about it?'

'Not really, no. I'm afraid that would make it worse. I just feel I need a break from school, or I'll go mad.'

'I couldn't agree more. We could go away somewhere, first thing tomorrow morning...'

'You don't understand. I mean a complete break from the school, maybe just for a few hours, each week. I've got to do it'.

'And I'm part of the school.' My face fell.

'I'm sorry, Henry. It's just for a while. I feel smothered by it, there's so much extra work to be done, this term.'

'You can blame your precious Stephen Green for that. I didn't want to do weekly assessments on each pupil.'

'And you don't have to. Although I don't know why heads of department should be exempt...'

'Now, don't you start that seditious talk in the common room, or I'll be really cross with you.' To my own ears, my affected jollity rang very hollow, but Dorothy seemed to take it at face value. Perhaps she was too absorbed in her own predicament to notice my hurt.

'We'll always be friends, Henry, whatever happens.' She gave my hand a reassuring squeeze. It reminded me of Jonathan Lander's gesture in the doorway. What do people mean when they touch you like that? I think they want to steer you somewhere.

'I hope we'll be lovers, too! I can't imagine us not!' Again, the little, reassuring squeeze on the hand, but this time it was the kiss of Judas in the Garden of Gethsemane. 'Can we? Do you mind awfully, Henry? I really and truly don't want this to be the end.'

I minded dreadfully, but I knew no useful purpose would be served by saying so. 'Well I've certainly got a lot on, this term, especially with casting this Anouilh, or whatever it is we're going to do. And *Othello*, next term, if you're going to let me have one last go, before I shuffle off.'

'Don't talk nonsense, Henry. You're not shuffling off anywhere yet. Dramsoc's your baby. It always has been.'

My baby. Is that what she came to tell me? And I too dense and self-pitying to understand? I must find out. I must know the truth .

I counted the months, like a silly teenager having 'got into trouble'. A baby that arrived in May or June could be mine after all.

We had our separation, as she wished. Only it did not end, as intended, in the Christmas Holidays, but goes on to this day.

She enjoined me to silence, for the sake of her reputation as well as mine. How could I refuse? And it was as if our love had never been. She nodded and smiled as we passed in the corridor, we discussed the occasional pupil's progress from time to time, but the intimacy was gone. I asked her about Green directly:

'You're not starting it up with him again, are you? If you are, I'd rather know now'.

'No, I'm not ! I'd tell you if I was. I'm not that much of a coward!'. Her indignation almost convinced me. But then I remembered how she had been as my lover. Her ecstasies. Was I expected to believe that she would not make love with me because she had too much paperwork to do? It was ludicrous. But I pretended to believe it, and wished her good night with chaste kiss on the cheek, and hoped, oh, hoped against hope that she would come running back and tell me it was not true. I should be as strong as Othello, and blow my love away to death:

'All my fond love thus do I blow to heaven!'

Name: *Lord Harry Barra*

Perfectly

Form: *-ed*

Book 6 : For Gold

Effingham School
Effingham, Glos.

'Much have I travelled in the realms of gold' wrote John Keats, *'On First Looking into Chapman's Homer'*. Well, I have done my share of travelling by means of books, and there is certainly gold to be found there. Literature is liquid gold, the purest knowledge of the tribe.

The accumulated wisdom of whole lifetimes is poured into books. Or so I always thought. I wondered why others did not share my passion, why everyone did not spend their lives as I did, searching in books for wisdom.

It is only now, at the very end of my life, at the reckoning-up of what I have done well, what poorly and what I have not done at all, that I discover there are many easier ways of getting wisdom. I am like a prospector who, having spent his life panning poor streams for a few grains, meets a newcomer who has stumbled across a nugget of the pure metal.

Perhaps we find only the gold that is strewn in our path, that is pre-ordained for us. I do not believe this: God gave us free will, so we have choices to make: we can turn this way or that. We can choose to uncover the gold we are offered in our lives or choose to lose it or ignore it. Is it truly better to have loved and lost, than never to have loved at all?

I cannot deny it. For the brightest gold I have found has been in the arms of women, in their eyes, in their hair, in their inscrutability, in their exquisite unconsciousness of their own perfection. Loving opened my eyes to the multitude of possibilities that my life could open up to me. It made me believe it was in my power to make a choice that would lead to happiness and fulfillment – and yet it omitted to warn me that the same choice might lead to pain and desolation.

I have known men who have read less than a dozen books in their entire lives, who have a far greater store of wisdom than I. Every one of us is free to find his own gold. One man's treasure can be dross to another.

There are many more exciting ways of living than by sticking one's nose in a book, but for whatever reasons, that is how I have spent most of my precious allotment of time.

'And what do you have to show for it?' I hear Mother demanding, petulantly, and of course I have nothing. I have knowledge that is of less practical use than a rudimentary understanding of plumbing. I have been a high priest of a religion without a God. I have instructed the young in enjoying the greatest pleasure (after sex) that I have known – reading. That is my gold, and it shines as brightly as any.

The low value that our society places on teachers has always astonished me. I am not bleating about higher pay, although that is an unavoidable yardstick, in our culture. In any other society, those who nurture the next generation are revered and honoured: their contribution is respected and their place at the council of elders assured. Whereas we work our teachers into the ground; we make it impossible for them to do their jobs properly and then complain because they have failed.

I am not fond of pontificating about the greatness of the British Empire: our assessment of its worth must be tempered by what we now understand of its cruelty, atrocities and cultural blindness. But whatever gifts it gave the world were based on intellectual acuity.

We had the best minds and so we achieved what others could not. We wore the mantle of leadership, which we have now ceded to other nations. And that leadership was fostered by the British education system. Any comparative analysis shows us now lagging well behind many of our erstwhile colonies in educational standards: economic standards are bound to follow this avoidable decline. It is regrettable that the lesson is lost on our leaders, most of whom never listened to their teachers in the first place.

It is no longer my axe to grind, but it still shocks me that education, the only real hope of enduring prosperity for our nation, should be so disregarded by politicians.

What other gold has there been in my life? Relationships, I suppose, even though Shakespeare had no need of the word. I once thought my relationship with Dorothy was one of the supreme treasures of my existence, but now I see the lead showing through the glitter. All my happiness then was an illusion, a mirage in a desert life, conjured up by my own longing – and by Dorothy's permission.

Why did she permit me to suffer? They shoot dogs that are fatally wounded: did I not deserve the same consideration? You see how easily I slide into self-pity. I know it is unattractive, but I no longer hope to attract. I am a dead man, a hollow man, *'headpiece filled with straw'*! Or, if not quite dead, I am a man under a self-imposed sentence of death. I view the world from the tumbrel, on my last journey that only the guillotine will end.

It was not always so. With Fanshawe, I would roar with laughter until the tears rolled down my cheeks. Our friendship was a golden time. I have rarely recaptured that mad eagerness for life, that voracious appetite for experience. Surprisingly, Fanshawe spurned the College's offer of a research fellowship, writing in his letter, I thought unnecessarily, that he was not yet ready for Madame Tussaud's. I warned him that Fellows have notoriously long memories, but he was set on throwing away his brilliant academic career, and as things turned out, he would have no need of it.

He went into advertising, of all things, and worked in London. He said it allowed the showman in him to shine, after being curbed at Cambridge. We met many times to go to the theatre and to dine and drink more lavishly than ever I did at home. He never lost that spark of originality, that irreverent view of the world that made life such a source of fascination for him. To my surprise, his work in advertising seemed to sharpen his wit. He always spoke of writing something of more lasting value, but all his time was taken up and it was not to be.

Going home one night to his country cottage in Oxford, he fell asleep in the train and missed his stop. Awaking, he left the train in haste, failing to observe that the platform was on the other side. He fell on the track in the path of an oncoming train and all that wit and wisdom, all that zest for life and fun was snuffed out in one awful instant.

I heard the news by letter from a friend who did not know how I had loved him. That was the official version of Fanshawe's death, the friend added, but he had heard darker rumours of a gang of drunken youths on the same train. There were suspicions of an attack; the guard had called them 'a bunch of poofter-bashers' but no witnesses came forward and, in the absence of any other evidence, my dear friend's death was judged to be accidental.

I mourned his loss, but it was my own loss that I felt most keenly – and the world's. Here was a mind untapped, a supreme talent gone to waste. That Fanshawe, the golden boy who had promised so much, should be reduced at the end to verbiage for a few jingles to distract the mind and sell goods, seemed a profligacy that typified our time. As Yeats observed:

'The best lack all conviction,
While the worst are full of passionate intensity.'

The blessed release I promise myself at the end of this self-imposed penance was to have taken place on a railway line, in homage to Fanshawe, but I have read about the effects on train drivers of frequent suicides. It cannot be pleasant to be the cause of a man's death, however unwittingly, and I have no desire to leave pain by my departure. There is no-one else left alive to be hurt by it, thank God. It is nearly time to take the Steppenwolf's emergency exit from life and end this farce. How to dispose of this body I no longer need is a question that has been exercising my mind – as it must the mind of a murderer. Suicide is self-murder, after all, not sanctioned by the state. This absurdity is presumably a throwback to feudal times, when we poor serfs did not even own our bodies.

There is a dreadful, sickly taboo about death in the West. We hide from it and try to wish it out of existence. This is a primitive response, unworthy of what we call our civilisation. New Guinea tribespeople are said to put their corpses up in a tree for six months, so that death and the deceased shall continue to be a part of everyday life. In this way, they overcome the fear of death that holds us in thrall.

I considered leaving my corpse in a tree on the school's cricket field. Doubtless, Colonel Pepper would summon the janitor to cut me down before Morning Prayers; the headmaster would make my departure the occasion for a moral homily, but my point would have been made. Not my style, I am afraid. I am not so much of a showman. Nor would I wish to inflict such an image on the boys. My quarrel is not with them. So, with whom am I quarrelling? With Dorothy? With Stephen Green? No, only with myself. I quarrel with my own reluctance to accept the destiny that I have already embraced.

I will not continue to live as an empty shell, discarded on the sidelines. I declare, with all the bluster I can muster, that it is not good enough. I say to myself Keats' words to the Nightingale:

'Thou wast not born for this, immortal bird!'

And what of immortality? What of my hope of resurrection? What of my faith, at this most testing time? What do I find in my Bible to sustain me, to convince me that life is truly, after all, worth living, despite such persuasive evidence to the contrary?

I find Job, covered with boils but still crawling towards the Light. I find the Song of Solomon, extolling the erotic delights that are now closed to me. I find the Psalmist, like Keats, *'half in love with easeful death'*. And I find Christ himself in the Garden of Gethsemane, trying at all costs to submit to God's will, and forcing himself to take the decisive steps that he knows will lead to the Cross. Cold comfort there.

So what in my life has there been of true gold? My love for Dorothy had its golden moments, for all the pain it brought me. I remember also snapshots of pure joy in my childhood, most of them before my father died. That first sight of the sea, driving down to the South coast for the annual summer holidays. My father, sweeping me up in his arms when I ran full pelt down the garden path to meet him. And I remember a strange moment with Mother, when we watched Grandmother nodding off in the middle of a game of Scrabble; then she woke with a start and peered round to see if either of us had noticed. We stared at our tiles and pretended we had not. That was a sweet complicity. Gold enough for a quiet life.

Cambridge, recollected in tranquillity, was pure gold. We had three years in which to read the books of our choice, with warm encouragement and help to make that choice wisely. What more could a bookish, young, would-be aesthete desire?

What Cambridge gave me above all was fellowship, a sense that we were all comrades in arms, going along roughly the same intellectual path and able to help each other along the way. Neither at school nor, later, as a teacher, have I had such comradeship, and I am the poorer for it.

I was never particularly good at going out and making friends. I dislike public houses and most sports bore me. I tend to let people make the first move. If they want to talk to me, they are welcome, but I will not impose my views uninvited. I know it is contradictory, but I confess: I am chronically shy and too old to change.

What was unique about Cambridge, for me, was the way my contemporaries simply ignored my shyness. They bounded into my room wanting tea and hot buttered crumpets, toasted by the gas fire. They chipped the Royal Doulton teacups, they knocked over my tapestry footstool, they spilt biscuit crumbs, they trampled the mud of Grantchester Meadows into the faded, long-suffering College carpet and turned my sanctum into a sanctuary for themselves.

Some of the liveliest and finest minds of my generation came to discuss matters of importance. Literature and Life. In that order. I was entranced by the vigour of it all, the energy and originality of thought.

I was simply not allowed to be alone at Cambridge. There were ten of us reading English under Dr Rice's benign tutelage. We went in pairs for weekly supervisions but met at mealtimes, at lectures and at many other functions we devised to legitimise our frequent convocations. We took elevenses between lectures, sherry before lunch, coffee after it, afternoon tea, butter-soaked toast or crumpets courtesy of the omnipresent, hissing gas-fire, pre-prandial drinks, post-prandial port or coffee or even Ovaltine before retiring…

We had no end of excuses for sitting down convivially and continuing the discussion that began on our first day in College and continued unabated until we went down three years later. In a way, I think the dialogue continues in each of us, long after that – we are all Cambridge men, like it or not, for the rest of our lives.

We had a cast of mind, I think. We are investigative by nature, ready to challenge, but we respect scholarship and precedent. We are aware of being links in a chain that stretches back for centuries. We are privileged: accordingly, much is expected of us. You know you will get a fair hearing from a Cambridge man. No idea will ever be banned by sheer bigotry: intellectual liberty reigns supreme and we would die for freedom of speech.

Yes, thanks to Dr Rice and my colleagues, the Cambridge years were my years of gold, never to return, our hey-day, our high days and holidays. I missed the joy of it, alone again as a teacher and back at school – from which I had only just escaped! I never succeeded in establishing anything more than a very superficial communication with the other members of the teaching staff. I have an unfortunate manner, I know. They suspected me of being pompous and priggish, a snob.

For my part, I found the minds of my colleagues generally lacked the depth required for meaningful discourse. So perhaps they were right to suspect me. They probably saw me as a PEPSIPITA – the acronym we had for one of our less charismatic lecturers. What did it stand for? Ah, yes, a Pompous, Extremely Pedantic, Self-Important Pain In The Arse.

I see it clearly now. The Cambridge years were indeed my years of gold. I see myself strolling in Spring through the first crocuses beside Trinity Bridge or scuffing the crisp brown leaves along the Backs in Autumn, marveling at what CS Lewis was reputed to have called 'the finest view in Western Europe', from Kings Bridge across the lawn to the majestic sweep of Kings College Chapel. In a moment, I am eating cherries with Fanshawe by the river after the exams. Or a small group of us are reading aloud all of Eliot's *Four Quartets* through the night. We fall upon each movement in turn, ravenous to detect nuances and shades of meaning, but above all to imbibe what this great seer has to tell us about the condition of twentieth century man.

Of what significance was it for our small coterie to improve our understanding of TS Eliot? The world would be no poorer, had we shirked our duty. It seemed important to us, at the time. It was our job, I suppose. It was our part in the interminable wrestle with words and meanings. We were Eliot groupies; we practically danced and sang Hare Krishna before his lotus feet. Metaphorically speaking, of course. We were English, after all.

And has our erstwhile idol proved to have feet of clay? – Not at all. No contemporary poet has his breadth, his stature, his wisdom or his originality. He speaks for our century, an Einstein of the spirit. He is a great teacher. Not least, he taught us a new way of thinking, about the world and our place in it. Dr Rice brought him to life for us, reading aloud. *The Love Song of J Alfred Prufrock*, a party piece for which he was justly famous. His sonorous tones shrank to a plaintive whisper at the lines:

"I grow old … I grow old …
I shall wear the bottoms of my trousers rolled.
Shall I part my hair behind? Do I dare to eat a peach?
I shall wear white flannel trousers and walk upon the beach.
I have heard the mermaids singing, each to each.
I do not think that they will sing to me."

The pathos of it. On the contrary, one gathered from Dr Rice's ever-twinkling eyes that, for his part, all his life, the mermaids had practically shimmered up and down his erect member, uttering shrill cries of intense delight.

Rice was a medieval Irishman, robust, hearty and delighted with the richness and diversity of life. He had served as a Brigadier in the war and had taken a wound that shortened one leg. Still a tall man, with white hair and a ruddy smile, he towered over us, leaning heavily on one stick, to select unerringly the book that would prove whatever point he was making at the time. He had a kindly, quizzical, sideways look that assessed us, weighed us in the balance, as if, I felt, wondering if in the final analysis we would come up to scratch and get the first class degrees that we and he deserved.

There was an implicit understanding that if Dr Rice paid you the supreme compliment of inviting you to join his complement, you would be expected at some stage to deliver one of the slim volumes of elegant verse or mighty tomes of scholarship that appeared on his table at the beginning of each Autumn term. As he would gruffly mention, with some pride: 'One or two volumes written by your illustrious predecessors – generously dedicated to me.'

Rice had no great expectations of me, I am sure. He saw me for the teacher I was, and am. *'Deferential, glad to be of use, Politic, cautious and meticulous.'* A link in that mighty chain of which he himself was a more important link. For if there were no teachers, there would be no students, and if there were no students, no progress. He did not undervalue our roles, but he paid more homage to those who dared to create, rather than merely criticise.

'Those who can, do. Those who cannot, teach. And those who cannot teach, become critics.' That was Dr Rice's view, often stated, with a pugnacious glance around the room in case any brave soul cared to take up the cudgels on behalf of those beleaguered souls, the critics.

Rice did not live to be disappointed by me, or by Fanshawe, of whom he had the highest hopes. As he would undoubtedly have wished, a heart attack took him before he could grow frail. Strong men should not grow old. I was glad Rice had been spared the final, forlorn 'Rage against the dying of the light'.

He was famous, in his younger days, for riding a horse along the towpath while coaching the College Rowing VIII. By the 1930s, a bicycle was the conventional means of transport for this activity, and it ended in tears, as all those oarsmen must secretly have hoped it would, when on one occasion he abruptly parted company with the horse, flew through the air until gravity reasserted control and then found himself up to his neck in the River Cam.

Dr Rice set up two Cambridge institutions of which he was justly proud. On alternate Sunday afternoons in term-time, he and his wife would give formal tea-parties. Mrs Rice, a woman never lost for words, was a hostess from a bygone age. She rang a tea-bell every

15 to 20 minutes during the tea ceremony, so that she could rear-range her guests on the armchairs and sofas.

The result was that one had a few minutes' conversation with everyone there. Attractive young women were always present, a welcome novelty in male-dominated Cambridge. One, the blonde, dewy-eyed daughter of a Professor of Chemistry, was bright and striking enough to awaken Fanshawe's heterosexuality for a week or so, until he met her younger brother.

The tea-parties were the setting for another of Dr Rice's famous practical jokes, of which I was the butt in my first freshman term. A dozen or so guests were generally seated in groups of 3 or 4, with one young lady as the focal point of each group. Dr Rice sat at a high chair that was easier for his leg and had just one guest seated beside him. I felt honoured to be invited to take this chair at the second sounding of the tea-bell.

I attended to Dr Rice's inner man, to the extent of refurbishing his teacup and passing him the larger half of a home-made scone, with which he took an inordinate amount of strawberry jam including, I noted, the last two strawberries. The great man wiped a few crumbs and a smear of jam from the corners of his mouth with a crumpled white linen napkin:

'Settling in all right, Barraclough?'

'Thank you, sir, very comfortably. Good to get one's books on the shelves.'

'You can't read them on the shelves, you know. A few on the desk as well, I trust, and a healthy pile of references on the floor? You've got to cast the net wide, do you see, if you're going to make con-nections? The whole point of studying widely is to cast fresh light on the everyday. Intellectually, we are at war; in the ferment between Light and Darkness, we are warriors on the side of Light. Remember Goethe's last words?'

'I can't quite recall them,' I confessed.

'*Mehr Licht! – More Light!*' He paused to let his words sink in. I racked my brain for pithy and apposite famous last words, but found the cupboard bare. Dr Rice continued to regard me genially, eyes twinkling behind wire-rimmed spectacles. 'You should take up a sport, Barraclough. *'Mens sana in corpore sano'*, you know. Motto of the Army Physical Training Corps. As fine a body of men as I've ever encountered. A healthy mind in a healthy body. What exercise do you take?'

'I generally walk after lunch, sir.'

'Not enough, for a man of your age and physique. You need a proper work-out. Why don't you have a word with the Captain of Boats? Drop a note in his pigeon-hole and ask him to organise an outing in a tub for you. See how it feels.'

I was as likely to join the rowing club as I was to fly to the moon, but I refrained from mentioning this, bearing in mind Dr Rice's well-known love of rowing and the river. I tried to assume an expression of sympathetic attention, but fear I did not convince.

'Doesn't have to be rowing. Any sport will do. Anything that gets your lungs pumping, your heart racing, blood coursing through your veins – something elemental, visceral, to remind you you're alive.'

Again, he paused to observe the impact of his words, before deciding which course to set next. He leaned forward confidingly, beckoned me to do the same and tapped my knee with a long, bony forefinger.

'Tell me, did you notice my flies when you came in?'

I gazed at him open-mouthed, transfixed like a rabbit caught in the headlights of a car. What did he mean? Had me been trying to tell me something by extolling the virtues of manly sport? For a hor-rifying instant, I thought this great man, my hero, whom I idolised, was going to turn into a slavering old pederast and invite me to put my hand down his trousers. My world was on the point of shattering.

He stood with some difficulty, leaning heavily on his stick, and motioned me to follow him through the room, threading our way past laden tea-tables and literary chitter-chatter to the door. I clumped along behind him with reddening face and leaden footsteps and was too late to open the door for him. He hooked the handle with his stick and twisted it. We were in the hall. It was dimly-lit. He led me to a glass-fronted cabinet and groped about beside it to switch on a light.

''I tied them myself. Rather proud of them. My wife had the cabinet made to display them. In Ireland, you see, the trout go for different flies according to the weather, the season or the time of day. I wrote a short monograph about it, kindly illustrated by a friend, and published by another.' He opened the cabinet to pass me a slim booklet, entitled *Fly-Tying in Southern Ireland*. His eyes twinkled mischievously. I could almost see the boy he had been, fifty years earlier. 'It's said to be the seminal work on the subject.' He rattled on with various details about the beautiful little bundles of coloured feathers that filled the cabinet. They danced before my eyes. I took in none of the details. Dr Rice had moved on to the subject of casting the flies now, and was waving his walking stick around in an alarming manner, to demonstrate particular methods of swooping the little lures precisely over the tip of his quarry's nose.

I had a shrewd suspicion that Mrs Rice would hold me personally responsible for any treasure that may be broken or, worse, any injury that might befall the good doctor during our *tête-a-tête*.

At last, I succeeded in steering him back to the sitting-room and was thankful when the tea-bell interrupted our progress back to the great man's eyrie. Mrs Rice seated me next to a plumpish, friendly girl who was reading Modern Languages at Newnham. She said she was Dr Rice's god-daughter, but I took in little that she said. I was still in a state of bemused wonder at the trick that had been played on me.

Later, I sat next to a third-year English student who had suffered the same fate two years earlier. He told me the trout-fly game was a favourite party-piece, trotted out once or twice a year to be practiced on selected innocents.

Dr Rice's other great contribution to College life, apart from his legendary slide lectures on the relationship (that word again) between iconic art and literature, were his Monday Evenings. Monday Evenings deserve capital letters because they were an Institution.

Modelled on the Friday evening sessions arranged by Yeats and his friends, Monday Evenings were simply the best discussions I heard in Cambridge. Aristotelian in their simplicity, they consisted of students sitting at the feet of a master. I have a certificate naming me a Master of Arts, but beside Dr Rice I am a pale shadow, no master, barely even an apprentice. The breadth of his knowledge was phenomenal.

We would arrive at Dr Rice's suite of rooms just after High Table rose from dinner, with the gowns we had to wear to dine in Hall now draped over our shoulders. A butler would serve small cups of coffee and sweet biscuits. Dr Rice would pass among the company offering cigarettes from an inscribed silver box, presented to him by his regiment. Occasionally, he would persuade either the favoured or the foolhardy to take a pinch of snuff.

This in itself was something of a test. The undergraduate of the nineteen-sixties, no matter how great his pretensions to Edwardian dandyism, was generally more familiar with the ritual of rolling spliffs or joints than with the finer art of pumping snuff up his nostrils. Those few who were accomplished in the skill received an appropriate compliment, while the inept were left floundering and spluttering in Dr Rice's wake.

I remember one particular Monday Evening. Dr Rice took his accustomed high armchair by the fire and his deputy the smaller armchair opposite. Other, lowlier dons and research fellows sat on lesser chairs. We undergraduates, also following some semblance of seniority, sat on even lower, less comfortable chairs, leather pouffes and cushions against the walls, all around the room. Every seat, you may be sure, gave a good view of Dr Rice.

The butler flashing the lights on and off was the signal for all of us to find our places. The room was left bathed in soft candlelight. Faces were visible, but not distinctly. The flames played tricks and threw off unexpected colours, but one soon acclimatised and relaxed. It was an ideal light for listening, for focusing exclusively on what was being said.

And the candlelight was enormously helpful to any of us who had the temerity to speak in this august symposium: the listeners were often obscured in flickering shadows and therefore less threatening, with the result that one was able to focus very clearly on what one wanted to say, and often to enunciate it with surprising clarity.

On this Monday Evening, the usual expectant hush fell, as everyone settled into their seats. Dr Rice appeared to savour it for a moment longer than usual, before purring into action:

'There was a scientist dining with us in Hall tonight, a world-famous biochemist, one of the leaders in his field. And we fell to talking of clouds...' He beamed around the room as we all imagined clouds. I fear mine were probably great, grey, smoky mountains, rather than light, white, frothy strands of cottonwool scudding across a clear blue sky, but no matter.

On to this shared background, Dr Rice proceeded to weave a dazzling tapestry of clouds. Pausing briefly to examine the cloud's place in Greek and Roman literature and classical Chinese painting, he went on to consider the Cloud of Unknowing, through which the medievals believed the individual soul must pass on its journey to God.

'There is no union with God until the soul has cast itself utterly adrift. Alone. Without faith and without God. What image are we given to help us visualise this limbo? A cloud. We enter it, and at once we lose all sense of place and direction, all that is familiar to us. Perhaps we even lose our selves. We enter a state of unknowing. And only from that vulnerability can we rebuild our understanding...'

He tracked the cloud through the work of the Elizabethan dramatists, the Metaphysicals, the Rosicrucian tradition, Indian art, the Romantic poets and the Victorian novelists, via the life-saving effect of clouds for World War Two pilots, to Turner, who, he ventured to suggest, knew considerably more about clouds than anyone before or since.

It was an extraordinary *tour de force*, a brilliant dance through scholarship and cultures known and unknown to us. Rice presented it with the dexterity of an orchestral conductor, hearing all the instruments separate and distinct and then blending them, fusing them seamlessly into a new rhapsody.

He drew on the phenomenal array of knowledge he had acquired through a lifetime of eclectic reading, with the apparently effortless skill of the conjuror, teasing out now a card, now a coin, now a pocket watch, now a live pigeon for his delighted audience, dazzling us with a bewildering display of confluences of which he was both creator and conductor.

Dr Rice's deputy, who spoke next, wisely deferred to his Head of Department and contented himself with adding the odd footnote to his Master's dissertation. One could understand his reticence. It was an impossible act to follow.

The rest of us, having more time to prepare our responses, were quite galvanised into action. For once, almost everyone spoke, and all seemed to feel that Dr Rice's wonderful ramble through human knowledge and perception of clouds had struck a personal chord. Everyone had points to make, comparisons to draw, anecdotes to offer. Truly, it was *a feast of reason and a flow of soul'* such as I have rarely experienced, before or since.

Of the substance of the discussion, alas, little remains in my accursed memory, but I recall vividly the exhilaration, the level of concentration, the sense of almost thinking as a group, in unison. Perhaps it was something akin to what the Americans, with their penchant for fusing nouns and turning them into verbs, call 'brainstorming'.

By the fire, Dr Rice sat back and observed us genially, savouring the flow of ideas he had stimulated. He reminded me of an old coachman giving his team of horses just a few deft flicks of the whip to steer us hither or thither.

A precocious freshman made a promising debut that evening, with an offering only loosely related to the subject in hand, but so elegantly turned that no-one minded. His final reference to Queen Victoria as 'an ageing Teutonic fertility goddess' scored a genuine laugh as well a rumble of scholarly approval.

The best measure of the success of a Monday Evening was how long we would sit up talking afterwards. At about 11 pm, the official proceedings would come to an end, fortunate visitors from other Colleges would be escorted off the premises and we would re-convene in our own rooms. As an aid to such truly educational processes, the college kept an excellent wine cellar from which we could purchase quite cheaply and pay at the end of term. Often, I remember, convivial conversations went on long into the night. Surprisingly, the Monday Evenings were not inhibiting: certainly, there was a sense of speaking in public, in a situation where one's words would be weighed and judged and might well be found wanting. But there was also a feeling of being at a private gathering, in College, with a group of people who worked together and knew each other well.

Younger members brave enough to speak were given a very fair hearing; many found a voice and the confidence to use it. The candlelight was a great inspiration, in that it made a formidable audience seem warm and inviting. Only a couple of tyros suffered a serious mauling over the three years I attended, and I thought they richly deserved it, for bringing pomposity and pretension into a gathering that could sniff out such anti-intellectual bad habits at fifty paces.

Well, I have dwelt on Dr Rice at some length in the golden part of my *Apologia Pro Vita Sua,* and with good reason. This man showered me selflessly with gold, like no other person I have ever met. He asked nothing more than my full attention to his words and six hours of academic work on five days of the week, More, he believed, was counter-productive: body and spirit needed the remaining time for other activities, in order to develop to the full.

He gave much more than information. He showed us by his example that it was possible both to love literature and to live a full life. Like the heroes of the Renaissance, he combined the contemplative with the man of action. Now, with the benefit of hindsight, I can see what a poor figure I cut, by comparison.

He tried to show me I had the precious gift of youth, but I chose to ignore it. So he returned to his job, the job of opening my eyes to the wisdom that is occasionally to be found distilled into works of fiction and artifice.

Rice was a sublime teacher, with the gift of opening young eyes. I suppose he thought that if I understood what all the poets and novelists were telling me, really understood it, then I would realise that I, too, had a life to live, and would close my books and go and live it. If that was his aim, it was never fulfilled.

I salute him, with all my heart, as a man who did the job I tried to do, and did it very much better than I could ever have done. Teachers teach by example. If they have flaws or inconsistencies, they may be sure their pupils will be acutely aware of them. For any teacher, purity of heart is vital. There can be no dissembling. It may be that Jonathan Lander read my heart more truly than I.

There is another, greater experience that belongs in the annals of gold. I hesitate to commit it to paper. In thirty years, I have never attempted to write of this, although it has probably been the most fundamental and formative influence in my life.

It was the summer before I went up to Cambridge. I had followed the usual middle class, Anglican routine of christening and confirmation followed by doubt. I had attended Sunday School religiously: I had collected coloured stamps in booklets and I had formed the desired image of Jesus as the Good Shepherd in cleanly robes, while lambs and children frisked at his feet and listened to his stories: I had consumed my share of bloater paste sandwiches, sausage rolls and orangeade at interminable Sunday School picnics and I knelt to pray or stood to sing at all the correct intervals.

But in the months between leaving school and going up to Cambridge, I found myself questioning the very foundations of that tired old set of assumptions I called my faith.

At the beginning of those summer holidays, as I cleared away the last vestiges of boyhood in preparation for my change of status, I asked myself, perhaps for the first time, what if it were all a gigantic hoax? What if there was no Heaven and no Hell, no resurrection of the body and no life everlasting? Normal people ask themselves these questions in their early teens and either decide that the mystery is credible or adopt a materialist view of existence. Those who opt for the mystery then have to investigate its nature and decide which mystery to believe in, but there is first the fundamental decision to make, between Holy Ghost and unholy hoax, between Christ the Redeemer and Christ the deluded victim.

I had accepted Christianity unquestioningly from Sunday School to Catechism, or so I thought, but I had never truly addressed the idea that I might be alone in the universe, with no Father-God to care for me. This may seem hopelessly naive, but I was nurtured in blind faith and had never considered the alternative. As a teenager, once I imagined myself without God, it suddenly seemed clear that there had been no God all along, and only now was I strong enough to acknowledge it.

I consulted church elders about my loss of faith and received only platitudes in reply. To be frank, I enjoyed my apostasy: it was, until now, the only time in my life that I ever felt truly rebellious. I considered Kafka's theory, that if there is a God, what He probably enjoys most is playing practical jokes on us. But I found blank nothingness suited my mood better. I became caustic and sharp with those good people at church who had been so proud of me. I even refused to go to Communion with Mother. And stood my ground against all her direst threats and entreaties and blackmail. Unknowingly, I was adrift in the Cloud of Unknowing. Two or three days before I went up to Cambridge, I woke before dawn with some words swirling around my mind. Unable to sleep again, I slipped out of the house and walked, to the next village. I was hoping, as nineteen-year-old, budding students of English do hope, that a poem would form itself in my mind and allow me to write it down.

The words eddied back and forth, caught by ripples of ideas or patterns of sound. I fell into an easy rhythm of walking, teasing the phrases into lines. First light stole softly over the landscape and showed me my way. I suppose I was seeking inspiration (from the Latin, *inspiro*, I breathe in). It is curious: when someone inspires us, we are said to breathe in that person, or at least the spirit, or breath, of them.

Did I breathe in Dorothy's spirit? Indeed, I was intoxicated by it, by her. When we made love, there were moments when we shared each other's breath, squeezing the last atoms of oxygen from the exhausted air. I drew her sighs deep into my heart and breathed back my life into hers. We became one; we inspired each other to greater heights of passion. Inspiration is pure gold: it cannot be bought or sold.

My early morning search for inspiration was rudely interrupted, first by an early morning lorry, rumbling past and away into the stillness, then by an early morning tractor, grunting and clanking its way up into a field. My words dissipated, no longer hung together, no longer sounded fresh or interesting, even to me. The air tasted stale with petrol fumes. I was suddenly discontent. I wanted more isolation for my reverie.

I turned in through the gate of a churchyard, first pausing at the thought that I no longer belonged there, and then continued, reflecting that if there truly was no God it did not matter.

I felt liberated. I looked at the church with a different eye, as a piece of architecture, a meeting place built on a false premise. The ground around was no longer sacred; it was merely an English garden, grassy with yews and a tall oak towering over all, spreading its branches so far, it seemed to overshadow the whole churchyard with its reddening canopy of leaves. With God or without, the oak was still magnificent, a massive expression of power and confidence.

I strode up the path to the church door. In my mind, I was the renegade returned to challenge hypocrisy, cant and humbug. Surely, I reasoned, it is better to face the truth than to hide from it in fantasy! I had the idealism of nineteen years and the world at my feet.

A poor-box was built into the pillar beside the church door. On an impulse, I put all the money from my pocket into it. The coins rattled hollowly. I had promised myself a decent breakfast on the strength of that two shillings and sevenpence halfpenny, but there it was. And there it would stay.

I questioned whether this charitable gesture betokened some lingering religiosity, but I convinced myself there were sound sociological reasons for redistributing that particular, modest share of wealth, and walked on, round the church.

Here were some of the older graves: Joseph and Martha Matthews died before the Civil War; Judith Coombes, Spinster, went to the Lord when Shakespeare was alive. I wondered about these people, tried to imagine them, walking every Sunday up the same path I had walked. They had belonged to the church all their lives. Belonged. So the church owned them. And now it owned what was left of their bodies. Their very dust had become real estate. What had I in common with these people?

I was a mid-twentieth century man: I had grown up with the knowledge that all of humanity could be destroyed in an instant by nuclear bombs. I lived in an age that was on the verge of developing instant telecommunications. I lived in a century when hundreds of millions died in war, a century that went on to allow starvation to wipe out many millions more in Africa. An age with great pretensions, but lacking a very acute sense of morality.

Joseph and Martha and unmarried Judith knew all about morality. The Rector would have thundered at them from the pulpit about the hellfire and damnation awaiting sinners who did not repent. They may not have obeyed all of the Ten Commandments throughout their lives, but I bet they knew them by heart.

They belonged to the church also in a sense of willingly being a part of it. They had heard the same stories I had heard, about the Fall from Grace in the Garden of Eden, about Jesus feeding the Five Thousand and raising Lazarus from the Dead. Why, I asked, did He not look down from Heaven and raise Joseph and Martha from their eternal slumbers, too?

They must have looked up, as I did, during services, at sunlight streaming through the same fragments of stained glass in the windows. They prayed the same prayers in the same words that I used, asking for forgiveness, for strong children to carry the torch, for good harvests, for health, wealth and happiness. They died in the faith and were slowly subsumed into the very soil around the church that was the centre of their moral and spiritual universe.

I tried to recapture my sense of superiority over these simple folk. I looked down on their graves, but I found I could not look down on their lives. I wished instead that I could share their comfort. I envied them their sense of security, their knowledge that God was in His Heaven and all was right with the world. And so I simply asked to be allowed to share it. TO WHOM WAS I ADDRESSING MY RE-QUEST? The thought struck me with the force of a blow. I had spoken it aloud in the empty churchyard, paused to make sure I meant what I was saying, and repeated it. I was a declared atheist, and yet I was speaking to God. I had prayed for the greatest blessing of all, the gift of faith.

Such a request carries its own inevitable answer. The soul that truly seeks God, finds God. Uttering a prayer simply reveals our belief that it will be heard. With each prayer, we re-define God for ourselves. We use our individuality to appreciate the divine power behind creation. It is what we were born for. *'It is Margaret you mourn for.'*

Our images of God mature as we do. The old greybeard in an armchair in the sky will not do, past eight or nine years old. God is Love. That is still the best and purest definition. How can one speak to Love? Can we ask Love to answer our prayers and make our wishes come true? God is the embodiment of Love, the spirit of Love, which, if we are very lucky indeed, we may breathe in, to inspire us, once or twice in a lifetime.

That September morning in the village churchyard, I was inspired. I came to know the God of my adult life. I saw the power and the glory of the God-spirit and accepted it as the guiding principle of my life, the creative force behind it. I am composed of an incredibly complex chain of DNA, according to a predetermined pattern. My highest potential achievement is not self-knowledge, but to pass through it, to God-knowledge.

The prophets wrote that an encounter with the living God was a fearsome thing, inspiring terror. My encounter with my loving God was gentler but still cataclysmic. All my ideas and preconceptions were turned upside down in the light of that faraway dawn. I realised that I am a being created by God in his own image, so that He may know Himself.

Alan Watts pointed out in *The Book (On The Taboo Against Knowing Who You Are)* that periodically we hide from God and pretend we are alone in the universe. Now, that is a truly fearsome game, for the soul is lost without God and has no guiding spirit. The realised soul finds its way through the Cloud of Unknowing and back to God before death.

I asked to be shown, to understand, and I was shown, I understood perfectly. I looked over the cemetery wall at a field full of football pitches. In my mind, I was lifted up high above them and saw that the patterns of the pitches were made up of millions and millions of individual lives, all over the world. I could see the pattern as God sees it. And then I went very closely into some of the individual lives, their thoughts, their hopes and fears. And I understood how it can be that God is conscious of the totality of creation at the same time as He cares for each individual life.

I understood that God is in us, in all of us. We are His children and we carry a piece of His immortality: it is up to us whether we acknowledge it or not, but His life-force itself is present in every breath we take.

It seemed so clear in the first rays of sunlight. I thought that afterwards I would be able to explain what I had learned, and help others to see God as I had seen Him. But it was not a calling, it transpired. A few late-night companions at College listened politely, some sceptical, some sympathetic, according to their lights. So I learned my transformative experience did not provide illumination for others. It was a private revelation, and I have accepted and treasured it as such.

Later that morning, I tried to re-create what had happened to me, physically. At the moment of asking for enlightenment, I was walking around a corner of the church. In St Paul's terms, I was struck blind: at least, I saw nothing I can remember until some time later (twenty minutes? an hour?) When I came to, on the other side of the church, having walked through the graveyard and past the football pitches, I leaned against a railing, catching my breath.

In that time, however long it was, my view of the world went through a revolution. In my young man's nervous distaste for company, I had seen the world as a rat heap, with humanity squirming and scrapping and betraying one another in the endless struggle for survival. Now, I understood that we were not just brothers and sisters, but parts of the same organism. We were no more separate from the earth than the oak tree. Our roots were subtler but no less sustaining, no less binding. We are bound to this Earth: we are made of it, we came from it and we will go back to it. There is only one thing that separates us from it, and that is our spirit, our breath of life.

Cynics said I had not found God at all, but a definition. I felt that finding a definition of God that I could accept, emotionally and intellectually, and by which I could guide my life, was a worthwhile achievement. But by and large, people stick to their own views, in such discussions, and I made no converts, so far as I am aware.

The second part of my vision, for such it was, was an acceptance of Jesus, the man, the Son of God, as my personal Saviour. I understood for the first time that Jesus was truly a man, with a man's fear of death. He was not God pretending to be a man, knowing all along that he had divine powers. He was God made flesh and blood. He felt pain. He was afraid. And yet He gave everything. He gave His life for a dream.

What I believe is that because one man's spirit was strong enough to challenge Death and defeat it, we who share that same spirit can follow his example and also rise above death, to enjoy immortal life. One perfect oblation was all that was required. For all time. Jesus is an example of perfect manhood. If we love Jesus, we are inspired with his spirit, which is Love itself. Christian Love is very different from Buddhist Compassion: it is not compassionate but passionate and revolutionary. It is universal – it embraces all humanity. Jesus says: 'Change your ways: do good now and you will do good forever. But do wrong and you will embrace evil forever.'

Hell, for me, is not eternal fires and vindictive demons. Nor is it, as Jean-Paul Sartre suggested, other people. Hell is absence from the presence of God. There is no greater punishment. Many inflict it on themselves. They choose to live in Darkness because they cannot bring themselves to trust the Light.

The final mystery that was unfolded to me, that astonishing morning of thirty years ago, was the relativity of Time.

The central tenet of our lives is that Time marches on, from birth to death and beyond, from the past towards the future, always intersecting at the present moment. This is a necessary condition, for sentient beings: we are constructed to focus almost exclusively on the now. Past grief, hunger and pain are mercifully forgotten. Past joys fade, too. Only the gold remains to comfort us in our old age.

At the moment of death, time ceases for each of us. Atheists believe that time continues, the wave goes on, leaving us floundering in non-existence. I believe we merely step out of the trap of time, into a zone where all moments of time are equally present, where whatever has been has its own existence, forever.

So the supreme moments of our lives, in particular, are not lost to us. Ecstasy is not trapped in time: moments of sublime emotion escape into the ether, and we escape with them. Those times when we are most fully engaged in the immediate moment soar into the stratosphere, and we soar with them.

We are not trapped in time; we merely pretend to be trapped there, for a lifetime. Our task is to climb the mountains, write the poems and songs, dance the dances and love the love that is our bridge to eternity.

That, my dear Dorothy, is why I loved you, and why I have never ceased loving you, because a denial of love would have been a denial of life. No matter that it took place in the past; if my vision was true, and at death we step out of time, then the moments when I held you in my arms and we loved each other will still exist: we will look at our lives and know that we spent together the highest and the purest and the sweetest moments of all. I can never believe that those moments are gone forever.

You scoffed at my belief before, and shot it full of holes. Perhaps you would do so again, but in spite of myself, I wish you could read these words. I wish I could read them to you. Would you not see the justice of my cause? If I laid my soul bare to you, as I have tried to do here, for myself, surely you would not condemn. If you understood that my love for you was true and pure, could you not, would you not – love me again?

'Here I am, an old man in a dry month,
Being read to by a boy, waiting for rain.'

Love me? Love me? I am becoming a sick joke, even to myself. And yet I dare to hope: once hope dies, the flame of life is snuffed out.

A cup of tea with the local newspaper is what passes for intellectual companionship, these days. Surprisingly, on this occasion I have found valuable information in its grubby columns. Dorothy's production of *Othello* is to be given at the local theatre this week. Good seats are still available to members of the public at £5 a head.

I suppose I am still a member of the public. A pariah dog, perhaps, to the PTA, but nonetheless a human being and entitled to buy a ticket like anyone else. I should like to see Lander's Othello. No doubt, she will have given Iago to beefy Thomas. His military bearing will suit the part splendidly.

Dorothy herself said I should get out more, only the other day. She probably meant to invite me to the play. It must have slipped her mind. I shall not make a scene. If she appears too busy to talk to me, I shall simply stay in the background, sipping my gin and tonic and studying the programme notes. If I did happen to speak to her, I could mention the writing project in which I am engaged. She would be interested, politely at first, but more sincerely on hearing she is one of the *dramatis personae*... Perhaps she would be interested in reading the work, when it is complete. If she cared to, she could cast an eye over the six books that are all but completed, now: I can finish this one with an account of the play and our meeting, at the interval, say, or after the performance.

She would be delighted. Flattered, that I should think so highly of her opinion. She would take great care of the manuscript, if I would like to drop it round - or she could collect it from me, yes, that would be easier. She could call in at tea-time...

I must stop these self-indulgent fantasies. It is absurd to think that all could he made well at this late stage in the affair. But is it absurd? We make our own reality, to a large extent. Can I not seize the moment,

*'Squeeze the universe into a ball,
And roll it towards some overwhelming question?'*

I have a right to be heard. I am no longer willing to take my punishment like a dog.

*   *   *

Well, now; I have made an even greater fool of myself, if that were possible. I have shredded the last remnants of my reputation and I am no longer fit to be received in society. So be it.

I dressed respectably, in a suit, and arrived at the theatre in good time for the performance. I purchased my ticket and a programme and headed for the theatre bar. I saw no-one I knew there and found a seat at a small table in the corner.

I began to read a rather patronising account of the provenance of *Othello* written by Dorothy Pargeter-Green (Director), but I was interrupted by Mrs Jowett, single parent of Terence, tottering a little on unaccustomed high heels and attempting to deal simultaneously with a large handbag, her overcoat, a programme and what appeared to be a glass of port and lemonade.

'It's Mr Barraclough, isn't it? I wonder if you'd mind...'

'Not at all.' I helped her into the adjacent chair.

'Oh, thank you. You're so kind. Don't know if you remember me – Sandra Jowett. My boy Terence is doing his GGSEs next term.'

'Of course I remember you, Mrs Jowett. And Terence. Are you pleased with his progress?'

'Oh, yes, he's doing ever so well. You were such a help with his reading. I don't know what we'd have done without you, really I don't.'

I remembered a dull, overgrown, slightly dyslexic boy with spots.

'You're very kind, Mrs Jowett, but I rather think Terence deserves the credit for putting all that hard work in, don't you?'

'Well, you were the first to notice the problem, Mr Barraclough. None of his other teachers spotted it.'

I saw Dorothy come into the bar, in a purple dress which did little to hide her condition. She started to walk towards us and I waved to attract her attention, but she did not seem to see me and went through a side door to the dressing rooms.

Mrs Jowett, turning to follow my gaze, gave me an encouraging nod:

'Fancy, you letting someone else organise the play, this year. You must have a lot of faith in her. Terence is in her class, now. Nice to see a woman getting a chance, I say.' In vain, I tried to explain to Mrs Jowett that I retired from the school before Christmas. She was intent on discussing Terence's prospects of doing 'A' level English:

'You see, he reads a lot better than he used to, but he's still not what you'd call a bookish boy, not really, not like my Mum, she always had a book in her hand, round the house, on the bus, everywhere. I like a nice romance, myself...'

It was a relief when we had to take our seats. I realised how impatient I have become with other people's chit-chat, after more than three months of solitude. Fortunately, Mrs Jowett was seated in another part of the auditorium. Otherwise, I fear she would have favoured me with a whispered commentary throughout the performance. I had no time to look at my programme before the lights dimmed and the curtain went up.

To my astonishment, Jonathan Lander appeared, not as Othello, but as Iago. Most amateurs overplay the evil, but not this one. Civil, suave, ever the diplomat, the only hint of his villainy was an occasional glance aside to the audience, whom he treated as his confidant, or inner self. Never obsequious, he was the loyal lieutenant, the honest man in a wicked world, innocent of blame. He played the part to perfection. I recognised it – I had seen him play it before, in the Headmaster's study.

Beefy Thomas was a credible Othello, a little stiff in the lyrical account of his love for Desdemona, but nicely authoritative, born to command, with the inner strength needed to make his threats chillingly convincing:

'Put up your bright swords! for else the dew will rust them.'

I confess, I concentrated little on the first three Acts. Lander's duplicity was so obvious: the Headmaster, Stephen Green, Dorothy, everyone must have seen the significance of it. He flaunted his ability to deceive in front of all of us. I looked around, once or twice, to make sure other members of the audience saw it too. If so, they gave no sign of it.

At interval, I caught up with Dorothy on her way to the bar. The opening was unpromising:

'Henry, what the devil do you think you're doing?'

'I imagined I was a paying customer. Do you want to see my ticket?'

'Don't be obtuse. It doesn't suit you. I mean, why are you here?'

'To see your unusual casting. Most revealing, I thought.'

'You never saw that boy for what he was, did you?'

'He's an absolute piece of slime. But I didn't think that entitled me to ruin his life. Or yours.'

'I understand that. I'm grateful to you, I've told you. So, what are you doing here?'

'I don't mean to embarrass you, Dorothy. I've been doing some writing.' I fumbled with a large brown envelope containing these six exercise books. 'I wondered if you'd be kind enough to cast an eye over it.'

'I'd love to, Henry, but I've got such a lot on at the moment. You know how it is. I'll read it after the baby's born, with pleasure.'

'It's not very long. I thought, if you read a few pages each day... I've no-one else to show it to, you see.' My voice tailed away as Stephen Green joined us, putting a proprietorial arm around Dorothy's shoulder and planting a proprietorial kiss on her cheek.

'Congratulations, darling.' He gave a curt nod in my direction. 'Barraclough. My dear, the Headmaster's delighted. Why don't you come and speak to him?' They left and were quickly swallowed up in the crush around the bar. I secured the gin and tonic I had ordered in advance and avoided Mrs Jowett, who had buttonholed Colonel Pepper. She was one of those parents who collect members of staff like trophies – give me the ones that stand at a respectful distance and forget your name, any day.

General Thomas, Beefy's father, stood with his back to me, accepting congratulations on his son's performance,

'Professionally? No, no, I wouldn't permit it, for a moment. Far too hand-to-mouth. The boy's got a place at Oxford and we'll see if he can't come down with a Rugger Blue and go straight into Sandhurst. Graduate entry's the fast track, these days, you know.'

The lady with him murmured something inaudible to him and he turned to look at me:

'Bless my soul! Barraclough! You've got a bally cheek, coming back here, haven't you?'

'I don't wish to speak to you, General Thomas,' I said, mustering some dignity.

'I should, bloody well think you don't! If I had my way, you'd be horse-whipped and thrown off the premises.'

'I'm sorry you feel like that.'

'Sorry? It's a bit late to feel sorry, isn't it? After you've interfered with a young chap. Could have ruined his life. And how many more have there been over the years, eh, that we don't know about? Your kind of scum make me sick!'

'I am innocent of all those charges, General Thomas, and if you do not stop defaming my character, I shall take you to court.'

People were starting to look round at the noise. The Headmaster came over, with Stephen and Dorothy a few paces behind.

'I think we'd better discuss this in the ticket office, Mr Barraclough, if you don't mind. Thank you, General Thomas, I'll take charge of the matter now.'

'If you have anything to say to me, Headmaster, you can say it right here.'

I stood my ground. General Thomas poked me hard in the chest with a bony forefinger:

'Do as you're damn well told, you filthy pervert.'

I raised my hands and backed away. The brown envelope fell from under my arm and scattered my exercise books all over the floor. I bent to pick them up, narrowly avoiding General Thomas' up-raised knee. The Headmaster snatched one from my hand.

'If this is school property, Barraclough...'

'It's not! It's mine. It's private.'

'Exercise Book Four: For a Boy!' What are you playing at, man?'

General Thomas was incensed: 'If you think you can bring your filthy pornographic writing and hawk it round at a school event, you've got another think coming!'

He seized one of my arms in a vice-like grip, with the evident intention of throwing me bodily out of the theatre. It was Dorothy who intervened, taking the last exercise book from the Headmaster and restoring it to me.

'It's quite all right. Mr Barraclough was kindly bringing these books to show me, in connection with the Creative writing strand. Henry, would you mind taking me out to the foyer? I'm feeling a little faint.'

'Certainly.' I noticed that she looked a little pale. Moreover, as Dorothy took my arm and allowed to me to steer her through the crowd, the General's grip on my other arm loosened. I tried to catch Mrs Jowett's eye as we passed her, but she pointedly looked away from me and Colonel Pepper adopted an aggressive stance and glowered at me.

Once in the foyer, Dorothy quickly let go of my arm and faced me, eyes blazing:

'How much more humiliation do you want, Henry? Don't you understand? You don't belong here any more.'

'I feel as if I never did.'

'Then why are you here?'

'I came to see you, I suppose.'

'Well, don't! It doesn't help anyone, least of all you. Fancy making a scene like that, and throwing your brooks all over the place. What were you thinking of?'

'I didn't start it: it was General Thomas…'

'Well you might have known standing next to him like that would provoke him. I think you did it deliberately. You're very cruel to me, Henry. It's dangerous for the baby, for me to get upset like this…'

She started to cry and dabbed her face with the clean handkerchief I offered her. She shrank away when I tried to put my arm around her

'I'm sorry. I don't want to upset you. I'll go. I just wanted to see you. See how you are.'

'I'm fine. And I'll be a lot better if you go home now, before General Thomas raises a lynch-mob of parents to track you down and tear you limb from limb.'

'Yes, of course. Thank you. You will let me know, won't you?'

'Let you know what?'

'When the baby comes. You know, names and things. Just a line to let me know you're all right. Mother and triplets doing fine, that sort of thing.'

'All right, Henry. If you'll go now, I'll let you know. Only I don't want to see you until after the baby's born. Would you do that, for me?'

'After the baby's born? Well, if that's what you want.' I made to kiss her cheek, but she stiffened again and I held back. I left the theatre and walked home in the rain, carrying my overcoat. So, I shall go and see her after the baby is born. It is agreed. It was not a wasted journey, after all.

What else have I learned from the evening? That people can be very cruel, in presumed defence of their young. But I knew that already. That I should move away from this neighbourhood. If I were not already firmly committed to moving out of this life.

Above all, perhaps, for my own peace of mind, I have learned that Dorothy understood Jonathan Lander's nature and potential far better than I did. Giving him Iago was inspired casting. I know now that my downfall was deliberately engineered: I can no longer pretend it was misfortune.

I cannot resist fantasies of taking my own revenge: what if I turned anarchist and dispensed my own rough justice? They would call me a madman and tighten security in schools. At least I would have made a stand, fought back against the gross injustice done to me...

But no. It would not be Christian. My path is to turn the other cheek, to endure the stoning, the pillory, the stocks, even the cross, without complaint.

It is Easter next week. I shall go to a Catholic church for the ceremony of the Stations of the Cross, to meditate on our Lord's progress to the very gates of death and beyond.

I remember going with Fanshawe, one Easter Vacation, to the Stations of the Cross at a small church in Brittany. He was entranced: the incense, the candles, the droning voices, the Latin, above all the sense of community delighted him. It was the closest he came to Christianity, for all my gentle persuasion. Beautiful frescoes for each part of the story made it almost a cinematic experience: I can visualise now the woman Veronica, or *Bérénice* as the French have it, wiping the Face of Christ with her veil.

I was determined to fast from 3pm on Good Friday to Easter Sunday morning. Fanshawe was sceptical about this seasonal self-denial. We stayed at the cafe in the village square, opposite the church, until nearly midnight, and he did all he could to tempt me, with French bread and *patés* and cheeses and red wine, which he savoured with what I felt was unnecessary gusto, in the circumstances.

'Let me see if I've got this right,' he said, leaning back in his chair until it was balanced on the two back legs, 'Jesus made the supreme sacrifice, so no-one ever has to do it again. Is that right?'

'Something of an over-simplification, but that's the general idea. It doesn't mean no-one ever has to suffer again.'

'No. I've noticed that. Pity he didn't sort that one out, while he was about it, don't you think? No concentration camps, no genocide, no starvation, no terminal diseases. Hmm. Missed few tricks, didn't he? Even you have to admit that.'

'Christ never claimed to create Heaven on Earth. We still have to deal with all the challenges of life: what Christ brought us was a promise of an after-life.'

'But not for everybody!' Fanshawe objected. 'With strings attached. Automatic entry only for the godly and the good, like you, not for old perves like me!'

'There is a moral dimension to it, yes, but no-one is excluded.'

'I don't think it's fair, God coming down and intervening in the game. It's like the referee scoring a goal. I think, once He set the universe up, He should have left it to run its course, not come down and stood around in the pub, pretending to be one of us.'

'He didn't pretend. He became Man. He had to experience the isolation from God that we sometimes feel. That's the whole point of Him crying out *My God, my God, why hast thou forsaken me?* when he was dying on the Cross. He was really, totally, one of us. And He conquered Death for us. I can't give you any proof. I can only tell you what I sincerely believe to be the truth.'

'I don't doubt your sincerity,' declared Fanshawe, pouring another glass of red wine and dragging another bowl of olives across the table with his forefinger. 'But my original point stands: if all the necessary suffering has already been completed, why on earth won't you try some of these *rillettes du Mans*, with a crust of bread? They're delicious – the garlic is unbelievable!'

I smiled and took another sip of water, savouring my strength of purpose: 'I'm fasting for the good of my own soul, no one else's. I'm surprised you take it as such a personal affront.'

'You know what Huxley says, in *The Doors of Perception*, about monks undergoing sensory deprivation, in order to induce a psychedelic high? Well, if that's what you've got in mind, Henry, I'm sorry to tell you, I don't think thirty-six hours is going to be enough. I daresay you'll tuck into your Easter eggs all right, but I don't imagine you'll get another private audience with the Almighty by Sunday morning. Have you considered scourging? I gather that used to work quite well, for the monks. I could help you there, if you like...'

I declined his offer but could not hide my fondness for him. He was such an engaging companion: life would never dare to be mundane, when Fanshawe was around. He would challenge it, wrestle with it, take it by the throat... And even Fanshawe, the liveliest of us all, would not live out his days. Well, that is all the dear, dead past, and I must deal with the present. I have to perform. I shall give three months' notice to terminate the lease of my house. I shall sell some books and paintings and close down my building society and bank accounts, insurance policies and pension funds.

Ironically, it seems I have the means to be reasonably well off, if eighty thousand pounds can be considered well off, in these days of lottery lunacy. I will try to do some good with what is left of my share of worldly possessions. I may give it to a charity or bestow it on some stranger in the street. If Dorothy's child is mine, then he or she shall have it. I shall leave this life tidily, as I lived.

I am well aware that I am going against the dictates of my faith in proposing to take my own life. I have questioned my conscience closely and prayed for guidance on the matter, but I am not deterred. If a dog were in extreme pain, I would have no hesitation in putting it out of its misery. Shall I deny myself the same consolation? I have the right to impose suffering upon myself, and I have the right to end it.

I have discovered that there is a land-fill site, a few miles away from here, where people take their rubbish and old furniture and household appliances and garden waste. I shall take out a licence and purchase a gun. Late at night, I shall go there, wrap myself in black garbage bags and half-bury myself at the bottom of a pit. I shall place the gun in my mouth and pull the trigger. I imagine I will be completely buried, quite early the next morning. If they find the body first, it is no great matter. But I would prefer it otherwise.

Now, at the completion of my sixth labour, I feel very calm, unemotional. It is decided. Only the birth of a child and one more exercise book stand between me and eternity. I have what I want. I need no-one to pity me. I can carry my own cross, these last few steps, having come so far.

Name: *Prince Hal of Barraclough*

Form: *Harry, England & St George!*

Book 7: For a Secret Never to be Told

Effingham School
Effingham, Glos.

A boy came up to me in the playground when I was about eight years old. Perhaps it was a rare event, for me to recall it so vividly.

'Hey, Barraclough!!' he demanded, 'Can you keep a secret?'

'Yes, of course,' I replied eagerly.

'So can I!' he chortled, pushing me hard, so that I fell on the ground. My spectacles flew off and wet mud splashed all over my uniform. When I tried to explain to my form master, he accused me of 'telling tales'. In vain I protested that it was nothing but the truth: he advised me that truthfulness was no excuse. I was under an obligation to keep the matter secret.

I have taken that lesson to heart. When I have been blamed for the crimes or misdemeanours of others, I have kept 'stumm' and taken their punishment 'like a man'. And much good it has done me. I am still an outcast, whether tale-teller or villain. It makes little difference: the result is loneliness and Isolation, either way.

What I still do not know, after half a century of wondering, is whether I truly chose my own lot in life or whether it was chosen for me. Could I have chosen to break into the circle and be part of the group? I came closest to it at Cambridge, but I fear I was still regarded as something of an oddity, studious, bespectacled, with neat, Brylcreemed, ginger hair, when all around were growing flowing locks after the favoured fashion of the times. I wore tweed suits to their crushed velvet and the sensible brogues Mother had bought for me while they sported 'winkle-pickers' with 'Cuban' heels.

I could have joined them but I lacked the *élan*, the daring that might have brightened my clothing, my spirit, my life. When we all came down from Cambridge most of those supposed friends of the heart fell away all too quickly. Only Fanshawe remained, the most glittering personality of all, to remind me how to live, to shake me out of my lethargy.

Love makes demands in unexpected ways. My love for Dorothy required me to sacrifice my own life, rather than ruining hers. Was it love – or cowardice? Did I shrink from the conflict? I do not think so. In the teeth of all the evidence to the contrary, I cling to the belief that it is possible for love to be genuinely altruistic. So shall I die for love? And no-one will know: that is the cruellest twist of the knife.

'I've bent over backwards for you, Barraclough,' said the head-master, gesturing expansively around his study.

I reflected that forwards might have been a more appropriate di-rection, in view of the charges laid against me, but I said nothing. My dark sense of humour has too often been misunderstood.

'Can't you see how it looks? You've admitted drinking alcohol with seventeen-year-old boys, late at night, and reading love poetry with them! Now, I've nothing against – er, bachelors, in the teaching pro-fession. Some of you chaps are among the most dedicated masters we have. And there's been no scandal before in – how many years have you been here? But you must see how it looks to an outsider.'

'There's no reason to bring in outsiders: it's none of their damned business! Thomas and Lander were studying English literature as members of my Oxbridge entry group. If they're going to write essays about poetry, don't you think they should be encouraged to read it aloud? Otherwise, how will they ever appreciate…' The Headmaster had stopped listening, I could see. Now he cut me off in mid-sen-tence:

'I suppose we don't have to bring in outsiders – so long as Mr and Mrs Lander don't want to take the matter any further. Might be best just to hush the whole thing up, as you suggest.'

'I suggested nothing of the kind!' I snapped indignantly.

'You said you didn't want outsiders brought into it.'

'Naturally, but that's not the same as hushing things up! I have nothing to hide, Headmaster. If I had committed any breach of my moral duty to those boys, I'd be happy to offer you my resignation on the spot!'

I felt like a half-dead rabbit brought in by the cat, waiting for the merciful blow on the back of the neck.

'Would you? Would you really?' He brightened up for a moment. 'Well, let's hope it doesn't come to that. Buck up, man, we may yet contain the damage here: the Chairman is going to see the Landers this afternoon. I'd much prefer to manage the problem internally, without too much unpleasantness.'

The unpleasantness took the form of a cadaverous Scotsman named Neil MacPherson, senior partner in a large firm of accountants, who had wheedled his way to the position of Chairman of the Governors by cheating the community of the Income Tax that should have been paid by wealthy parents. He had the pleasure of being a lay magistrate in his spare time. I was called to a meeting with MacPherson, the Head and Graham Swinton, the school chaplain, a pale, nervous man, always fiddling with his dog collar, as if doubting his vocation.

Macpherson questioned me about my Oxbridge entry groups in previous years. He had been on the governing body long enough to know my record. I said that many past pupils were still friends.

'"Friends,"' he rumbled, 'do you normally make "friends" with your pupils, Mr. Barraclough?'

'I beg your pardon?' I played for time, but ineffectually, realising I may have said the wrong thing.

'It's a simple enough question: do you or do you not think it appropriate for a schoolteacher to befriend his senior pupils?'

'In certain circumstances, yes.'

'And what circumstances would those be?'

'They're maturing adults: they don't need to be treated like children. The Oxbridge interview is probably the most crucial test of a boy's career; parents and friends can't be expected to understand the level of concentration required. So, yes, as the time approaches, one becomes their most fervent supporter. One tries at all costs to build up their self-confidence. And friendship can be a lot more useful than authority.'

'"Useful"' - it's just a teaching technique, then, this friendship, is it?'

'I wouldn't say that. It's got to be sincere, or you'll do more harm than good. One cannot just invent or pretend a friendship, to serve a purpose, any more than one can honestly like all of one's pupils. It's very important to be genuine.'

'And were you "genuine" with Jonathan Lander?' he kept turning my own words against me, and they sounded foul and sordid in his mouth. 'When Lander went up for his interview, did you feel emotional about it, or were you just doing your job?'

'I've told you very clearly that I was not emotionally involved with Jonathan Lander, but naturally I wanted him to succeed.'

'Apart from preparing him for the exam, did you do anything to ensure this success?'

'Well, I... I...'

'Go on, man!'

'As a matter of fact, I prayed for him to get a scholarship.'

'Well, that's very constructive! You know, Barraclough, our parents pay upwards of £12,000 for the privilege of sending their kids here. And the best thing our Head of English can do for them, after five years and £60,000, is to pray for their good fortune!'

'Correct me if I'm wrong, Mr Chairman, but I understood this school was a Church of England foundation: is praying no longer encouraged?'

'Of course it is, Barraclough. In moderation,' the Head cut in, 'but you don't want to go overboard with it. Academically, prayer is no substitute for good, hard work. I've always believed that God helps those who help themselves.'

'Headmaster, I said nothing about prayer being a substitute for hard work: I was asked what I did in addition to preparing them for the exam. And if cost is a factor, I might point out that I prayed in my own time.'

Swinton, the Chaplain, butted in: 'I've always worried about praying for an advantage for a particular person, you know. One presumes it can only be at the expense of someone else.' Swinton had endured the meeting in silence, fidgeting all the while with the apparently unbearable restrictions imposed on his breathing by his badge of office. Now that we were on ground he felt he could call his own, he spoke out for the first time, in a rather quavering voice that had always annoyed me. 'One never knows how the other person may be situated; he may be deserving in some way. So, I think one can only pray for one's own candidate to do his best, and then submit to the Almighty, say "Thy will be done"...'

'Thank you, Reverend.' MacPherson was clearly unimpressed. 'Do you mind if we postpone the purely theological aspects of this case to a later discussion?'

'Yes, of course. I just felt, you know...' Swinton fluttered away into a corner, perspiring gently.

'What about this London jaunt, the weekend before the exams?'

'It wasn't a jaunt!' I bridled. 'We went to the West End to see an outstanding performance of *An Ideal Husband*. By Oscar Wilde.'

'I see. And you think that an appropriate preparation for what you call "the most crucial test of a boy's career", do you? What on earth was the time, when you all came home?'

'About two o'clock, I should think. We caught the last train. It stops everywhere along the way.'

'Two o'clock in the morning?' MacPherson was either genuinely shocked or pretending very well. I remembered hearing that he rarely watched the *Nine O'clock News* because of the lateness of the hour. 'What about their revision?'

'I advise them not to overdo revision. Reading or studying for six hours a day is quite ample. Any more can be counter-productive.'

'At least, they managed to put in six hours on Saturday and Sunday, did they?' The Headmaster seemed keen to find a crumb of comfort in the whole sorry state of affairs.

'Theoretically, yes. We caught the train up at three-thirty.'

'To see a play?' MacPherson still regarded my behaviour as lunacy of the first order. 'What did you do, all that time?'

'We had dinner in Soho. Nothing elaborate, just a Greek meal.'

'With Retsina?'

'Yes, as it happens.'

'Did the boys drink any of it?'

'Just a glass each.'

'You were, of course, aware of their ages?'

'They were both within two or three months of their eighteenth birthdays. I knew their parents allowed them to drink at home.'

'At home, yes. Not quite the same thing as drinking in Soho with a bachelor schoolmaster, is it? At seventeen.'

'I don't believe my status as a bachelor has anything to do with this.'

'I fear it does, Mr. Barraclough.' MacPherson was heavily impassive. 'I fear perhaps it does.'

'With respect, Mr. Chairman, I think that remains to be seen.' The Headmaster was not used to playing second fiddle to anyone, but nor was MacPherson: 'This Oscar Wilde was a well-known homosexual, was he not? Sent to prison for it.'

'As a matter of fact, as a married man, he's thought to have been bisexual. Either way, it makes no difference to his plays.'

'How can you say that? Do you think he'd have written the same plays if he'd been sexually normal?'

'Probably not. He'd have written different plays, possibly better, maybe inferior.'

'Do you think it appropriate to take schoolboys to see the work of a man like that?'

'Why not? Wilde was a comic playwright of genius. His sexual preferences were his own affair, no-one else's.'

'And I suppose your sexual preferences are also your own affair, are they?'

'I think everyone's sexual preferences are their own affair.'

'Well, there I take issue with you, Barraclough. I think if you're entrusted with the care of young minds and bodies, you're obliged to be of impeccable moral character.'

'Indeed. Are you suggesting I'm not? Because I'll sue you for defamation, if you are.'

'Look here, there's no need for that sort of talk.' The Head tried to take charge again. 'This is just an informal inquiry into one or two allegations. A private matter. No point in dragging the school's good name through the mud.'

'And what about my good name?' I was indignant and beginning to feel persecuted. 'It's all right to besmirch my name, is it? "Poor old Barraclough – never married, you know, must be getting his kicks from touching up the sixth formers!" If you have any evidence for these totally unfounded claims, please present it. Otherwise, I demand an apology.'

'The boy's parents are naturally very concerned. He went to them immediately after the interview and said he was afraid he hadn't done as well as he might because of his "emotional involvement" with you.'

'There was no involvement.'

'These Thursday evening - what did you call them – "tutorials" at your home...'

'Supervisions' I put in rather curtly.

Macpherson brushed the correction aside impatiently: 'Whatever. The point is, young Lander has said he stayed behind on a number of occasions after Thomas left. Is that true?'

'Yes, but purely as a matter of convenience. Thomas had a bus to catch. Lander lived much closer.'

'You say you found that "convenient".'

'Please stop twisting everything I say! As a matter of administrative convenience, I sometimes went through Thomas's essays first so that he could catch his bus. That's all. It gave us ten minutes more to play with.'

'To play with?'

'Look here, I'm not prepared to be treated like this...'

'Ten minutes more.' Impassively, the Chairman took a note. 'Lander also told his parents that on at least one occasion, he returned to your house on his own, after Thomas had gone home. Why was that?'

'I think he forgot one of his books.'

'Oh, highly original,' muttered MacPherson, but I caught what he said.

'What do you mean by that?' I snapped.

'Mean by what?'

'You said "Oh, highly original." What did you mean by it?'

'What I mean is, if this was a clandestine meeting, which is not yet proven, I'd have expected a Cambridge First and a scholarship candidate to concoct a more convincing cover story.'

'May I speak, Mr. Chairman?' The Chaplain had located another persistent itch under his dog-collar. 'Surely the lack of originality, as you put it, speaks more to the innocence of the parties than their guilt. Guilty men would, indeed, have dreamed up a much more original excuse.'

Support from an unexpected quarter! I could have kissed him, but I judged it unwise to mention such an impulse.

*   *   *

The inquisition went on, but I found my mind drawn irresistibly to that last evening I spent alone with Dorothy, early in the Autumn term. After dropping her initial bombshell about wanting a break, both from the school and from me, she seemed more cheerful and relaxed, while I was plunged into a black storm of introspection and doubt.

'Don't take it to heart like this, Henry.' She squeezed my shoulder, whether for emphasis or to give me strength, I hardly knew. 'It's not the end of the world.'

'It may as well be, for me.'

'Can't you give me a little time? It's not much to ask, is it? And I've told you how I need it.'

'I'm afraid I don't believe you. I think you've had enough of me, only you haven't the courage to say it. I can't blame you for that. I'm only surprised it didn't happen earlier.'

'Look, if you're going to be in one of your self-pitying moods, I really will get fed up with you. Can't we just enjoy the evening?'

'Not very easily, no. Do you expect me to shrug this off and carry on as normal?'

She was quiet for a moment. 'No. I suppose that's too much to ask. I hoped you would. I know I'd love and respect you more if you did. But it's asking too much of you. I see that now. I'd better go.'

She stood up and looked round for her coat.

'No, please don't.' I stood with my hands raised in surrender. 'I'll try and stop being such an old bore. It's a bit of a shock, that's all. Made me realise how much I've come to rely on you - on your company, these past few months.'

'I know. That's another reason why we should - well, cool off a little. Try and get things into perspective.'

'It all sounds far too sensible to me. What happened to love?'

'Love changes. It grows. What did you expect?' She took a step or two away from me and then turned almost venomously. 'Only I tell you, Henry, if you put me under pressure like this, you'll destroy everything. You really will.'

I went to take her in my arms. She submitted to my embrace without responding – I felt helpless.

'I'm sorry, it's just too sudden.' My arms fell to my sides.

'I've been so looking forward to being in bed with you again. I'd give anything...'

She stroked my cheek. 'Poor Henry. I didn't realise it would be so painful for you. Do you really want to take me to bed?'

'Desperately.'

'If we do, will you promise me something?'

'Anything.'

'Well, you know how this whole thing has been our secret?'

She looked at me wide-eyed; I nodded, unable to hold her gaze for long. She always seemed so naked, when I looked into her eyes. She watched me now, coolly, assessing my reaction. 'Could you bear it, if it stayed our secret forever?'

'I suppose so.'

'Will you promise me now, never to tell another soul?'

'What about Green? He's seen the photographs.'

'Yes, but I told him we didn't have an affair. He'd have hated you, otherwise. He's terribly jealous. He'd have made your life Hell! Trust me.'

'But that's a lie!'

'I said we had a very close friendship, but we didn't sleep together. In fact, I said I wanted to make love with you, but you refused. I told him you were a man of honour and principle. Which you are. Believe me, it's for the best!'

I was stunned by her words but by now her perfume was assailing me and I felt the softness of her hair on my face. My grasp on reality began to slip. She kissed me on the cheek and paused: 'What are you thinking?'

'That this is the way Judas betrayed Jesus - with a kiss.'

'Look, if you don't want to, just say!'

Her flash of anger was genuine enough, at least. I hoped the kiss might be so, too.

'Of course I do!' I held her as tightly as I could. 'I'll do as you wish. As I always have. If you want it to be secret, then secret it shall be. You have my word.'

She sighed. 'Thank you, Henry. It's for the best, you'll see.'

And then we made love, for what may well have been the last time. Or rather, we did not make love: we made anguish.

We did nothing to increase our store of love, that night. For me, the pain far outweighed any pleasure. For her – how would I know? She gave me her body to plunder, but her spirit was away, already far away. It was a sordid bargain, self-serving on her part and desperate on mine. I was like a drowning man, fathoms deep, making a last lunge for the air, the light, for a life that had already slipped from my grasp, for a woman who already belonged to another.

Afterwards, we lay still for a long time. Then she slipped from the bed, taking care not to disturb me. She dressed quickly, with her back to me. I imagine she hoped I was asleep but feared, correctly, that I was awake and watching her through half-closed eyes. Her haunches gleamed in the damp light from the landing. She would not stay to take a shower.

'I'm not asleep, you know.'

She jumped, I noted with satisfaction.

'Don't mind if I wallow in this humiliation, do you?' I muttered from under the bedclothes.

'I'd rather you didn't, actually. This isn't easy.'

'Good. There is an alternative, you know.' I threw back the covers and patted the pillow. 'Let me make you a drink.'

'No. I must go. Please don't make a scene. Don't make it impossible for me to come back.' She pressed the lapel of her coat against her cheek. I leapt from the bed with what I hoped was a vigorous, friendly gesture, but succeeded, I fear, only in looking ridiculous. She backed away from me. I put on my dressing gown.

'Sweetest love, do you go, for weariness of me?' I deliberately misquoted one of our favourite passages from John Donne's exquisite Song:

'Sweetest love, I do not go,
For weariness of thee,
Nor in hope the world can show
A fitter love for me,
But since that I
Must die at last, 'tis best,
To use myself in jest
Thus by feigned deaths to die.

Yesternight the Sunne went hence,
And yet is here today;
He hath not desire nor sense,
Nor half so short a way.
Then fear not me,
But believe that I shall make
Speedier journeys, since I take
More wings and spurs than he.'

The first time I quoted these words, on parting, she found it charming. I fear I lost my ability to charm with repetition. It is the scourge of teachers: we are never content to say things once, because we know that our charges never remember the things we say once — or only those things we would prefer them not to remember. So, I exhausted the power of the charm, out of habit. I still remember my delight when, on one occasion, she replied with the final lines of that same poem.

'Thou art the best of me.
Let not thy divining heart
Forethink me any ill;
Destiny may take thy part,
And may thy fears fulfill.
But think that we
Are but turned aside to sleep;
They who one another keep
Alive, ne'er parted be.'

I see her sweet face now, smiling as she presented me with this gift, smiling as we returned at once to the bed from which we had so recently risen and smiling again as I stiffened against her. And then there was a rolling eternity of Love: how can I ever be ungrateful for that? How can I ever doubt that she loved me?

*   *   *

I was startled when Jonathan Lander quoted that same poem, late one evening, shortly before their interviews, when we were catching up on one or two of the Metaphysical poems that Beefy Thomas had omitted to study earlier in the term.

'Do you think he meant it, Sir?' Lander's question startled me.

'Meant it?' I echoed.

'Yes, did he really believe in this ideal love, or was it just a literary convention?'

'Of course he believed in it: otherwise he wouldn't have written about it!' offered Beefy, who liked Donne, possibly because the poems are so short: indeed, he once observed with pleasure that he had a better chance of boning up on Donne than Dickens in the run-up to his 'A'-levels.

'He was certainly writing within a very strict literary convention,' I said in my 'suggest-you-take-a-note' voice. 'But I must say, I've always felt there's a freshness and immediacy about Donne, that makes me think the poems probably did spring from genuine emotions. That may be fanciful, but I've certainly found in my own life that when one is in the midst of a turbulent romantic experience, there are few poets who express one's own thoughts and feelings more accurately than John Donne.'

Beefy nodded at this while Jonathan tipped his head to one side and then pounced: 'Have you had a great number of turbulent romantic experiences, Sir?'

'Well, it would be surprising if I had reached my great age without doing so, but fortunately they are not on our syllabus, are they, Jonathan? You won't be required to answer questions on them, at any rate.'

'But you told us Dr Rice asked questions of a rather personal nature.'

'Yes, in the context of a scholarship interview. That's a little different, don't you think?'

'I thought you said it was what the study of English literature was all about!' returned Lander. 'What about *The Flea*?' And he picked up his volume of John Donne, opened it at a marked page and began to read:

'Mark but this flea, and mark in this,
How little that which thou deny'st me is;
It sucked me first, and now sucks thee,
And in this flea, our two bloods mingled be;
Thou know'st that this cannot be said
A sin, nor shame, nor loss of maidenhead,
Yet this enjoys before it woo,
And pampered swells with one blood made of two
And this, alas, is more than we would do.'

He snapped the book shut, giving me an insolent stare.

'Lines that have fuelled many a literary seduction, I'm sure.' I noticed Thomas was looking a little nonplussed. 'You should remember them, Beefy. They may be useful at the conclusion of the Rugby Club Ball, don't you think?'

'I doubt it, Sir!' grinned Beefy. 'But thanks for the thought!'

'Pretty well irresistible, I'd say.' Jonathan sat back in his chair and brushed his hair from his forehead. 'I'm sure I couldn't refuse anyone who said that to me.'

'You won't need to refuse anyone!' threw in Beefy. 'No-one'll ever ask you!'

'Coming from you, you great ugly brute…'

'Gentlemen! We seem to have exhausted the fascination of Metaphysical poetry, so I'll leave you to continue this absorbing discussion on the way home. We don't want Mr Thomas missing his bus.' I felt I'd given them enough leeway and started to shepherd them out of the house.

'But I didn't read my favourite poem!' Jonathan was still protesting as he piled books into his briefcase.'

'Another time, eh?'

'You know, sir, *The Good Morrow*'. This time, Lander quoted from memory, looking at me again.

But this: all pleasures fancies be.
If ever any beauty I did see,
Which I desired and got, 'twas but a dream of thee.'

I was polite but brisk: 'Plenty of time after your interviews.'

'I hope so, Sir.' Jonathan took his coat from me and I opened the front door for them both.

'Sure of it. English literature isn't going to go away just because you've been offered your places, you know. Wait till you see the reading lists your colleges send you.'

'I can't wait,' groaned Beefy, sarcastically.

'No, nor can I,' said Jonathan, and we made our farewells and they went down the path. Should I have been more alert to the boy's feelings? Did I understand what he felt for me? Not fully, or I should have done something about it. I suppose the truth is that I did have some inkling but thought it best to ignore it.

Schoolboy crushes are not so uncommon: I have rarely been the object of them, but I have always felt it my duty to deal gently with anyone suffering from unrequited love of any kind. That is very glib. It is not so easy to deal gently without being misunderstood, if one is the object of that love. Should I then have acknowledged Jonathan's feelings more openly? That might have made matters worse. It might have made it more difficult for him to retreat gracefully. And what if he had denied it all? I would have looked pretty silly.

Perhaps I should have reported the matter to the proper authorities. Once again, there would have been a real danger of being taken for a deluded idiot, or worse. I could hardly take my concerns to the Deputy Head, in the circumstances. And what sort of teacher would I have been if I had gone to the Headmaster or his parents, just a few days before the boy was to go for his interviews? I had no hard and fast evidence. Better let sleeping dogs lie. Or so I thought.

*　　*　　*

The end of the Autumn term at Effingham was enlivened by numerous House parties, or excuses for the boys to let off steam before the onslaught of Christmas. The emphasis was very much on home-made entertainment, which I am bound to say was of variable quality. My days as a housemaster had long since come to an end: I never took Dr Rice's advice to develop an interest in sport, and I found the petty nationalism of inter-house rivalry very artificial, if not downright sinister.

I only attended House parties when I had forgotten to arm myself in advance with a suitable excuse.

Except that Dorothy had become deputy house-mistress of my old house. Was that why I went? If so, I deserved the comeuppance I received. The entertainment was better than usual – not too many painful violin solos and a staff-room skit which gave the boys a chance to perform their impersonations of members of staff for a wider audience than usual. The caricature of myself I found woefully inaccurate, but one boy had caught the Headmaster to the life. He huffed and puffed his way through a vigorous peroration in praise of the school:

'There's nothing wrong with Effingham, you know. I love Effingham, and so does my wife. We've been Effingham for years. If a prospective parent seems a little reluctant to send his boy here, I say to him, I say: "Why don't you try Effingham, try it for a term and see how you feel!" Oh, yes, I believe in Effingham. I promote it at every opportunity!'

The reception was rapturous. Tears rolled down cheeks and sides were held to stop them splitting. Personally, I found it hard to credit that the humorous potential of the school's name had never been appreciated by 90% of the audience, but as a guest, one must not be too critical. The mood was infectious. I myself was even enjoying a quiet chuckle at the impersonator's bravado, when I noticed Dorothy staring at me. She inclined her head towards the door. In a moment, we had made our exits, while the applause went on unabated.

'What's the matter?' I went to hold her, but she shifted away.

'Nothing. Nothing at all.' She squeezed my forearm to soften the moment, but this time neither of us was deceived. 'I wanted to tell you myself, before you hear on the grapevine. You know how it is - tell one person, and you may as well announce it at Assembly!'

'Announce what?'

'Sorry. There's no easy way to say it.'

'Are you - are you ill?'

'No, no, quite the reverse. I've never felt better.'

'Then what?'

'Well, I didn't know if you'd heard: I've been seeing Stephen.'

'Not again!' I must have looked disgusted. She became defensive

'It's not the same as before. He's divorcing his wife.'

'Isn't that what they all say? Don't tell me: she doesn't understand him!'

She turned to go. 'I'm sorry. Forget I mentioned it.'

I put out a hand, blindly, to hold us back from the abyss.

'I'm sorry. Tell me.'

'We're engaged.' She did not turn to deliver the blow. Her words were muffled. I hardly heard them. But for the life of me, I could not ask her to repeat them. I released her arm, but still she did not go. Instead, now she turned very slowly, to observe the impact of her words.

She would not have been disappointed. My face felt formless, like the centre of Hiroshima, a second after the bomb dropped. It was some time before the atoms could compose themselves into a new format, and longer before words formed in my brain and found their way to my tongue.

'I suppose congratulations are in order.'

'I didn't call you out to congratulate me.'

'No? Then why?'

'I thought you should know. I'm sorry. I didn't mean to make such a mess of it.'

'You did it very well. If I didn't know better, I'd have been quite convinced you cared.'

'I do care about you. You know that.'

'You know what puzzles me?' I could look at her now. The worst had happened. There was no more to fear. 'Did you ever really love me - I mean wholeheartedly, as you said? Or was I just a device to lure him back?'

'Of course I loved you.'

'Then how could you stop?'

'I don't know. It happens.'

'Do you love…' It was an effort to get the blasted name out – 'Stephen – in the same way?'

'She considered. 'No, in a different way.'

'Less?'

'Probably more, if you insist on analysing it.'

'How could you? – How could you?' I sat on the stairs with my head in my hands. At last she came to me. Perhaps she saw I was no longer a threat. It was safe for her to put her arm around my shoulders as they began to shake, uncontrollably.

'Believe me, Henry, this is the last thing I wanted to happen, to see you like this.' It was some time before I could speak, so she continued: 'I didn't think I could ever love anyone again, after Stephen. But I did love you. You were different. You made no demands on me. At first, I could say anything, do anything, be anything. So I became the woman you wanted. But then I met Stephen again, and saw a chance of my own happiness.'

'Rather than mine.'

'It doesn't have to be an alternative. You'll find someone. Now you've remembered how to love.'

'I don't know that I want to love. It seems a curse.'

'It's not. It's the greatest blessing. You know that. When you're yourself.'

'I hate being myself. I hate being in love with you. I wish I could turn back the clock, but I can't.'

'I can't help you.' She was very close to me now. I felt the familiar softness and fragrance of her hair brushing against my face. 'Somehow, you've got to find the strength to start again. I can't give you that, Henry. You can only find it in yourself.'

'There's nothing left of myself. I gave it all to you. I am a hollow man, a stuffed man, *"headpiece filled with straw."* How can I make a fresh start, after this? I work here. I practically live here. I see you every day.'

'You've just got to close the door on the past, Henry.'

'Confess and be absolved, you mean? It's not as easy as that. There's no divine grace involved in retreating from love to normal life again. In any case, you're asking me to base this brave new life I'm supposed to have on a complete falsehood.'

'How do you mean?'

'Denying my love for you.' I flapped my arms at my sides, not so much a shrug, more a gesture of complete hopelessness. 'If you're serious about this, I think we both deserve a fresh start. And that means facing up to the truth about the past. For all three of us.'

'No! Henry, you promised!' She seemed genuinely outraged.

'What are you afraid of? Much better Green should find out now, than later.'

'There's no reason he should ever find out. You don't know him; he's a perfectionist; he couldn't handle it. Besides, you promised!'

She seemed to be on the verge of hysteria. For all my distress, I was calmer than she, and I tried to take control of the situation:

'Green deserves to be told. The truth is important.'

'You'll ruin my life if you tell him!'

'And mine if I don't.'

'If you really loved me...'

'You know I do.'

'You said once you loved me more than life itself.'

'So you want me to commit suicide for you.'

'Of course I don't: I want you to live! And I want you to give me enough space to live, too!'

But there is not enough space for us to live apart, my dear. Not in the wide, wide world.

*　*　*

And already it is June. The sun warms the earth but it does not warm me. On an impulse, I telephoned the Maternity Hospital and asked if they would be taking care of a Dorothy Pargeter or Green. I was her uncle, I said, long estranged, but I cared about her. The best lies always contain as much truth as possible. But the girl refused to give me any information.

Two days later, not to be deterred, I rang the school, claimed to be the East Midlands University arranging a date for the Deputy Head to visit us, and asked if I could check what dates he had booked for maternity leave. The secretary consulted a diary and told me it officially started from the last week in June, but his absence could begin 'any day now'.

My heart leaped at the news. So the child was conceived in September, and must be mine! Unless she betrayed me almost as soon as Green arrived at the school. Surely not. Did I count for so little?

Stephen Green will be at the birth. That is what matters. Then so shall I. Not at the bedside, mopping the young mother's fevered brow and soothing her cries. But not far away. Unseen. It may be my child. They shall not exclude me.

It occurs to me that Dorothy may well be right: my exile is probably warping my view of the world. Society creates outcasts at its own peril. A man who is consistently rejected must come to feel himself no longer bound by that society's moral and legal rules.

I am not about to turn into a monster and take a sub-machine gun to Effingham School, nor even to its Deputy Headmaster and Acting Head of English, but I begin to understand how such monsters are made. Continued oppression, whether real or imagined, must lead to a breaking point: we should not be surprised if the reaction is sometimes not commensurate with the treatment that provoked it.

Dorothy said I should get out more, and for the past few days I have been taking her advice. A little park adjoins the modest bungalow where she and her lover conduct their still adulterous relationship. I have taken to spying on their comings and goings from the shrubbery. I know their routine, so I shall know when they go to the hospital.

Green is an early bird, always scrubbed and shaved immaculately with 'gleaming morning face'. She sees him to the door in a dressing gown and offers her upturned face for a chaste kiss.

She holds the door to hide her swollen body from public view. He is solicitous, uxorious – but then, he has experience in the art of being a husband. He carries a bulging briefcase to work and brings a bulging briefcase back; to what extent the contents change, from day to day, I am not aware.

I do not approach the windows until well after dark, half past ten or eleven o'clock, these warm summer nights. I am not a Peeping Tom. I am merely keeping a legitimate eye on what may well be mine. Nine times out of ten, the curtains are closed.

Once in a while, I am vouchsafed a glimpse into their lives. I see how they look at each other, how they behave when they think they are quite alone. I need to know these things. It is an intrusion, but I have suffered much. Oh, very well, there is no excuse. I have no reputation left to lose.

I have watched them sleeping, as a breath of wind blows back the net curtains. They are restless, covered only by a sheet. Now she hugs his shoulder; now she presses her face against his back. They do not make love. Perhaps that is the way, when the egg is about to hatch.

On the other hand, perhaps he knows the baby is another man's and has rejected her.   No. Not so. He is every inch the expectant father. And she – she is radiant. Her skin glows, her eyes shine, she bursts with life. I would love her, too. I still do, with the remaining fragments of my heart.

For him, I feel only a deepening, implacable hatred. If he did not exist, I would be the man lying beside her at night. I would watch over her, not snore and fart inconsiderately, as Green does. Soon, he will begin to take her for granted. She will become 'the wife' and he will secretly prefer the golf club. He will not love her as she deserves.

I should rescue her like a knight of old. I should save the damsel and slay the dragon. As Claudius killed Hamlet's father, I could easily pour poison in his ear as he sleeps.

Or even as he wakes! Why did I not think of it before? Dorothy did. That is what she feared, that I would use the only weapon I had, to poison his mind against her. What was it she said? That he was a perfectionist, that 'he wouldn't handle it', that he was terribly jealous.

I will talk to him. I will be Iago and lead him by the nose. Iago had to tell lies: for me, the truth will suffice. I will tell him I have been 'tupping his white ewe'. I will tease him into such a rage that – that what? Am I trying to provoke him to destroy the woman he loves, out of jealousy and wounded pride? That would hardly serve my purpose. If only I can induce him to destroy the love and leave the woman. Surely that is not beyond my wit.

It is curious how the information one gathers, apparently at random, sometimes coalesces to form an apparently pre-ordained pattern. When I took Lander and Thomas to see Wilde's *An Ideal Husband*, Jonathan Lander was particularly taken with the evil Mrs Cheveley, who tries to blackmail a government minister.

'I thought she was divine!' Lander declared, as we sat with coffees, while waiting for our train.

'Mrs Cheveley?' protested Beefy. 'She was a malicious, old snake!'

'Yes, but she knew what she wanted. She wasn't especially malicious: she just didn't give a toss what happened to anyone else, so long as she got her money. She had a power and she decided to use it.'

'Yes, but she only had that power because the man's wife was such a perfectionist. She was exploiting someone's weakness.'

'That's what weaknesses are for, isn't it – to be exploited?' Jonathan gave me a sidelong glance. 'Mrs Cheveley breaks the rules of society, just like Oscar Wilde did. It doesn't matter whether she's right or wrong: she just does it.'

I thought it was time I interjected: 'Every play needs a moral universe. It may well create its own, but it has to have one. Essentially, drama is about the conflict between the forces of good and evil – light and darkness, as Dr Rice saw it.'

'Not necessarily.' Jonathan shook his head. 'It can be nihilistic. The playwright doesn't have to approve of the society he describes. His job is just to portray the world as he sees it. It's up to the audience to make whatever moral judgments they see fit.'

'Well, the moral judgment in *An Ideal Husband* is pretty obvious, isn't it?' put in Beefy, 'She doesn't get away with it.'

'That's not the point.' Jonathan fired back quickly, 'The point is, he shows us someone trying to do something totally evil. And why? – Just because she can. Like the dogs licking themselves. There's no better answer. What Wilde's saying is that human beings can be selfish and greedy enough to behave like that.'

'Not exactly hot news, is it?' I remarked drily, thinking Jonathan's argument was heading in a fruitless direction. 'Of course, Wilde himself had a taste of man's inhumanity to man, not long after writing this play.'

'You mean, in Reading Gaol, Sir?' For once, Beefy had done some of the background reading.

'I was thinking of the journey there. Did you read about it?'

'Well, not all of it, Sir.'

'It was a harrowing experience, by his own account. The prison guards paraded him up and down Paddington Station in his convict uniform, while waiting for the train to Reading. Apparently, when they found out who he was, quite a crowd gathered to scoff and jeer.'

'That's disgusting,' observed Beefy. 'He may have deserved to be sent to jail, but he didn't deserve that. It's extra punishment.'

Lander was first off the mark: 'What do you mean, "he may have deserved to be sent to jail?" Homosexuality's not a crime! Personally, I think they should have given him a pension: he was a national treasure.'

Throughout the day, I sensed that Jonathan might be trying to show off to me, to monopolise my attention. My response was to try and involve Beefy in all our exchanges. It was not until halfway through the rail journey home, when Beefy was demonstrably asleep, that Jonathan took advantage of an empty carriage to be more direct.

'Do you find me attractive, at all?'

'I'm not a homosexual.'

'Oh, pull the other one.'

'It's true. And even if I was, you're my pupil.'

'I won't be your pupil for much longer.' As if to underline the point, he adopted a rather matey, much less formal tone. 'No more supervisions. Pity. I enjoyed our Thursday evenings together. Beats me how you do it, year after year.'

'What do you mean? I'm paid to do it.'

'How can you stand it? The level of intellectual companionship in that staff room must be well below zero.'

'Jonathan, I really can't listen to this sort of talk. You are still a pupil at the school and I am still a member of staff.'

'I know, but honestly, aren't there times when you want to tell them all to fuck off?'

'I can't say I've ever felt a desire to use that expression. Not exactly witty repartee, is it?'

'You just don't believe in breaking the rules, do you, Sir? I must say, it's one of the things I admire about you, but I wish you'd kick over the traces once in a while.'

'I'll celebrate your scholarship, Jonathan, with pleasure.'

He pouted and quoted Shakespeare at me:

'Come live with me and be my love,
And we will every pleasure prove.''

'Not that sort of pleasure!' I tried to laugh, but it rang rather hollow.

'It wasn't a quotation, it was a proposition!'

'In that case, the answer is very definitely no.'

'What if I ask you again, once I've left school?'

'The answer will still be very definitely no.'

'Don't you fancy me at all? I've seen you looking at me.' His mock-serious tone invited me to play along with the game, but I felt it had gone beyond a bad joke.

'Jonathan, I'm going to wash my hands, sit in another carriage and forget we ever had this conversation.' I said sternly, then collected my briefcase and left. As I went, I felt his parting shot between the shoulder blades.

'You think you've got everything, don't you? You think you can play with people's emotions like you play with books! Well, I'll get you, you bastard. Wait and see!'

As the door closed on his words, I took a breath of air from the next carriage and reflected that Stephen Green's point about holding my supervisions at the school had been a sound one after all, and worth following up, next year...

I blamed myself for Lander's outburst: I should have been more aware. I should have seen it coming long before he embarrassed himself like that. I did not take his threat seriously. Clearly, that was an error of judgment.

I ignored the warning, as I have ignored warnings all my life. I do not seem to see them. A thoroughgoing knowledge and understanding of English literature is not, after all, the best preparation for the twists and vagaries of fortune. There is a lot to be said for low cunning.

That is a valuable lesson. I shall be more cunning now that the trap is about to spring. I have been to the Maternity Hospital with a bunch of flowers, to see the lie of the land, and I have purchased the disguise and props I shall need. It is a pity I was not more cunning in my dealings with the Headmaster and Chairman MacPherson. They waited till the last day of the Autumn term to administer the *coup de grâce*.

'It's a very generous financial settlement, Henry.' said the Headmaster, as I looked through the papers he had pushed across the desk. 'A lump sum payment, in lieu of all entitlements.'

'Very generous, I'm sure. But I don't wish to take early retirement.'

'You've no choice in the matter, Barraclough.' MacPherson sat at the end of the desk with his arms folded. 'And frankly, neither had we. I'd no wish to sign that cheque, believe me.'

'We've got to give the Landers what they want, you see, Henry. And what they want – what they've agreed to, after a number of meetings, the minimum they'd accept, is for you to leave the school and for there to be no publicity.'

'What if I refuse to cooperate?'

'They'll hand the matter over to the police for criminal investigation and take out a private action against you and the school.'

'Let them. I'm innocent.'

'I'm not saying they'd win the case: our lawyers feel they probably haven't got enough evidence. But the publicity would be disastrous, both for you and the school. Not to mention, I suppose, for young

Jonathan Lander, as well. You did say you once had a genuine regard for the boy…'

I was silent for a moment. I could see no way out. I felt outraged
at being falsely accused, and yet I had no stomach for the fight. I
could call on Dorothy to give evidence as to my heterosexuality:
would she tell the truth? Probably. If not, I had her letters. I could
call on her, but only at the cost of breaking my promise and, as she
would put it, ruining her life.

I certainly had no stomach for a fight when the weapon that would
win it was out of my reach.

'Sign between the two pencil crosses. Both copies. And just initial
the other pages.' Macpherson handed me a fat fountain pen and,
practically in a trance, I did as I was told. They gave me an envelope
containing the cheque and the Head shook my hand. I hardly took
in what they were saying. The Head rubbed his hands together and
extolled, I think, the virtues of spending days on the golf course.
MacPherson put the documents away in a folder and looked at me
as if I were something very unpleasant that was about to be swept
under the carpet.

'I know you don't believe me, Mr MacPherson,' I said, as the
Headmaster opened the study door for me, 'but I am completely
innocent of all these charges.'

'That, Mr Barraclough,' sniffed MacPherson, 'is for yourself and
your conscience. As far as the school is concerned, the matter is
closed. But as far as I, personally, am concerned, if I ever hear the
merest suspicion that you have been trying to corrupt another young
person, I'll take all the evidence from this case straight to the police.
You're paid off for the moment, but you put one foot out of line and
you'll have your day in court after all. Now clear your desk and get
off the premises.'

I hovered on the threshold, desperate for some sign that at least
one of them believed me. The Headmaster took my arm and gripped
it just below the shoulder. 'For what it's worth, I do believe in your
innocence, Henry. Perhaps you've always been a little too innocent.
You've seemed to live in another world, sometimes, another age.

Schoolteachers need to be wily old birds, you know, just as they were when you and I were at school. I think you suffered a failure of your pupil management system, frankly. I don't mind admitting, I wondered, when I first heard Lander's story, but on reflection I'm satisfied it was all pretty one-sided. That's why I pushed for the full settlement for you.'

I looked to MacPherson for confirmation. He nodded curtly.

'I suppose I should be grateful. I must say, I don't feel it.'

'There's no need. I have to do what's best for the school, you see, that's what they pay me for. My hands are tied.' He mimicked a man with his arms tied tightly behind his hack.

'Really, Headmaster? I've never seen the attraction of bondage, myself. Where's the pleasure in that?' I watched for a second or two as their jaws hit the floor, then pulled the study door closed and walked smartly down the corridor.

As soon as I turned the corner, I felt physically sick. My head was spinning. I leaned against a radiator for support. Then I thought: Dorothy! She would never stand by and let me suffer this injustice. I swayed on my feet and lurched forward, like a man about to pass out, but instead, found my balance and headed for the staff room. It was empty.

Her usual coffee mug was on the table, with a smudge of lipstick near the rim. There was still half of the coffee left. I took a sip. It was very sweet. And still warm.

I ran blindly to the car park, as if my life depended on it. If she knew, she would not let this happen to me. She would not only release me from my promise, but would speak up freely on my behalf. Green would understand the need for it. There is no reason why he should love her any the less, because she once loved me. Is it such a disgrace?

Panting at the unaccustomed exertion, I reached the school drive just as Dorothy's car emerged from the car park, about fifty yards away. I stopped running and waved to flag her down. The car seemed to stutter for a moment, then sped up. I held up my hand again, as one does at a serious road accident, claiming the right to force someone to stop.

But she drove on towards me. I saw Stephen Green, sitting in the passenger seat, winding up the window. They both looked away from me. I moved my feet swiftly, to avoid being brushed by the front wing, but she swerved a little at the last moment, and so the collision was averted. I should have thrown myself under the wheels, when I had the chance. Let her taste the blood of a real human sacrifice. My body is of no further use to me.

I remember Green's white face staring back at me as they careered through the school gates and turned out of sight.

I could have followed them. I could have put on my bicycle clips and cycled the three miles or so. I would have been only half an hour behind them. I could have denounced her as a shameless hussy, or pleaded with her to speak the truth and save my worthless skin. But I made my mute appeal for help in the school driveway, and I received my answer.

I went home, I know not how or why. I stopped at a pub to buy a bottle of whisky, which I drank till it made me sick. It was several days before hunger forced me out again. – Well, not exactly hunger, for I still had no desire to eat. I wanted fresh milk for my tea. But all the shops were closed. I knew it was not Sunday, or thought I did. It was only when I found the garage shut as well that I realised: it was Christmas Day.

I think that is when I felt most truly alone. All the world was inside in the warm, celebrating, in name at least, the birth of Christ, while I, who claimed to be His follower, trawled the streets in ignorance. I was so wrapped in my cloak of self-pity that I had denied my Saviour, and forgotten the significance of His birth.

That was probably the shock that jolted me back to reality and awoke my instinct for survival. I began the long process of throwing away my papers. I found these seven exercise books, and with them at least a transitory sense of purpose.

But now they are nearly complete. They were not wasted after all, though they may as well have been. I realise how foolish I was, to think that she might spend her golden time perusing my fearful mid-night ramblings. I am a beaten man, I admit it, whipped like a dog, so accustomed to pain, I can scarcely howl.

It is the now the middle of June. Still, he goes to school each morning and returns each night. Still, she stays at home, broody and brooding, unaware of her lover's eyes watching her unseen, roaming freely over her face, her neck, her arms, her shoulders, when she bares them to the warm air.

She is more confident now. She reclines in the back garden, sunning herself, stretching like a somewhat ungainly cat. I watch from my hide in the shrubbery, hardly daring to move, for fear of spoiling this precious moment together. For who knows how many more such peaceful moments we shall have? The wheels of the tumbrel are rumbling in the distance.

She has made her preparations and now she waits. I too am prepared. I too wait. I have obtained a gun licence and a pistol with surprising ease; the shop assistant showed me how to fire it. I have reduced my possessions to bundles of banknotes, many more than I originally thought I possessed.

I always admired the panache of Phineas Fogg, in Jules Verne's Around The World In Eighty Days: Fogg's packing for the journey consisted of putting £25,000 in cash into a Gladstone bag. Well, I have bought my own Gladstone bag, now, and filled it with nearly five times as much. Where to bestow it, I am still unsure. Perhaps it will pay for my child's education.

But this is fantasy, and I must deal only with reality. Any other way, madness lies. How much longer, Lord? *I 'gin to grow a'weary of the sun.'*

For all my long vigil, when it happened, I was stunned by the suddenness of it. Lights were switched on again, almost as soon as they had been extinguished. I had not yet moved to the windows. I was hiding like Priapus in the shrubbery, drinking a cup of coffee from my flask. Green emerged first, to put a bag in the car. He returned to help Dorothy down the steps and they were away, leaving me to pack up my picnic like a late reveler.

In their haste, they left the bedroom window ajar. It was the work of a moment to climb inside. The air almost stifled me. It was the air they had breathed, my woman and the interloper. I gasped for oxygen and headed blindly for the front door. On the way, I stumbled over a teddy bear that must have fallen from her bag, and picked it up. It was to prove a passport.

Outside the Maternity Hospital, I waited most of the night. As soon as the nursing shift changed, I went in. I passed the reception desk unchallenged. I simply tucked the teddy bear under my arm and walked briskly, as if I knew precisely where I was going. I often used the same trick, when crossing the quadrangle at school, with a sheet of plain, white paper tucked under my arm. It looks official and fends off predators.

I found the delivery room and watched through the small window in the door. Green crouched by her at the head of the bed. Dorothy's face was grey and gaunt between spasmodic pains which stretched her on the rack. Her expression was strangely familiar: I wondered when I might ever have seen her so absorbed in a physical sensation. Then I remembered.

'Can I help you?' The woman's voice at my elbow was sharp and accusatory.

'No, no, it's all right, thanks. I brought this, you know, for the couple in there.' I thrust the teddy bear into her arms. 'It fell out of her bag, on the way. You don't mind giving it back to them, do you? I think it's a sort of good luck charm.'

'No, of course not.' She smiled. 'Won't be long, now.'

'How long, would you think?'

'Three quarters of an hour, maybe. Are you the grandfather?'

'Not exactly.'

'Come back in visiting hours. You'll be able to see the baby, then. Starts at ten o'clock.'

I thanked her and made my way to a small storeroom used for cleaning equipment and materials. The state of it suggested it was rarely used. I waited a further hour or two, then took some trouble to put on the wig and false moustache I had brought with me and finally re-emerged into the corridor wearing a white coat and carrying a camera. The official hospital photographer now had an elderly, unpaid apprentice.

I found the ward quite quickly. Dorothy lay propped on pillows in a bed in the corner, with the ever-faithful Green continuing to display dog-like devotion, wrapped in a blanket in the chair beside her. They both seemed fast asleep. On the other side of the bed was a tiny cot decorated with a blue ribbon.

I walked as quietly as I could towards the cot and peered in. I had left off my glasses, for the sake of the disguise, and I see little at close range without them. Moreover, a corner of the sheet covered most of the baby's face. As I reached in gently to pull the sheet aside, Dorothy woke with a start:

'What's the matter? What are you doing?'

'Hospital photographer!' said I with as much hearty good cheer as I could muster. 'Nice snaps of the little fellow...'

She interrupted me with a piercing scream: 'Stephen! It's him! He's after the baby – oh, stop him, for God's sake!'

As Green fought to disentangle himself from the blanket, I held the camera at arm's length over the cot, pointing, I hoped, at the baby, and pressed the button. Dorothy was still screaming so I ran to the door and out into the corridor. An orderly and a nurse were running towards the noise.

'She's in there. Hurry!' I shouted at them perhaps it was the white coat, perhaps that tone of authority I have been practising for thirty years. They ran on, towards the commotion in the ward, and I made good my escape down the back stairs and cycled to town to have my film processed.

I have the photograph in front of me as I write. It is not a masterpiece, but it tells me all I need to know. The baby has a wispy shock of ginger hair. Mother would recognise it at once – 'That's just Aunt Lucy's colour!' she would say. What a splendid surprise for two dark-haired parents!

I feel quite calm, now. Whoever said revenge is a meal best eaten cold was absolutely correct. The little boy will take my revenge on

Dorothy for the rest of her life. Now she will never forget. She can never again deny my love.

I could almost be content to leave the matter there, but presumably the happy couple will not concur. I have entered the holy of holies and defiled it; I have ruined their shadow play of pretence with a dazzling shaft of truth.

No doubt, I will now be branded as a baby-snatcher, as well as a perverter of teenagers. Soon, the police will come to the door and take me away for questioning. If I am not considered too great a danger to the community to be released on bail, my neighbours will shun me in the street. Urchins will throw bricks through my windows. My life here will rapidly become untenable.

No matter. It is a trifle. I am ready now, Lord, ready to serve you by giving up the life You gave to me.

Did You expect me to make more of it? So did I.

I have loved and lost. That is about the sum of it. I have not been a gracious loser, for I staked my life on this love, and now I have lost it. I cannot take back the bet because the result is not to my liking, any more than I could save my own skin by breaking my promise.

The Headmaster accused me of being innocent. He was too kind. I have been arrogant, fatally inflexible. My downfall is of my own devising. Could one not say the same of most of Shakespeare's tragic heroes? Now, there is fascinating thesis to test with a programme of reading. I suspect they are not so much tragically flawed, as AC Bradley contended, as active architects of their own downfall.

So, is it better to have loved and lost, than never to have loved at all? Of course it is. Is it better to have lived and died, than never to have lived at all? Again, of course it is. I freely exchange the final twenty or thirty years of my natural life for those few bright moments, those timeless ecstasies in which my love and I melted to the very essence of ourselves and flowed as one. That was the purpose of my life – and I fulfilled it.

My darling Dorothy, when we conceived our child, there was a point at which my seeds were alive inside me. They were a part of me: in microcosm, they were me. I was alive in the seeds, we pulsated and poured into you, wave upon wave, and your body received us, welcomed us, drew us deeper inside until I (one I, which I, I know not) plunged at last headfirst into my destiny, to melt and merge with you and grow into this brand new life. I am the Resurrection and the Life, and this is our continuance.

Observe the pineapples, how they grow: they emerge from the spiky crown of their parent, grow a spiky crown of their own and so, the process continues, ad infinitum. Their chain of being is plain to see. Our own is nonetheless real for being somewhat concealed, but we should never forget that we are merely links in that chain, nothing grander.

Against all likelihood, my genes will live on, in this little boy, as he grows to manhood and beyond. I wish him well, but I shall play no further part in his life. Having one father is enough of a misfortune: having two – smacks of carelessness.

Now I must go, before the police come to delay my exit. I will go to conduct my final reconnaissance. I shall see where the bulldozers are working on the land-fill site, so that I shall know where to bury myself tonight. I will take the pistol, the roll of black, plastic garbage bags that will form my shroud, and the Gladstone bag containing my worldly wealth and hide them behind a little shed on the site, in readiness.

I will leave these exercise books here, just for the next hour or so. When I return, I shall hole up in here till nightfall, ignore the doorbell, if it rings, and read through this drivel before consigning it to the fire – and myself, perchance, to the fires of Hell.

I have still not decided how to dispose of the money. Perhaps the Buddhists are right, and all human possessions are merely an encumbrance. I may bestow it on a charity shop as I cycle through the town, just to be rid of it. I regret, now, that I did not squander much more of it on wine, women and song, or indeed, on sex, drugs and rock 'n' roll, to use the modern parlance.

I hear Fanshawe telling me it is a little late in the day to realise such an obvious, fundamental truth. And yet, he counsels, it is not too late. Too late for poor Fanshawe, but not for wealthy Barraclough.

At last, I am free. Free of my memories, free of my misbegotten love. At this moment, I even feel free of the great weight of self-pity and sorrow that has beset me, all this year. It is true. I am free to live, if I wish. Why not? It is an absurd idea, but I suppose I could, even now, buy an air ticket to Australia and start a new life, as a new man, with my Gladstone bag for company. I should put my passport in my pocket – and be free as a bird, to fly away…

Just another fantasy. I shall stick to my plan. How can I live without my love? I shall cycle to the land-fill site, complete my reconnaissance and return to read my story, in these pages. I always thought I might write a book – and now I have. How sad, that I am destined to be its only reader. But that, I will do. I was always assiduous with my reading assignments.

Once I have read and burned these books, I shall return to the site, going the long way round, so as not to pass that woman's house. I shall never speak or write her name again. Then, I shall take one deep breath and put a merciful bullet through the final, sorry chapter of my wasted life.

Unless, for almost the first time, I choose to do something entirely on impulse, and find a completely different way of leaving my old life behind. In which case, this seventh chapter would not be the end of my story…

Mick Le Moignan is a Sydney-based writer and tv producer and a consultant on fundraising, marketing and communications.

He grew up in Jersey and read English at St Catharine's College, Cambridge University. After working as a tv newsreader and tv critic for *The Stage*, he moved to Australia and reviewed

tv, theatre and film for *The Australian, The National Times*, and *The Sydney Morning Herald*.

For ABC-Radio, he wrote *The Poet's Tongue*, adaptations of *The Tree of Man* by Patrick White, *The Fortunes of Richard Mahony* by Henry Handel Richardson, *The Waves* by Virginia Woolf, *Middlemarch* by George Eliot, the *Gormenghast* trilogy by Mervyn Peake and dramatised documentaries on the life and work of Franz Kafka, Hermann Hesse, Aldous Huxley and Patrick White.

For Corroboree Films, he produced several films on contemporary Aboriginal life, including *Eora Corroboree*, and won two Australian Writers' Guild AWGIE awards for dramatised documentaries, one on Aldous Huxley and the other on drug and alcohol awareness in indigenous communities.

In the UK in the 1990s, he was Story Editor on *Eastenders*, Script Editor on *The Bill* and an independent producer for BBC-TV, producing over 100 documentaries on a wide range of subjects, including the popular series *Turning Points*, in which celebrities told the story of a pivotal moment in their lives.

He took a Diploma in Law in London in 1995 and was for two years Artistic Director and General Manager of a large provincial theatre. An unexpected career change led to five years as Deputy Director of Development at Gonville & Caius College, Cambridge. He came home to Sydney in 2009 to join the Sydney Conservatorium of Music as General Manager, External Relations.

His book on the international outreach of the University of New South Wales, *UNSW Sydney – Australia's Global University*, was published by NewSouth Press in 2017.

From 2005 to 2020, he edited *Once a Caian…*, the annual alumni magazine of Gonville & Caius College, Cambridge. He currently writes a regular column on Australian life and politics for *The Jersey Evening Post*. *The English Teacher* is his first novel.